About the Author

Olivia Levez lives in Worcestershire, where she divides her time between teaching in a secondary school and writing. *The Island* is Olivia's debut novel and she is already at work on her second book, which Rock the Boat will publish in spring 2017. She writes mainly in her caravan in West Wales and was inspired by the coast to create the desert island in this book.

You can follow Olivia on Twitter **@livilev.**

WITHDRAWN

WITHDRAWN

The ISLAND

Olivia Levez

ROCK THE BOAT

A Rock the Boat Book

First published by Rock the Boat, an imprint of
Oneworld Publications, 2016
Reprinted, 2016

The moral right of Olivia Levez to be identified as the Author
of this work has been asserted by her in accordance with the
Copyright, Designs and Patents Act 1988

All rights reserved
Copyright under Berne Convention
A CIP record for this title is available from the British Library

ISBN 978-1-78074-859-7
ISBN 978-1-78074-877-1 (ebook)

Printed and bound in Great Britain by Clays Ltd, St Ives plc

This book is a work of fiction. Names, characters, businesses,
organizations, places, and events are either the product of the
author's imagination or are used fictitiously. Any resemblance
to actual persons, living or dead, events, or locales is entirely
coincidental.

Oneworld Publications
10 Bloomsbury Street
London WC1B 3SR
England

Stay up to date with the latest books,
special offers, and exclusive content from
Rock the Boat with our monthly newsletter

Sign up on our website
www.rocktheboat.london

For my mother, Judith

Dog Breath

They all know what I've done. Of course they do. That's why they leave me well alone.

Hi I'm Rufus! is fascinated, like I'm some frickin sideshow. You can tell because his eyes are on me every time I look.

I stare boldly at him – *I won't use my freezing power, not yet* – till he flinches away.

So here we all are, on a plane the size of my shoe.

The plane is tracking along the runway at Ptang–Plang Airport, bracing itself for take-off.

Outside there's the shimmer of bluesky and brightlight and palm trees.

Inside is a dog, curled up in its travel bag, panting. Even across the aisle I can smell its breath, warm and stinking in the close air.

Hi I'm Rufus! has one of those posh voices that owns a room. It cuts through Ella Fitzgerald as she yearns through my earphones.

'Pilot's dog,' he's saying.

Lucky me that he's sitting right in front. He twists so that I see the nasty yellow of his TeamSkill shirt that does nothing for his complexion. He's wearing his TeamSkill name badge with its happy rainbow colours.

Rufus reaches a freckled arm over to stroke the dog's head.

'Hello, old boy,' he says.

Old boy?

I shoot bolts of ice at him before he flinches away but I've already seen what he's thinking: *It's the monster, the one in the files.* He doesn't give up though; he remembers his TeamSkill training and says, 'I like dogs', as the dog beside me pantpantpants.

I glance out of the window, then wish I hadn't. Looks like we're heading straight towards the sea.

I turn down Ella.

'Why d'you keep looking at me? You some kind of perv?'

I hurt almost without thinking these days.

'Do you have any friends, Fran?' Sally-the-Counsellor's voice, ever calm and ever concerned.

'My name's Frances,' I say. 'Only people I like call me Fran.'

There were friends once, but they melted away. Things are different now I'm a monster.

Medusa Girl

That's the first time I've spoken since yesterday.

I'm Medusa Girl. Cold as rock, hard as stone.

Medusa was a monster who turned flesh into stone. A useful skill. I think of all the people I would turn to stone, and whether it's the hate that does it, bleeding out of your head through your eyes and puddling towards people like poison, or whether you shoot out white-rage like a spear of lightning.

I think of Angela with her I-really-care eyes; imagine freezing her so all of her endless questions drop like pebbles

2

through the air.

Angela is my social worker.

She's got one of those voices that goes up at the end of each sentence. It irritates the frick out of me. If only I'd discovered my Medusa powers when we first met, maybe I could have stopped all of this from happening.

Maybe.

At Heathrow she had to have one last go at saving me.

'You know this is such an opportunity? I mean, an island in the Indian Ocean? Everyone's rooting for you, Frances?'

I watch the other social workers fade away, but not Angela. She still hovers. Holds out her hand.

'Well, goodbye, Frances. Hope you enjoy the experience? Even though it'll be tough?'

When I shove my hands in my pockets she looks disappointed.

I stare at Angela, and she can't hold my gaze; she flinches away. Doesn't stop her talking though.

'Frances, remember what we discussed – before? When you come back, I really think you should visit her. She understands why you did it. She –'

My snakes hiss and spit.

'Shut up. Just shut up,' I say.

My gate is called, and I turn to follow the rest of TeamSkill.

'She's asking to see you?' calls Angela.

I don't look back.

Just then our little plane gives a great lurch and bounces into the air.

Makes my memory snap shut like a book.

Are You Sitting Comfortably?

I clench my fists as the plane curves over palm trees and parked cars and miniature buildings, then veers over the coast into the sea.

Ella Fitzgerald tries to calm me with her caramel voice but it's not working. I grip the armrest because that's going to help. Then I try to focus on the other passengers.

There's Tiny, real name Paul. Fourteen, but looks three years younger. Only clue to his age is the bumfluff that pokes through his zitty chin: those head-phone's he's wearing are bigger than him.

There's Coral, screech-laughing to the boy beside her. When she shifts position, I can see the silver stretch marks on her belly. On her arm is a badly-drawn tattoo of a baby's face.

Next to her is Joker. Sixteen-ish, cap yanked high on the back of his head. He's jiggling his knee, all pent-up fury behind the gags. Like he'd slam your head down on the point of your pencil, Heath Ledger style, if you provoked him. He mutters something to Coral and she screams with laughter, showing her tongue piercing.

Our survival kit is in the hold. It's all been packed for us. They think we can't be trusted to pack for ourselves because:

we'll fill our backpacks with knives and vodka and smack

we're city kids so haven't seen a frickin tree before, let alone a coconut.

'Are you really nervous?'

Hi I'm Rufus! is still trying hard. Has he forgiven me yet for spoiling his stupid team game back at the Centre? Probably wants to write a report on me or something. Fran Stanton: Special Case Study.

4

He has pale skin, the sort that looks surprised to be out-side. Eyes blue as a Tory boy. Everything about him is soft: soft skin, soft fringe, soft life.

'Here, have a sweet to take your mind off it.'

He hands me a wrapped boiled sweet which I shove into my pocket just as the plane gives an alarming shake. Everyone cheers except me.

'I flew one of these once, a Cessna two-seater. My father gave me lessons for my eighteenth birthday. Fantastic things. Really robust, you know –'

'You don't have to practise on me,' I say.

'What? I mean, pardon?'

'All your TeamSkill training. You don't have to practise on me. It won't work. I'm not listening.'

I watch his flush deepen.

I take a swig from my bottle and try to ignore the stink-pant of the dog. Outside, the world is all wrong: everything is edges and angles.

The co-pilot turns round to us and smiles. 'OK, you guys. Hope you are all comfortable back there.'

But I'm staring at the plastic-coated escape plan which is stuck to the seat in front. Cheerful passengers bobbing about in the sea and blowing whistles.

And now we are rising, high over the ocean, away from the land.

The plane lifts and my stomach drops.

Indictable Offence

'Frances Stanton. You understand why you are here in the Children's Court today?'

Shrug.

'It is my duty to pass sentence on the following crimes. You have been found guilty of, amongst other things, inflicting criminal damage to a public building, causing damage in excess of two hundred thousand pounds. We believe that there are many circumstances that make this case an indictable offence...'

Shrug.

'...aggravating factors...'

Don't think. Don't think about it. Watch her mouth work and twist but don't listen to the words coming out.

'However, in view of your age...and other mitigating circumstances...'

I am panting with rage, running, running. Running down the stairs, past the caretaker. Left down the corridor, up the passage. Outside, the sound of the loudspeaker. Inside, the clink of bottles in my bag.

I start to shake. Try to shove the memory back where it came from. Freeze it out. Freeze it out.

'...more focused approach...'

What is she saying? I fix on her purple glasses as her mouth works, blah blah blah. They are interesting glasses, for someone who must be at least fifty. They've got glittery bits in them. I imagine her choosing them, maybe with her daughter. 'Get those, Mum,' her girl would say. 'They're well cool...' I read the designer label on the side: Paul Smith. So she's got money then. Plenty of it, from sorting out crims like me.

'Frances Stanton?'

Stone stare.

'This scheme works by offering an intense three-month course that gives offenders the opportunity to focus on team-building skills...'

'What?' I say.

Sigh. 'Since this is your future we are discussing, Frances, it would be nice if you would pay attention. We've decided that we'd like to avoid a custodial sentence in a juvenile detention centre if at all possible.'

'Three months?' I say. 'I can't be gone for three months – my brother needs me!' I am shouting now. My Medusa thing isn't working. Sometimes it doesn't; sometimes I can't seem to turn it on.

Purple Glasses leans forward then.

'We are aware that you do have a close relationship with your half-brother, Johnny Bailey.'

A hand is restraining me as I struggle. My breath's coming quick and fast in my throat.

Remember you are rock. Remember you are stone.

'What of it?' I say.

'If you take up this opportunity we are offering, you avoid a custodial sentence, which means you will be able to have regular access visits.'

Then a man with white hair, who's been quiet all this time, shifts round to speak to me.

'Basically, Frances, if you get yourself locked up, you may not get to see your little brother for up to two years.'

Yogurt

Derek-the-co-pilot is tanned and relaxed. He winks at us all and dips in a spoon, slowly. He's eating blueberry yogurt. I watch that yogurt like hell because as long as he's eating it, everything's just fine.

'Our journey to the island will take around two hours. We hope you enjoy the flight, kids.'

The heat shimmers and the little dog grins and pants beside me. Coral nudges Joker and giggles. Tiny looks out of the window; hardly moves as he takes it all in.

'Carob-coated Brazils, everyone,' sings *Hi I'm Trish!* She starts to throw bags of nuts and bottles of ice-cold water to us all.

Joker catches some nuts and chucks them at Coral, who shrieks. My water rolls under my seat but I ignore it. Twist the lid of my own bottle instead.

'Tiny, not for you because of your nut allergy,' *Hi I'm Trish!* says.

Nice Trish. Wonderful Trish. Thinks of everything.

The other TeamSkill kids have quietened down now. They're swigging water and opening packets.

Coral has her head on Joker's shoulder; his hand, I notice, is under her top, stroking her back. Tiny's still staring out at the sea. As Coral yawns and stretches, her sleeve falls back, showing her tattoo. Too late, she sees me looking.

'My kid,' she says, and smiles.

She rolls her sleeve higher to show me.

'Tia. She's eighteen months. Just started walking.' She sighs. 'Got anyone you'll miss?'

So I stare at her tattoo, at this baby that crawls along her arm, one hand after the other, little fingers grasping the plumpness of her flesh, and I'm thinking…

I'm thinking
of another baby,
smiling
as it makes its way trustingly towards me.
The little inked face wobbles closer, closer.
Stare. Blink.
Turn away now.

Starfish

He's all scrunched up and angry-looking.

But I don't mind.

I am nine and I like babies.

'Can I hold him, Mum?'

Cassie's all woozy with wires. She's talking sort of bendy because she's had a difficult labour. That means there was trouble getting the baby out. I know because my best friend Priya's mum's just had a baby too.

Cassie nods, smiling through her blurriness. She watches me place my arm under the baby's head so he doesn't loll, and lift him, as carefully as I can, in my arms.

I sit on the chair and we both look at him.

He's all sleepy-warm and his hair's kind of yucky with my mum's blood and stuff but that doesn't matter.

What matters is that he's mine.

He gives a sort of snuffle and stretches one hand out like a starfish.

'Look, Mum,' I say.

He's smiling in his sleep; his eyes roll back and forth under their lids as his little mouth laughs silently.

'He likes you,' Cassie says.

I am enchanted. I trace my finger over his cheek, and it's firm and new. He's a conker just come out of its shell.

His eyes open then, and they gaze into mine, wise as an owl, thoughtful as time.

'Hello, Monkey,' I say.

Tarmac

I wonder when *Hi I'm Trish!* will notice that half her vodka's gone from the bottle in her duty-free bag. I refilled the last bottle of water she gave me with vodka, after pouring the water out over the hot, hot tarmac. Stood there for ages watching its steam shimmer and vanish.

The plane gives a jolt and I tighten my grip on the armrest. Take another swig and stuff the bottle into my hoodie pocket.

I take a quick look at the co-pilot. It's OK – he's licking his spoon and chatting to Trish, who is up at the front.

Poor cow. She doesn't know that she's only got twenty minutes left to live.

TeamSkill

First time I meet her is after I'm done screaming at the magistrate with her dry voice and glittery glasses.

Two police officers are gripping my arms through my school shirt. Angela said I had to dress up smart to make an impression.

'She's not stopping me seeing Johnny,' I pant. 'No way —'

I'm thinking they'll hustle me into a cell or something but instead I'm taken to a room that smells of air freshener and has a vase of fake flowers on a low table.

'Cup of tea?' asks an officer.

I scowl at her.

She leaves.

This room is small and bland and peach: peach flowers, peach walls, even a box of peach tissues in case it all gets too much. On the wall, a poster of a girl tells me that *Alone we can do so little; together we can do so much more.* Another has a bunch of teenage lads clutching each other and air-punching. *Coming together is a beginning*, it says. *Staying together is progress. Working together is success.*

Yay.

The door opens and in walks *Hi I'm Trish!* I know she's called that because she has a name badge with a rainbow logo on it pinned to her bright yellow polo shirt.

Trish is all sweetness and lies.

'Hey there,' she says. She's from Australia or New Zealand, small with shiny, dark hair.

The officer's back in the room, just in case I go wild and punch Trish or something. She places a cup of tea on the table, even though I didn't ask for it. It's in a mug with

Keep Calm and Eat Cupcakes written on it. I can tell without looking that it'll have tea stains inside because the handle's all grungy.

'OK, Fran – can I call you Fran? – I'm here to tell you more about the TeamSkill Enterprise for Young Offenders. It's a really exciting opportunity that will help in altering negative behavioural patterns…'

I hate fake flowers.

I hate how they're bright and cheerful and pretending to be something else while all the time they just sit there gathering dust, with their stiff petals and plastic stems. They don't even have a scent. What's the point of a flower with no scent?

'…and, consequentially, we find the challenge lowers the risk of reoffending. And of course there's an increasing body of research that indicates that contact with natural places supports both physical and mental health…'

She's really trying hard, is *Hi I'm Trish!* She's waving her hands around and smiling like she's got the best job in the world. When, really, she just gets to work with people like me, all the misfits and losers. I wonder what drives her.

She's pushing a leaflet at me. It's bright and shiny with the TeamSkill logo sweeping over the front.

'We're really glad that you're on board, Fran,' she says.

On board?

I'm staring at a picture of a desert island with palm trees and happy kids lighting fires.

'What's this?' I say.

Hi I'm Trish! looks pained. 'Like I said, it's an amazing opportunity for first-time offenders like yourself to learn how to build community skills and reduce lone mindsets –'

'Yes, but what is it? *Where* is it?'

She looks pleased I'm taking an interest.

'The magistrate has recommended you for our pilot

scheme for first-time offenders, Fran. You will take part in a twelve-week TeamSkill programme working with communities on a remote Indonesian island.'

'Indonesia?' The word sounds strange in this peach-washed room.

'It's in the Indian Ocean. There'll be a select group of other offenders on this scheme, all first-timers like you. The islanders will teach you the skills of survival in a natural landscape. You'll learn how to work with your hands, build shelter, live off what the island provides. In return, you will support them in rebuilding their environment after recent storms.'

I stare at the picture in my hands. The palm trees look unreal, like on a movie poster.

'You're taking the piss, yeah?'

Trish is delighted now. 'No. I mean, I know it sounds amazing, right? But we've worked together with the Indonesian government on this scheme and we really think it'll work. It's the ultimate in team building and community service. And all the young offenders we'll be taking will come home equipped with transferable life-skills, like...'

She's off again, blah blah blah.

The sky on the leaflet is bluer than blue. It's a colour I've only seen once before, and that was in a museum display case: a family of monkeys, picking fleas out of each other, frozen for ever under a bluer-than-blue sky.

I look at the blue and I think of the grey I see out of the window of Cassie's flat.

'Why me?'

'We've looked at your past history and you're a survivor, Fran. TeamSkill needs survivors. We give young people like you a second chance by providing outlets for risk-taking and facilitating social interaction. In return, you agree to let us use

13

your success story as part of our new marketing strategy…'

So they're going to use all us social misfits to prove their little scheme really works.

'Just a few photographs and interviews,'Trish is saying.

Ha.

Like I said, sweetness and lies.

They drag me off to get my tetanus and yellow–fever and typhoid jabs.

And that's how I get to be in this tinpot plane over the middle of the Indian Ocean.

Clouds

I stare out of the window.

'You're friendly, aren't you?' I hear Coral shift in her seat. 'What the hell's that?'

Hi I'm Trish! has also noticed the 'super' view.

'Cumulus.' She smiles. 'Cumulus clouds across the Indian Ocean. Look at them, all banked up like towers, like a forest.'

I am a rock. I don't have to look at rose-splashed clouds, kissing the afternoon sun like a garden of pink coral. But I do look. 'Course I do.

And for once the entire plane is quiet; even the pilot, it seems, has not seen a sight quite like this before.

Tiny is pressed up against the glass as if he wants to lick it; his breath makes little huffs of mist.

The clouds are beautiful.

'Come up, come up, Paul.' *Hi I'm Trish!*'s voice.

Tiny scrambles up and over the seats, skinny as string. Sits and gapes through the front window as Trish smiles and gives him a squeeze.

She's still smiling through the first lurch of turbulence.

We rise and fall, but only Joker cheers.

Derek puts down his spoon.

Fasten Your Seat Belts

Me and Cassie are watching old movies and eating popcorn on the settee. It's the one where Bette Davis turns from the stairs and tells her guests to buckle up 'cause it'll be a bumpy night.

Cassie is plump as heaven and smells of sweet cider and cuddles.

'Love you more than the moon and the stars and the planets,' she whispers, and gives me a swig ('Only one, mind!') of her cider.

'Love you more than all the fishes and birds and bees,' I whisper back, and the cider fizzes, sweet in my mouth.

'Sure you love me as much as that?'

'More than that.'

Bette Davis is right about the seat belts. It gets bumpy all right.

Crash and Burn

The plane is being seriously pummelled and it's like we're in an upside-down avalanche.

'Heyyyyyyyyyy,' whoops Joker. He'll regret that attitude soon.

'Sorry, folks. A bit of turbulence, that's all,' says Derek-the-co-pilot.

Up front, in the cockpit, the radio crackles. It seems the pilot isn't happy about something. He's sweating in his Hawaiian shirt and shades.

The plane rocks violently and, for a while, we're all quiet. Even Trish. Even Joker.

Coral reaches for Joker's hand and squeezes it.

Me, I turn my music up and Ella Fitzgerald shimmies into my head, singing about summertime.

A jolt, and Coral's Brazil nuts are thrown out of her hand.

She gives a little scream and Joker puts his arm round her again, which is what she wanted.

'Ohmygod,' she says. 'Ohmygod.'

And Joker leans to get the nuts but he can't quite reach, so he's unclasping his belt and squeezing between the seats.

Coral's scream is a full stop, but it's also the beginning: it sets everyone off and now the air is whipped with cries and moans and even laughter.

'Uh, we are hitting…a pretty bad…downdraught,' says Derek. His words are broken and his spoon has clattered to the floor.

But Joker spreads his arms wide and grins. Waves his hands around as if he's conducting an orchestra. Then Joker makes a bow so that everyone claps.

'What about my Brazils?' Coral shouts.

And then he

   then he

    hits his head during the turbulence and dies.

Joker is flung right across the seats, and there is a *CRACK* as his head makes contact with the metal armrest and he smacks against the floor and doesn't move and Coral is screaming.

And me? I've left my body and I'm crouching on the cabin ceiling, safe among the seams. I've left Other Me gripping that armrest, as the dog whimpers and whines.

I see:

Hi I'm Trish! – she's first aid trained, of course she is – swinging her head round just as *Hi I'm Rufus!* starts to unclasp his belt.

'Keep your belts fastened,' yells Derek.

The pilot is wrestling – wrestling with the stick and the weather.

'Stop,' shouts Trish to Rufus, and with this word she saves one life and ends another.

Because, as she rises to help, her foot is caught beneath the seats and at that moment the sky heaves our plane up and Trish lurches forward and *SNAP.*

There's her ankle broken.

She'll not get up again, but Rufus sits back down. Snaps on his belt.

I see:

Poor Trish writhing and gaping, but no one cares because the plane gives a little leap and *POP*, the propeller stops.

I see:

The pilot on his radio, listening and gabbling, fingering the rosary beads around his sun-scoured neck.

Brazil nuts begin to roll and the plane begins to drop, left wing first.

Words.

'We...lost...the...engine...'

The pilot checks the panel – for fuel? For God? – and white smoke pours in. And all the time, this high-pitched, whistling whine.

That control stick doesn't want to go forward.

'BRACE!' screams the pilot.

Other Fran shoves her head against her knees and Ella's voice in her earphones is plaintive as hell as she sings about spreading her wings and taking to the sky.

The suddenness of sea.

Time stops.

More Than

'Love you more than the stars and moons and planets.' It's a whisper.

'Whatever,' I say.

Cassie blinks at me through smeary eyes. Her nest is made of grubby bedding and tissues and *Heat* magazines.

I yank the duvet off her and she cowers into the settee, trying to hide her great, fat, useless body. She's wearing her business suit: a baby-doll nightie in black and red nylon. Her legs need a shave.

'Love –' she says.

'Move.'

She lets me shove her off the settee into a standing position. Stupid cow can barely walk. I watch her stumble over to the armchair and sink down with a sigh. She reaches for her Rizlas and starts to make a rollie. Her fingers shake with the shock of the morning.

I chuck the dirty sheets into a black bag and remake the sofa bed with fresh bedding. It smells of the outdoors because I used buckets of fabric conditioner.

Cassie looks around, bewildered, and I throw her the lighter, which was underneath a photo of some celeb flashing her tits.

Cassie lights her ciggie and sucks in her first breath of the day.

Unravelling

Sea is up over windows and it is not rain – it is sea. It is not rain – it is sea.

Fumbling to undo seat belts. Fumbling to get life jackets out of front seats.

'Life jacket –'

We are standing, clambering, unravelling. Legs, shorts, hands.

Sea is rolling down the floor of the plane.

Flip-flops, trainers, yellow rubber.

A flash of red hair and yellow plastic.

Where's my life jacket? Where's –

Sea is rolling down the floor of the plane.

I grab a package with the words LIFE RAFT and now I'm clutching yellow rubber.

Seawater swallows me. I should be cold, should feel the

shock of the cold, but I don't. Maybe it's because my face is being pressed up against the ceiling of the plane. And I'm floating now. Not just floating – I'm drowning.

Screams have turned to throbbing silence. It takes me some time to realise that this sound is my heart *whup-whupping*.

I have five centimetres of air space left. The last thing I will see is the seam of the ceiling; this grey vein curving away from my cheek. I clutch my rubber package and my shoe falls off and drifts away.

The water rises and I'm all covered, above and around and below. This is the way my world ends.

Something nudges my arm and I open my eyes and turn and it's Coral.

She gapes at me, her blind eyes bulging.

Her hair swirls and it rests and settles, stroking my arms, my face. She is water-whitened, but her hair is beautiful.

I cannot breathe.

I push her away with my foot; her belly is porridge-soft.

I cannot breathe.

Up

Soon all this will be over: this last, gasping, thrashing fight for air.

Saltwater fills my lungs and I am still fighting, banging on the ceiling with my weak, useless hands.

Burningburning suckingsucking chokingchoking.

Death is a struggle.

And just as the lights switch to black, the seam splits.

A searing crack of whitelight whitelight whitelight.
I claw through the opening
and I yank on the string of my yellow package
and something bursts
and I whoosh through the water, up like a rocket,
and am yanked up through the silver skin of the water into
air
pure and clean and cold like a
slap.

Burning

My throat burns.

I can smell talc and rubber, and sunlight is dancing red ripples behind my eyes.

I open my eyes. Stare at bulging, writhing walls.

I have no shoes.

I try to sit, and immediately vodka-waves rise inside me and I throw up, all over this strange, moving floor. At first I think I'm on a bouncy castle like the one in Brockwell Park, when the Lambeth Country Show is on. I retch and retch and wipe my mouth with my hand.

A spume of water hits the ceiling of my new, closed world and I cower back. Slide down, back into the puddle.

Everything on this raft is yellow: yellow walls and floor. Above me, a crack of white light behind a yellow flap. I shift round on my knees, lift the flap.

I look out and see:

Blue shimmering water.

Blue shimmering sky.

And nothing.

Lots and lots of endless nothing.

I am alone in the heaving sea.

I remember the whoosh and I remember the yank as the life raft inflated, as the nylon rope detached from the broken body of the plane. I look about, try to see the plane, but there's nothing: no smoke, no smashed-up metal lying in the sea. It's like my whole life has just evaporated: *poof* – just like that.

I think of Trish and Coral and Tiny.

I stare at the sea for a long, long time, and all the while the sun beats down and all the while my throat burns.

I must drink.

There's a plastic water bottle bobbing in the puddle of seawater; I feel it with my foot. I reach down and press it to my cheek. My tongue feels thick and swollen and I wonder if I'll even be able to swallow.

Oh God.

Vodka. It must have fallen out of my hoodie pocket.

Neat and mocking, it burns the roof of my mouth. I'm alone in the middle of the ocean and I have no water.

I put the lid back on the bottle; let it slide out of my hand.

After a million years, I get back on my knees and lift the flap again.

Outside, the ocean slops and swells, bigger than the world, bigger than my life, smacking me in the face with salt spray. When I zoom out of myself and look down, there is nowhere and nothing to cling to: I am a pinprick in the heaving sea, a scrap of yellow nothing in all that blue.

And that's when I start to laugh.

I'm still laughing when the first rolling wave hits me.

Dead Calm

Sun wakes me like a headache.

It beats down, heating up the yellow roof and the puddle. There is a lot more seawater inside than before; it reaches up to my thighs, my knees.

I trace my finger over the seams and now I see that the raft's skin is pierced in many tiny places. We are sinking, my life raft and me. The sea is killing it like it's killing me.

But I think the storm has stopped. All night it shrieked as I slid about the raft floor. I hid my eyes so I couldn't see the joins that criss-cross the body of the raft. I imagined the waves beating the raft so hard that the glue unsticks. Imagined it splitting like a watermelon.

I squirm upright and poke my head out of the roof.

Around me, the sea is milky calm; the sun drips on to its surface, warm as melted butter.

Exhausted, I flop my arms over the sides, sliding raw fingers down hot rubber. My throat burns. My tongue is fat and thick in my mouth.

I spin on my rubber island in all that wide, wide sea. Stare out at the ocean which the sun stabs with stars.

So thirsty.

How to Get Water

'This is probably the most important survival lesson you'll get,' announces *Hi I'm Steve!*

He's squatting in front of a sheet of grubby plastic and a bunch of leaves.

I need the loo because I drank too much coffee at breakfast.

Steve's got Tiny and Joker digging with spades.

'So you make a deep hole, about an arm–width across. Then you fill it with fresh, green leaves, just yank them off…'

It's started to rain: great fat splats of it from a muddy sky.

They start doing something with a plastic tub and a drinking straw and I pull my hoodie up against the rain. Open my mouth and catch it on my tongue.

'Are you listening at the back?' Steve barks.

Coral nudges me.

'What?'

'I'd like you to sum up to the group how to make a solar still,' Steve tells me.

I consider.

'Well. First you take the spade, which you've randomly taken to your desert island,' I say. 'And then you dig a great big hole with it – your own grave I s'pose, for when you die out there. And when the rain hammers down, like it is now in case you hadn't noticed, you drink the frickin water.'

Everyone sniggers.

And I kill him with my stone stare.

Red Nylon Bag

This water is fire.

As I drink the vodka, I see myself pouring cold-as-ice water on to the scorched runway. See the steam shimmer. See my water bottle rolling, rolling under the plane seat.

I lick my lips with my dead-wood tongue. The vodka scorches the back of my mouth and sinks into my veins heavyheavyheavy.

I sink back into my hollow pit of headache yellow.

I drink, hugging my knees, tracing the walls with my finger. There are thin trickles of water coming in now, seeping in behind the joins. The one by my left foot is different; the rest have an extra strip of rubber glued over them but this one doesn't. It's lumpy and bulgy and hard.

I push it with my foot and take another swig of vodka. Definitely hard.

It takes a long, slow time to rouse myself and get to that seam and feel it pull away with my hand.

Velcro.

It's a secret pocket and it contains the Red Nylon Bag.

'Ooh, look,' I giggle. 'Hello, Mr Red Nylon Bag. Welcome aboard.'

I crawl back on my hands and knees and close my eyes for a moment. It's sooo hard to get a grip – *Get a grip, Fran. Get a frickin grip* – because the floor's sliding and shifting bouncybouncybouncy.

I wave my bottle and slither about in the seawater. Quite a lot has come in now; it's swishing and sloshing all around me.

Then I remember the Red Nylon Bag.

Let's see what it's got for us.

There are loads and loads of things.

I spill them out all over the floor. Boxes, packets, sachets. Tubes and scissors and flares and a fishing line and a torch and whistles and plastic bags.

Hi I'm Steve! would love this.

I swirl them all around in the puddle. Take another swig of my vodka.

Then:

ohGodohGodohGod.

There's water.

Those fat little plastic sachets are labelled *Drinking Water*.

I can't pierce the sachets with the scissors.

'Oops,' I giggle. 'Don't want to burst the boat.'

They keep slipping and sliding out of my hands but I manage to stab one, pin it between my knees like it's a fish or something and then I hold it to my mouth and drink.

And drink. And drink.

And I have to take deep breaths and hold my tummy because I don't want to retch again. Mustn't lose all that liquid.

I drink three of the water sachets till my belly feels tight and full.

See? No need for solar stills.

I don't even know what to do with all the other stuff that's in the bag so in the end I have a little party.

Party

Ha ha.

I'm all on my own in my little bouncy-castle boat, bouncing up and down on my knees, waving my arms and blowing my whistle.

I blow up the solar stills through their tubes till they make balloons, and tie the bandages from the first aid kit round my head for a headband, and shine my torch as a lighter like it's a concert.

The radio's useless. Can't get a signal and can't make it work.

I down more vodka and that's probably a mistake because it makes me angry.

Angry so that I end up chucking the stupid thing out into the stupid, stupid sea.

'Cause what's the point of a party with no music?

It doesn't matter though because the smoke signal's amazing. I chuck it into the sea and it shoots up a jet of billowy grey smoke that turns bright orange and lasts for ages and ages.

I hang over the side and watch it forever. I just wish there were more of them.

Turns out I do have guests at my party.

They swoop low and follow my party boat, so low that I can see their bellies, all perfectly white with tucked-in red legs. The gulls don't seem to be moving but just shift slightly in the air currents, a nudge here, a nudge there.

I feed them all my emergency energy bars.

'Come on, birdies. Come to Fran.'

I'm not even hungry.

I am so hungry.

It's getting dark again but I have my torch, though it nearly slips out of my hand when I'm trying to dance on my knees.

But that doesn't matter because I have matches: twenty-five of them. I light them, one after the other, till there are only three left.

I save the best till last.

As well as the smoke signal, there's a flare. When I light it, a million stars shoot up into the sky, and my raft creaks and sighs in the black, black water.

I've never liked the dark.

The Morning After

What the Red Nylon Bag should contain:
- 1 fishing kit
- 1 radio
- 1 smoke signal
- 1 flare
- 1 safety knife
- 1 whistle
- 1 torch
- 25 waterproof matches
- 1 first aid kit: bandages, dressings, scissors, antiseptic cream
- Sun cream
- Plastic bags
- 2 solar stills
- 12 high-energy food bars
- 6 x 500 ml drinking water sachets

What it contains now:
- 1 fishing kit
- 1 safety knife
- 1 torch
- 3 waterproof matches
- Sunburn cream
- 3 x 500 ml drinking water sachets

Shit shit shit.

Team Games

Hi I'm Rufus! waits, flushing like a sunset.

He makes a big effort to start the team game and I make a big effort to stop it.

'OK, you guys, we're going to start with an icebreaker,' he says, and Coral and the others fall about, wetting themselves.

'Oy, Posh Boy, is your name Harry?'

'Yeah, man, how's the Queen, innit.'

I see his flush deepen and the colour clashes nastily with his yellow polo.

'He said to stand in a circle and clap,' *Hi I'm Steve!* barks. He looks like he's walked off a Tarantino movie with his bullet-bald head.

We're in a large hall somewhere in the New Forest. Everything's all fresh sawn from new wood and my DMs clump too loudly on the hard floor. Trish has the camera crew trailing behind her – one bloke, anyway, in flip-flops and a Blink 182 T-shirt. The camera zooms in on me, nice and close, and I freeze the lens with my stone eyes.

Only a tiny lad in too-big combats is paying attention to the game. He bobs about like a cork, listening hard.

Hi I'm Rufus! passes round a roll of toilet paper. 'Take as many sheets as you want,' he shouts. 'Then pass it round. Keep to the beat.'

We clap time, and this time I look into Rufus's eyes and they're blue as Fizz Bombs.

'Lovely game,' I tell him. I may be made of stone but I'm burning today.

These eyes of mine can shoot ice-fire at any moment, so watch out.

Coral starts arguing with *Hi I'm Steve!*

'No way,' she says. 'No way am I taking out my tongue stud. It'll close up, it'll get infected.'

'Now,' he says.

Hi I'm Trish! gives a little laugh as the camera lens swivels.

'I t's important that all the members of TeamSkill are stripped down to their basic essentials –'

'You're not stripping *me* down to my bare essentials,' hoots a boy called Kieran.

Coral shrieks and nearly bites her tongue.

'Come on, focus on the team game,' trills Trish.

'This is fun. What's the next one?' I say. I know my voice is too loud but I don't care. The room's rocking like a boat and I'm sinking, I really am.

When it's my turn, I pull sheets and sheets of toilet paper off the roll till it pools around my feet.

'Shall I take her for Team Out?' growls Steve.

I pass the nearly empty roll to a skinny girl, who shakes her head and hands it to Kieran-the-joker.

'No, leave her here,' says Trish.

'Who's she? The cat's mother?' I ask.

Rufus raises his voice over the noise. 'OK, right, you lot. Stop clapping and chanting now please. Um, the rules are:

each person must now take it in turns to tell the group a few fun facts about themselves…and the number of facts must equal the number of sheets of paper that the person holds.'

Everyone is looking at me: I'm holding twenty or thirty sheets.

'Facts must be new information to the group and only one very short sentence each,' he explains.

'I'm not telling you lot anything about myself,' I say, and my voice comes out all thick.

No frickin way.

Silence pulses, hot and prickling.

Freeze him with my gaze. Watch him crumble.

'So why don't you take your stupid game and use it to wipe your arse?'

And I crash out of the room to go and find somewhere that doesn't have a team in it.

Birds

The effort of climbing up to the observatory platform has made me feel sick and I hang over the railing and breathe deep.

I wish I had a fag.

I don't want a fag.

I still have bog roll in my hand and I rip off the sheets, one by one.

Fact: I destroy everything I touch.

Fact: I have done something so terrible it can't be undone.

Fact: I have snakes for hair.

Fact: Anyone who looks into my eyes gets turned to stone.

Fact: Cassie, my mother, shags for money.

Fact: I make the best Turkish coffee.

Fact: Out of all the exhibits in the Horniman Museum, I like the flying fish best.

Fact: I once had a little brother.

Fact: I don't like the dark.

Fact: There is nothing I don't know about vocal jazz and blues.

Fact: I am a rock. And I feel nothing. Ever.

I use the rest of the bog roll to wipe my eyes and let it all flutter down, where it hangs stupid and pink off the branch of a tree, and now I feel bad because it looks crap and the tree was nice before.

A dark cloud is heaving itself out of the tree tops. It spills and separates; it is birds, lifting and looping. I watch forever because it's crazy-beautiful; I wish Johnny was here to see it.

'That's a murmuration of starlings,' says a voice from behind me.

Hi I'm Rufus!

I don't turn round.

'Just before dusk is the best time to see them. They're performing their aerial dance as they choose their communal night-time shelter. In winter we get as many as a hundred thousand, all dancing together.'

The birds look like someone's moving a giant magnet through them. I could stare at them all evening.

He takes a picture with his phone. 'Trish sent me to find you.'

I scowl. 'Don't you have some more games to play?'

He shrugs. 'I don't think anyone was paying much attention. Where are you from?'

'Where are *you* from? Sound like you've swallowed a dictionary.'

It's getting dark, but I can feel his blush from here.

'Well, I'm actually from Surrey, but I went to school in the north of Scotland...'

I'm not interested; I watch the starlings swirl. I wish I had my music with me; their dance would go with one of Ella's improvised scats just perfect.

'...a boarding school called Gordonstoun. We learnt a lot about seamanship when we used to take the school's sailing boat out on expeditions. That's why they took me on at TeamSkill.'

I've got myself together again now.

I don't know why this boy's come up here. If I was him, I wouldn't get within ten metres of me for ruining his team game.

I lean my head against the railing and close my eyes.

Rufus's voice drifts in and out and the night settles like the tide.

Sun

Big mistake to fall asleep hanging out of the top of a life raft in the burning sun.

I unstick my cheek from the rubber and try to open my eyes.

Sun slices, burning the back of my neck raw. I lick my cracked lips and duck back inside.

Something rolls under my foot. The torch. *At least I've found the torch.* I flick it on and it gives a feeble glare.

I reach for another water sachet. Stop.

I stare again at the knife, the sun cream, the fishing line with its row of hooks.

The tiny plastic packet of matches nudges my knee. I pick it up and stare at them.

Three matches left.

Three water sachets left.

I don't know how many days that is to die.

I think of Coral's face, pale as the moon in the watery cabin; think of her billowing hair stroking my cheek.

I curl up tight at the bottom of my flickering world and close my eyes.

Nudge.

Something is butting against my hip beneath the raft. I jolt up, heart thudding.

Nudge.

Bigger this time; harder. More insistent. I draw my legs up and press against the walls, holding my breath.

Nudge.

And this time I think I see something pressing up against the base of the raft. It's smooth and muscled and solid. A whale? A shark?

Panicking, I grab the safety knife, then a voice in my head screams, *No, no — you'll puncture the raft.* I throw the knife down, trembling.

It's under the raft now and I drum with my feet to bash it, again and again, on its rocky head, its jagged back.

I huddle in the bottom of the sagging raft, shivering, too tired to fight any more.

And then everything stops.

Tree

Bump.

It takes me a moment to think what's different. And then I realise that I'm no longer moving.

The raft is bumping against something gently. The floor beneath my legs is still. The sound of the restless, tugging roof canopy has stopped.

I push up through the roof and shield my eyes against the sudden sunlight.

Something is waving at me; something with blurry fronds like hands.

A tree.

I blink. In the tree there is a bird, and below the tree there is a rock.

A rock. A bird. A tree.

The raft is caught up on the rock by its trailing rope, and the water around the rock is white-blue and shiversshiversshivers in the sun.

Before me, a long white beach lies open like a blank page.

Sea has turned to land.

I clamber inside to shove all the stuff into the Red Nylon Bag, and when I climb back up through the roof, I almost fall and the raft slides and bounces.

Then I slide off the side of the raft into warm water. When I try to stand, I can't. My legs are liquid.

I crouch in the shallows, the raft butting up against me, half-deflated. Somewhere in the back of my mind I know that it's useless now, that the sharp rocks pierced the raft as I slept, but I'm staring at the fronded shadows raking the sand, the clotted darkness of the forest's edge, the white-gold shore.

And like a dreamer, I leave the raft bobbing against the rocks and half swim, half wade through the lazy shallows, over the sucking sand and through the dragging breakers, stumbling, splashing, till I'm on the beach.

And I throw my bag down and fall to my knees and stare and stare.

First Steps

A million years later, I wobble to the forest's edge.

I don't know how long I knelt there in the sand.

I stare up at the palm trees; stare into the forest. At the other end of the bay is a cliff that looks like a mountain. And all this time, the sun pounds and throbs.

I crawl under a palm tree and try to think.

'So there are three things you should always do first in order to survive.' Steve's voice, with his Cockney twang.

I don't remember what they are.

I stare at my hands; untie my hoodie from my waist. Then I place the Red Nylon Bag on the sand and take out a water sachet. A lot of crumpled energy-bar wrappers flutter out.

I lay out all my things carefully. Line them up like a row of toys.

Then I strip off my filthy leggings. My feet are blistered. My legs are dirty and bruised. They have blood streaks down them where I must have scraped them trying to get out of the plane.

Don't think of that. Don't think of her hair.

I peel off my damp top. Lay it out in the sun to dry. Sit

36

in my bra and pants. Think about opening another sachet of water. Don't.

Instead I take out the tangled earphones from the pocket of my hoodie and put them in my ears. Remember I have no iPod to attach them to.

There's something else in the pocket: a little sweet wrapped in a twist of paper.

'Here, have a sweet to take your mind off it.' Hi I'm Rufus!'s voice, posh as plums.

When I put it into my mouth, its sweetness bursts and makes my cheeks ache with the sugar-shock of it; I suck and stare over the shifting, sighing ocean. Take the sticky sweet wrapper and press it to my tongue.

There's no antiseptic – *threw it overboard* – so I take the sun cream and squeeze it from its little tube and rub it in over my cuts, my grazes, my blood-streaked legs.

I take my damp hoodie and fold it into a pillow. I walk unsteadily over the beach and put my pillow down. Drain the last mouthful of vodka. Lying down on the hot, beating sand, I gaze at the seabirds wheeling over the sea and try to ignore the gnawing feeling in my belly. The last thing I ate was a sandwich on the plane from Heathrow.

But I have water.

'But only three sachets. What are you going to do when your water runs out? What are you going to do, Frances?' Steve's voice, in my head.

I lick my lips. Blink tears back. Blink them dry.

Rock girls don't cry.

I force myself to not cry.

I am an island.

Because that wastes tears, and tears are water.

I bet that's what *Hi I'm Steve!* would say.

Be Careful What You Wish For

I stab the sachet too hard this time and nearly lose half of it as the water spurts through my fingers out into the sand.

I press my mouth to the hole and glugglugglug till it's all gone and I'm just sucking air from the shrivelled plastic. It helps my thirst – a little.

Two sachets left.

I put them inside the Red Nylon Bag and stand up shakily.

My legs are jellified and sun-slapped where I didn't put the cream on properly.

Have to find more water.

I take deep breaths to steady myself and sway over to the forest's edge where it's shaded. Even that short walk makes me pant like a heart attack and I clutch my sides with my hands, as if that's going to help.

I lean against a tree that looks like a giant pineapple. Beneath, dry leaves crackle in the sand, and it's cool here in the shade. In front of me, the forest shivers with strange noises: *whoops* and *caaaas* and *kukukukukukk*-ing sounds.

I swallow the sand that's in my throat and move forward into the jungle. It looks dark in there. And I still don't like the dark.

I get about five metres because:

I have no shoes on my feet.

The ground is prickled with dead leaves.

Creeper things are barring my way in all directions.

Those screaming noises are creeping me out.

So.

I'm left with the beach and the sea and the mountain.

I pick all the prickles and dry leaves out of the soles of my feet and set off the other way.

The sun is high in the sky and flings my shadow sharp beneath me. I wonder if I should put my clothes back on, but it's too much bother and much too hot, so I just walk in my bra and pants, quick as I can because the sand is burning, burning.

But it's slow, walking over the sand, so I go to the sea's edge and let the water cool my scalded feet, and it's nice here, just me and the water. At some stage I untie my hair; let it straggle over my neck to stop the sun biting it.

I stare and stare over all that ocean, into all that blue. The horizon is milky where the sea and sky touch.

It's easy at first, climbing the rocks.

The bristly surface feels good on my bare feet and it's easy to grip. A tiny breeze freshens the hot air. I climb and climb because I've always liked climbing things.

I even get into a kind of rhythm, despite the beating sun.

After a while, I make it to an overhang, where a bent tree clings and grapples for the sky.

I hold on to the tree for support and look down across the bay.

For some reason my heart is stuttering and jerking. I take deep breaths to clear my head, tighten my hands on the tree trunk.

I see that I'm no way near to the highest point – not even a little. The mountain rears behind me, impossibly high. But I'm at the top of the cliff and I can see well enough, despite the sun-spots blinding my eyes.

I crouch on the dry, scabby ground and look over my new world.

There is only endless sea and sky and the huddled jungle.

The sun pulses. Below me, the sea winks and twinkles.
I am on an island.
It is small and high and rocky.
It is joined to another, smaller one.
No houses. No huts. No signs of life.
I am totally and completely

alone.

Would You Rather?

'Would you rather: sniff a tramp's bum or eat a dog-poo sandwich?'

Me and Johnny always play the same game going up Sydenham Hill. We get off at the train station and walk past the housing estate and the big posh houses.

As always, I wonder what it'd be like to break inside, to have a wander round, maybe drink a little something from the cocktail cabinet, make myself a salad from their well-stocked American-style fridge; have a little swim in their pool, use their gym.

'Would you rather,' Johnny repeats, 'sniff a tramp's bum or eat a dog-poo sandwich? Tell me, Frannie.'

'Hmmm…' I pretend to consider, but inside I'm in the kitchen of one of these houses, shoes off, Ella crackling out of the top-of-the-range speakers, a nice glass of Pinot on the go. 'The tramp's bum,' I say. 'Every time. Much as I like eating dog poo.'

Johnny goes off into gales of giggles and then falls silent as he thinks up another one. This takes him till we get to the play park, where he has to have a go on the witch's hat.

'Got one,' he says.

'OK, Monkey,' I say, spinning him. 'This had better be good. The last one was way too easy.'

'It is, it is. Would you rather: spend the night in a deep, dark wood all alone or…kiss Big Wayne with tongues?'

I stop the witch's hat and turn him round to face me. 'You've really thought about this, haven't you, Monkey?'

I'm keeping my voice light but inside I'm thinking of Big Wayne with his oily black hair and those hands that he's always shoving into bags of cheese 'n' onion crisps.

'You're gorgeous, you know that?' he said to me once, when Cassie was asleep, running his hands through my hair. 'You could be my backing singer, love. You've only got to ask.'

And he was playing his own music on the stereo, his own crappy band and crappy voice crooning away, curling round us like fag smoke. His cheese 'n' onion breath and cheese 'n' onion fingers.

'Kiss Big Wayne?' I say. 'Ugh. It's got to be the deep, dark woods. Anyway,' I say, ruffling his hair, 'I wouldn't be alone, would I? I'd have *you*.'

'No, no,' Johnny says, 'that's cheating. You've got to be on your own. *All* alone or it doesn't count.'

'We-ell, I'd be thinking of you and you'd be thinking of me and that would be the next best thing, yeah?'

'Yeah, Frannie. Spin me again?'

'Only if you let me on too.'

And I climb on and sit facing him and our legs are intertwined and the sunlight is spinning and our smiles are flying and, just for this moment, I am, we are, truly, truly happy.

Space Girl

The beach has a single tree on it, right in the middle and separate from the forest.

One Tree Beach.

My new home.

Climbing down the way I've come seems impossible in

this sun so I walk along the top of the cliffs instead, banked by the mountain on my right side and the endless sea on my left. If I crane my neck I can see the bright yellow paint-splodge of my raft, still caught up in the rocks.

There's a trail on the left that looks like it's been made by animals and which looks shady, so I take it and start to weave my way down. I soon regret it. Any animal that's made this track must be as small as a mouse because rocks and thorn bushes and brambles bar my way, and it's not as shady as I thought. Nothing stops this pulsing heat, and I'm tired and my feet are sore, so sore.

It's turning into jungle and what if I lose my way?

But then who cares, because there's nothing to go back for, is there? Only two sachets of water.

I lick my cracked lips with a dry tongue and walk on.

I must have caught my foot on something because, next thing I know, I'm falling, falling, and the thorn bushes are wrenched out of my hands as I grab them and rocks are skittering past and the ground has fallen away and there are no trees in this dry dusty ground and I

bash my leg on something and rip my nails and grab a root
    and
    hang,
    feet scrabbling on loose gravel,
    and all around me is
    air.

Marshmallow

Another metre and I would have sailed over the sheer drop like a shooting star.

Fran Stanton followed a rabbit trail and fell off a cliff. The end.

Shaking, I place one hand over the other on this over-hanging branch and use my feet to edge my way up the gravel to the firmer rocks. It's lucky I don't get vertigo; the beach swims below me. My hands and feet hurt like hell and there's something tickling my eye as it trickles down my face.

Somehow I get back to One Tree Beach.

I still haven't found any water.

I collapse under the palm trees by the edge of the forest, but not too close because there are things in there screaming and the shadows are stretching and the sun's all streaky like melted marshmallow.

So it's getting dark.

I'll have to spend the night here on this beach, alone.

I wade into the sea and drag what's left of the raft over the sand to the edge of the forest. There's flat sand and soft sand and sharp rocks, and I don't know if I should care about the sharp rocks, but the raft is ruined anyway so a few more holes won't matter.

I pull on my top and leggings then root about in the Red Nylon Bag for the torch. It throws out a thin beam and I swing it around the darkening beach and forest.

These trees aren't like the trees in Brockwell Park.

They're tall and swaying and hanging with green things that look like giant seeds. Fronds like ogre's fingers.

It's so dark in the forest.

I drag the raft over to One Tree and sit with my back to the forest so I don't have to see.

I arrange the life raft round me and stare over the ocean. It looks like someone's got a brush and dipped it in pink and orange paint and dragged it across the sky and the sea, streaking it all together. I may as well be on another planet.

I want my London sky back, blank and dull and grey.

I keep the torch on.

As the sun sinks, the noises rise.

Rats and Monsters

The torch beam is dying.

Something is behind me, rustling.

I hear it rooting around in the dry leaves.

I shrink further and further into my life raft, into my hoodie and, when that doesn't work, I slip outside of myself altogether and hover at the top of One Tree.

Dark shapes, squeaking and scrabbling in the leaves at the edge of the forest. I see one of them creep across to the life raft and scramble over to Other Fran's leg. Soon she'll feel its little clicking claws dig into her skin. I want to warn her but I'm scared to come down.

There are other things out there too. Howling and calling and screaming. One of them is restless and snuffling like a pig; it's giving low, mean growls as if it's warning off intruders.

The girl covers her ears and sobs, but silently – ssshhh, she doesn't want them to know she's there.

Make it all stop.

Voodoo

Hunting is a work of death, and it attracts death.

That's what the card in the museum says.

Of all the displays in the Horniman Museum, it's the one with the voodoo dolls and the bird hunters that scares Johnny the most.

The voodoo tribes of Haiti put plastic dolls' heads inside empty rum bottles. They squeeze them in tight and they stuff money into skulls and place them all on an altar. They believe it will connect them with their dead relatives and heal them somehow.

On the days Johnny's annoying me, this is the gallery I take him to first.

'No, no, get off me,' he wails.

So I grip his arm tighter and frogmarch him to the African room, where the voodoo altar shuts him up at once because he's so terrified he can't even speak.

Rum bottles and smiley dolls' heads and mirrors.

If there's a voodoo altar in this jungle I'll die, I know I will. And it'll be what I deserve. I deserve it all for what I've done. I know I'm a monster but I don't like the dark. I don't like the dark and it's creeping towards me. I can see its shadow from the forest, so make it stop.

Make it stop now.

I curl up tight on my side; draw in my knees and all the time the memories bleed and burn.

Wild Thing

Smoke is billowing out behind me; I can smell it, can feel it scorch my bones.

And now I'm running, racing past the playground, past the sports block, laughing and sobbing madly.

I don't stop till I've got to Brixton High Street. As I stoop down, panting, by the Tube station, two fire engines come blaring past, sirens wailing blueblueblue.

OhmyGod.

Oh my God.

I haven't finished yet.

Careless of passers-by, I start to run again. I'm free; I'm wild.

'Careful, love –'

'Out the way,' I call, my heart skidding, as I slam into the market, grab handfuls of fruit, of nuts, of mangoes – of anything, just because I can.

'*Losers*,' I bawl, swerving to avoid the stall-people shouting and grabbing at me.

I duck inside the arcade, head for the toilets.

I don't even want all this stuff; I leave it by the side of the sinks, where a woman is washing her hands. She stares at me open-mouthed.

I stare back.

'What's the matter?' I say.

Ha ha.

I leave the toilets. I'm in Brixton Village and no one's waiting for me outside; the coast's clear. I zigzag in and out of cafes, taking tips from tables, swiping half-finished drinks, toppling chairs.

'Oy, you –'

I whip a scarf from a vintage stand – just because it's bright, just because I can – and tie it round my head, laughing. I bomb it out of there because they're really angry now, they're coming running.

Duck under the railway arches and then out again, quick as you like, because Wayne's here; he's shuffling notes with some guy in the shadows, doing his deals.

Quickquick, before he sees me, I back away. I knock a kid off his skateboard and mouth sorrysorrysorry and swerve past the shoppers, the cafe owners, back to the Tube station. I race down the steps, three at a time, swiping some guy's Oyster card from his hand but not before I've vaulted over the barrier and I'm running and hooting; people are avoiding me, I'm a wild thing. I push past three layers of waiting passengers and into a crowded Tube train.

The doors hiss shut and I roll up and frickin
    kill myself
    laughing.

Thud

Sometime around dawn, I doze off, but it is then that the birds start.

Clacking and trilling and screeching. There are low howls that rise and rise into a wail, and all the time a clacking racket like ten thousand cars are getting into gear.

Where there are birds, there are bird hunters.

They stretch animal skin over a bird's skull and place it

on their heads to do their hunting dance. Makes them look the big man. Then, when the hunt is on, they wear their bird headdresses to trick and distract the real birds.

The howling I can hear won't go away. I shrink my legs up well inside my plastic nest in case a bird hunter taps my skin with his bird beak. Just before he draws his knife.

When I wake again, the wind is shrieking louder than the birds and I have to bury myself into the foot of One Tree and wrap the rubber sheeting of the raft around me to stop it from blowing away.

Dark noises surround me:

> *thud*
> *thud*
> *thud*.

One sounds just by my head and I scream.
I dare not look, I dare not look
    at what it is that is making that noise.

Stab

My legs are on fire.

It's like a million ants have buried under my skin and are having a party. I scratch my ankle and it feels so good, but I don't want to stop now I've started and my legs are *crawling* and there are hard little bumps all over my skin.

This time it really is morning.

The life raft has mostly blown away and I am buried into the base of the tree, clutching only the roof.

My mouth is dry.

I panic when I can't see the water sachets but it's OK – they're still in the Red Nylon Bag where I left them. I stab one open with my knife and suck the water greedily and it's lovely and plasticky and warm. I drink and drink and it takes only seconds to empty it.

One left.

Thud.

I spin around but it's only one of the green nuts falling from a palm tree into the sand. I always thought coconuts were brown and hairy but this one's green and sort of smooth. I pick it up and shake it.

Liquid.

Heart thudding, I prise at it with my nails but it won't split. The outer casing's thick and smooth like leather. It doesn't look like a coconut but I know I want what I can hear inside.

I scrabble around for the knife but my hand's so shaky it keeps slipping. Again and again I hack at the casing.

A few chunks of hard-as-leather skin fly off.

I'm drooling now, swearing. Nearly slice into my leg, I'm so mad.

Eventually, I turn the nut thing on its end and grip it between my bare knees. Stab over and over again with the stupid knife. Every time the nut moves, the liquid inside mocks me.

I lick my lips and try to calm down. The last water sachet I drank – *Only one more left. Only one more left* – has made no difference at all to the inside of my mouth, which feels full of sticks and stones and sand.

I hold the nut tighter between my knees and grip the knife in both fists. If I slip, it'll basically drive a spike straight into my thigh. I imagine the blood shooting up high and pretty like a flare.

Thunk.

The knife makes a tiny dent in the top of the could-be coconut.

In the end, it takes thirty stabs to split the nut open and all the liquid spurts out over my hands and on to the sand.

I. Am. Not. Going. To. Cry.

When I try to put my leggings on, the fabric scratches and snags on my burning legs. Each of my bites has turned into a watery boil so that my legs look like bubble wrap. They throb so much I can hardly stand.

I think of the spiky forest floor and rip off my T-shirt sleeves with the help of the knife. Then I bind them like socks over my feet.

There's a rock sticking out of the water that is curved just like a fang, so if I see it, I'll know I'm home.

One Tree Beach. Fang Rock.

I pick up my knife, limp along the beach, then take a deep breath and turn left into the forest.

I am going to find water.

Flying Fish and Torture Chairs

Children's shrieks explode like fireworks.

Two red howler monkeys bare their broken teeth.

Wellied mummies push their darlings to see the dead dogs' heads.

There's all sorts of stuff in here; you can never see it all because there's always something you've not noticed, in the back of some display, or maybe there's a different way of looking at something.

Down in the basement gallery, in among the crocodile death masks and the African puppets and the Japanese merman, is an actual torture chair from the Spanish Inquisition. It's made of iron and wood and stands by itself in its own display cabinet. Just in case you miss it.

The torture chair does spiking, racking and skull-crushing, so I suppose you could say it multitasks.

The people I've imagined being screwed into that chair include:

    Angela, my social worker.

    Miss Bright, my English teacher.

    Sally, the school counsellor.

    Big Wayne.

    And, of course, Cassie.

Me and Johnny used to come here all the time. That's where the would-you-rather? game started.

'Would you rather: sit in the torture chair or swim with piranhas?'

'Would you rather: sit in the torture chair or have a shark eat all your toes?'

Me and Johnny sit by the entrance to the aquarium, waiting for the guide to look away so we can get in without a ticket. We reckon he just pretends he doesn't see. He's nice; hums a cheerful song as he does his walkabout and helps the schoolkids cheat on their worksheets.

'See this here: it's a merman, see? Except it's not really. It's just a monkey's head stuck to a fish's body with little rat-claw front legs.'

The kids *ooh* and *aah* and we pretend we're with them for a bit till Johnny gets bored.

'Hungry,' he whines.

I give him half my Snickers. 'Shush. You can't be hungry already. Look at the ostrich, Johnny.'

He likes the baby ostrich best. This frozen baby gazes up at us with its Disney lashes. The stuffed bloodhound in the dog cabinet looks worried sick at all the attention he's getting.

I turn to show Johnny but he's gone.

He went a long time ago.

The Horniman Museum's only a train stop and a bus ride away. The main reason we came was because most of it's free to get into and they don't check your tickets at Sydenham Hill. But now I often come by myself and sit in the Natural History room and the African room and the Centenary room instead of going to school. Learning's learning, isn't it?

And, just for a moment, I smell smoke again.

I wonder if Miss has seen what I've done. I wonder if they've sent everyone home. All those teachers, getting an extra day off away from the kids. They should thank me, really.

Wish my heart wasn't still hammering.

Wish my stomach would stop flipping every time I think of it.

I take out the chocolate I've nicked from the gift shop and sit and watch the flying fish pretend to fly and the howler monkeys pretend to howl. And it's peaceful here because half-term was over ages ago and all the screaming babies have gone home.

'Shouldn't you be at school?'

The guide's standing next to me, looking over my shoulder.

'Left school, haven't I?'

'How old are you then?'

'Seventeen,' I lie.

'Don't look it.'

'What's it to you, grandad?' I scowl at him and move

away, deliberately dropping my Fairtrade chocolate wrapper on the floor.

He finds me in the Centenary room, staring at the jars full of stuffed birds.

'Old Freddie Horniman couldn't stop collecting things,' he says.

I ignore him and turn my attention to the brass hunting dogs' collars. They've got them on the pit bulls in Brixton, to make their owners look hard.

'In the end his house was so full that he and his family were forced to move out and live somewhere else. Christmas Eve, it was.'

'Oh yeah?' I say.

He chuckles. 'Turned his house into a museum, but still he wouldn't stop collecting, so in 1898 they pulled it all down and started building this place.'

I make myself look bored. 'What's this, a history lesson?'

The guide shakes his head. 'Cross little thing, aren't you?' He leans forward and whispers. 'I think, that if you're going to steal chocolate from our shop, the least you can do is listen to an old man give his guided tour. Haven't spoken to a soul all day.' He gestures towards my pockets. 'Come on, what else you got in there?'

I roll my eyes, but something about his manner makes me turn out my pockets. I have:

A walrus key ring.

A sachet of basil and strawberry bath salts.

A postcard with a photo of the baby ostrich on it.

The old man sighs. 'I think I'd better take these, don't you?'

I scowl, but my heart is beating African drumbeats *bangbangbang*. I don't want him to call Security. If I take the fire exit, I can be out of here in a blink.

'Used to be a policeman, didn't I?' the man is saying. He

puts my stolen goods carefully on his chair. 'So, shall we start with the hunters' headdresses?'

And I stand there like a kid in a classroom as he tells me all about the African bird hunters and their beaded masks.

Still, at least it kills time because I really can't

I really can't

go home yet.

Are You Listening?

Sometimes I imagine talking to her.

I imagine that I've done what Angela asks and have visited her.

The way I picture it, there'll be a glass partition, because of the risk of infection. There's always a glass partition in the films.

'*Miss,*' I'd say. '*Are you listening? Do you want to know why I did it?*

'*Well. It was you. You started it. You. Started. It.*

'*When they sent Angela round, that first time, I knew it was you. I knew what you'd gone and done.*

'*It was in your eyes, that last time I went to your stupid writing club. Your lying, purple-shadowed, traitor's eyes.*'

I imagine her looking back at me, and, because of the bandages, there'll just be her lips moving, forming those words.

'*What's that you're saying, Miss?*

'*Magnum frickin opus?*

'*Yeah, right.*'

Pool

I'm glad I have a knife.

The trees and creepers claw so thickly that often I can't get through and have to turn round. The whole time, I'm twitchy, waiting for something to come galloping out of the thicket or land on my head.

The forest floor is a rustle of dead leaves and, as I watch, a rat shoots out from behind some bushes. There must be snakes and spiders and frogs.

Crazy sounds, screeches and booms.

Somewhere, a bird is calling, over and over again. *Oh dear me*, it seems to say. *Oh dear* **me**.

Even though it's early, the heat presses in and sweat dribbles behind my neck and down my sides. I've passed the same log three times and am beginning to think I'm in that scene in *The Blair Witch Project* when the guy goes crazy and chucks the map away and the girl screams at him 'cause really, that's when she knows they're all going to die.

A muddy pool.

It shines dully through the trees like a badly cleaned mirror.

Water.

I hack at the few remaining creepers and slide down into the clearing. Run to the pool and crouch down. It's definitely water but I stop still when I see what's lying in it:

One dead rat, its mouth pulled back to show its little brown teeth.

Something nasty wrapped up in a spider's web.

Lots of murky brown stuff, which I suppose must be snake crap and worse.

But the water's still in my scooped hands and, even though it's warm and brown and smelly, I'm so thirsty after my trek that I nearly –

'If you drink dirty water, you die, plain and simple. You get sickness and diarrhoea, you lose any fluids your body has…'

Hi I'm Steve!'s sneering voice nearly makes me down it, just to show him.

Show him what? He's not here – nobody's here.

So I stand up again. Hold on to a tree when my head swims. I can't think clearly; my thoughts are all muddy, like the pond.

There's something niggling me; something that Steve said. Something about water. At least I can collect some, I think. I can take it back with me. But I can't even do that, can I? Because I haven't brought a bottle.

After a long time, I get up and wipe my eyes. It's steaming hot in the jungle.

Sweat runs down my bra and trickles into my armpits. I retie my torn-up T-shirt shoes, which are bloody and filthy.

There's nothing for it but to trek my way back to One Tree Beach.

Loser

I can't find One Tree Beach.

I break through the trees after what seems like hours of walking, only to find that there's a strange sucking swamp of tangled roots instead of the sea.

No Fang Rock. No One Tree.

I hiss in my breath. Wonder if I can somehow climb through the swamp and make my way through the roots to the sea. But when I put my foot in the mud, it squelches and bubbles and then I'm in up to my waist, arms flailing.

'*Help*,' I cry, but what a stupid thing to be calling, here in this gulping, sucking swamp. Of course there's no one to help me.

I crawl out of the mud myself, arms trembling. I've lost both of my T-shirt shoes.

This is a hateful place.

I think of Joker during survival training:

'*So will there be crocodiles then or what?*'

Steve smirking as he nods. '*There'll be crocs so big they'll kill a man quicker than he can grab his knife.*'

Joker fist-punches the air.

'*And can they climb trees?*' *Tiny asks, standing close to Trish, arms folded.*

Steve nods. '*Sure they can. And they're fast too. Faster than a horse at full gallop.*'

I trip barefoot back through the jungle. Everything looks the same. Something bars my way and it's a grove of fallen trees, criss-crossed crazily across my path. Have I been here before? I don't know if I have or haven't.

Panting and cursing, I clamber through the netted branches. Try another direction.

All the time, I'm listening for the sounds of galloping behind me.

Shall I?

Shall I? Shall I? Shall I?

I trail my finger over the sharp edges of my last water sachet; squelch its contents; hold it to my cheek.

Big mistake to lose my way and get tired and thirsty; stupid to go trekking in the forest and sweat out the rest of the water that was in my body.

I'm scratched and torn. My mouth burns.

Slumped under One Tree, I realise that I've done everything wrong.

I trace my finger over the plastic. It feels plump in my hands, smooth against my cheek.

Whatever happens, I will not drink that water till I've found more.

I drink that water with my eyes.

Countdown

- No. of water sachets left: 0
- No. of attempts to break into could-be coconuts: 8
- No. of times switched torch on in the night: 17

Thirst

I lick the condensation from the underside of the life raft, drop by drop.

It's over my head, bright and yellow. The sun is burning through it, into my head, into my brain.

I thirst.

I think about going back to the muddy pool. But I can't drink that. If I do, I will die.

I think about drinking seawater, just a little. But Steve's voice screams at me, '*Don't do it. Don't do it.*'

I look down at the green kernel in my hand. All around me are the broken shells of those that have split before I could get out the liquid. I don't think they can be coconuts because coconut flesh is hard and white – this stuff is green and wet and stringy. I decide to call them could-be nuts.

At least their flesh is wet. I sit surrounded by their skin as I've been scooping out the mush inside with my fingers. But I need their liquid.

Painfully, I reach again for the knife.

If I breathe through my nose, the heat is fiercer but at least I don't feel dry air sucking through the dry sawdust that is my mouth.

I sit gazing at the sea as it laps and licks at the sand. One Tree is against my back and the wind has blown the life raft on to the rocks.

I suppose I should wade in and drag it back to make my shelter.

I suppose I should find a way of pinning it down for the night.

I suppose, I suppose.

I'm staring at the sea, holding my torch and my knife, when I see a small, dark object in the shallows. It can't be a could-be nut because they're round and this is square.

After a million years, I get up the energy to stick my knife into the sand, make my legs stand up and walk across to the sea's edge. Each step is like wading through syrup; the heat pushes against me and my legs are treacle. I stop when I feel the warm water seep through my toes; kneel down and pick up the object.

It's a package.

It's wrapped tightly in white plastic and is the size of a shoebox.

I carry it carefully back to my tree and sink back down in the sand.

It takes for ever to get inside, almost as bad as getting into the could-be nuts.

I hack at the tape with the knife and tug and pull until all the tape is off and the package is exposed.

A small cardboard box with a picture of a sailing ship on the side. *SEVEN SEAS*, it says, stamped all over in blue and green. I pull away the perforated flap and lift the lid.

Inside it's crammed full with small white sachets, like a box of After Eight mints. I pull one out and look at it.

Seven Seas Eezi-Meal, it says, *Chili Mac with Beef*.

My stomach starts to growl. I haven't eaten anything but scoopfuls of mushy could-be nut flesh since I've been on the island. I pull out another packet. Tear it open. Sniff.

It smells faintly of cheesy-puff crisps.

Instructions for Cheesy Fish Pie, I read. *Simply mix contents with 150 ml boiling water and serve.*

I pour the contents into my mouth.

When I finish coughing and trying to swallow about five

tons of dried fish-flavoured sawdust, I pull all the sachets out and scatter them across the beach; kick the box across the beach; kick One Tree again and again with my bare feet and scream.

My voice is dry as a dust bowl but I don't care; I fall to my knees in the sand and

HOWL

Hello Kitty

Carefully, hardly daring to breathe, I place the tip of my knife over the could-be nut.

I've spent what seems like hours chipping away the hard shell, and there's the top of it, all ready to pierce. I'm not going to use the rock this time because I can't afford to let the liquid splurt out all over the sand again.

Not this time.

Not when there are hardly any could-be nuts left.

Wedged between two stones is an open packet of *Hearty Stew with Chicken 'n' Mushroom*. I've poured half of it out into a scraped-out could-be nut shell. All they need is liquid.

I lick my cracked lips.

Take a breath.

Cut away with my knife to make a small opening.

Now.

My knife breaks through and liquid sprays out and *quickquickquick* I shake the juice into the open packet, into the shell of dried food.

Then I press the could-be nut to my lips and drink and drink and drink.

It's heaven. It's bliss. It's fresh and clean and almost fizzy in my mouth, soothing my dry throat, plumping out my cracked tongue.

'Thank you, rock,' I say.

I take another could-be nut.

Crack, split, drink.

And another.

I'm getting good at this.

I count the could-be nuts I find lying on the sand. Seven.

The rest are clustered tight in their palm trees, high out of reach. But there are lots of palm trees fringing the forest. And I could get a stick.

The drink has given me energy again. I collect the nuts and pile them neatly by One Tree and think I could even have a swim later. The water shimmers whitebluewhite and is studded with stars like a gypsy's wedding dress.

White with a splash of red.

I blink.

There's something in the water.

Something small and bright and red, winking as it's nosed by the tide on to the wet sand. I leave the could-be nuts and wade into the water. The sea nudges its gift to my feet like a dog with a ball.

I pick it up and begin to laugh; of all the things the sea spits out, this has got to be the most useful, right?

It's a Hello Kitty washbag.

Inside:

Turquoise nail polish
Eyeliner
Vaseline lip balm with cocoa butter
A nail file
And a box of tampons, unopened.

It must be Coral's. No way *Hi I'm Trish!* would use that shade of varnish on her nails.

I think of swirling hair and shiver.

The cat's face on the bag blinks back at me.

But I have food.

Back on the beach, I find a stick and stir the mixture in the packet, then I stir the mixture in the shell. There. I have a starter and a main. With the could-be nut mush I even have dessert. So maybe my luck is finally changing.

Maybe the sea will just keep chucking me the things I need –

some cans of ice-cold Coke would be nice and a couple of
cheeseburgers and a Snickers bar —

and my life will literally be just perfect.

Eezi Does It

The Seven Seas package contains twenty freeze-dried
Eezi-Meals.

What they're supposed to taste of:
• New Orleans Rice with Shrimp
• Beef Lasagne
• Chili Mac with Beef
• Hearty Stew with Chicken 'n' Mushroom
• Spaghetti 'n' Meat
• Pink Blancmange 'n' Berries
• Apple Pie 'n' Custard
• Lemon Meringue Supreme

What they actually taste of:
• Cold puke
• Warm cheese
• Dry sawdust

I put a dollop of Hearty Stew on the stick and eat. I eat it all,
every last bit.

Yum frickin yum.

Bubbles

After I finish my breakfast of Apple Pie 'n' Custard washed down with could-be nut water, I look at the sea and know I have to get in there.

It feels so good just to wash; to splash around in the shallows and lie on my back with the sun on my face and the waves tickling my cheeks and forehead.

When I duck my head below the water, I can see shooting shoals of fish, zipping and zigzagging over the sandy bed and around the rocks. I try to touch one with my finger and it twitches away.

I take another breath and dive lower; swim further out to where the water deepens and darkens.

'Look at me, Frannie. Look at me!'

Johnny, standing by the pool's edge, skinny knees shivering.

'Watch me jump, Frannie.'

'I'm watching, Monkey, I'm watching.'

I've always liked to swim.

This sea is brimful of sky; it fizzes with bubbles of light as I swim and dive, heading towards the horizon. Now there is coral foresting the ocean floor. It's purple and red and mysterious. I drift in the water on my tummy, reaching my hands down towards it.

Fish flinch and shiver.

When I come up for breath I'm dizzy and alone. I could go on and on, could keep on swimming. There is nothing and no one to stop me. The thought nags me.

What if I just keep on going?

What if?

I hang in the water, pulsing. The sea holds its breath.

Then I turn, back to the white curl that is the beach, back to the island.

SpongeBob SquarePants

Maybe it's something to do with the tide, but it's happened again. The sea is feeling generous today.

The first gift is hanging off a rock, bright yellow and startling.

This time I recognise it at once.

My SpongeBob SquarePants bikini.

I sort of remember lifting it from Primark. It's turn-your-stomach skimpy. I don't know why I took it. I pick it up, and SpongeBob winks at me with his giant blue eyes. It's only the bikini bottoms. I'm hot though.

I have a wash in the sea, strip off my dirty clothes and put the bikini bottoms on. It feels weird being topless. I feel like I'm being watched, but of course there's no one here to see Fran Stanton's boobs. I push the water away and launch out and it feels nice, the bath-warm seawater on my skin. I should cover up soon though. Don't want to get sunburnt.

Imagine.

Then I find the second offering in the shallows. I pull it out of the water and it's fat and heavy and streaming.

A black rucksack.

It could be one of the boys' on the plane, I think. At first it seems to be empty, most of its contents swirled away by the sea. But right at the bottom is a red Nike T-shirt. It's XL, which is good. Means I'll have something to wear at night, and I can hug it over my knees when it gets chilly. There's half a packet of chewing gum and a Lambert & Butler fag packet, containing two wet ciggies. I lay these on a rock to dry. Not that I'm stupid enough to use one of my last matches to light them. But it's nice to know they're there.

And there's something in one of the pockets: a photo, much folded and refolded, and almost destroyed by the sea. I lay it out on the rock and look at what's left of it.

It's Joker – Kieran. The man that's with him must be his dad, because they have the same eyes and teeth. They're both grinning away at the camera and holding up cans of lager, even though Joker only looks about twelve in this picture. His dad has his arm around his son's shoulder, loose and easy, and Joker looks happy as hell.

When both the bag and the picture are dry, I refold the photo and zip it back in its pocket. Try not to think of Joker thrashing around on the floor of the plane.

Won't think of that.

The bikini top is strewn further up the beach, so now I have the full set.

Lucky me.

But next to it on the sand is something much more exciting. A pair of sunglasses. They may be fake Ray-Bans, like something swiped from Brixton Market, and they may have an arm missing, but right now they're worth more to me than all the fags in the world.

Well, almost.

I put them on, and it feels amazing, to not be squinting against the harsh sun. I tie my T-shirt over my head so it hangs over my neck, damp and cool from the sea. Then I take two pieces of chewing gum and they burst mint-fierce in my mouth. Make my cheeks ache with drool. Can hardly bear the cold-fire of it, not after so many could-be nuts.

Taking a deep breath, I go to the Red Nylon Bag and take out the little waterproof packet.

Three matches left. Only three.

I take one of the matches in my hand and my hand's trembling now –

blistering pages shrivelling in the heat, crinkling paper, curling, withering, dying –

and I drop the match in the sand.

Now I'm panicking as I can't find it; the sand's covering it. I'm frantically scrabbling in the sand.

'Oh God, no, no,' I moan.

But it's OK, it's here, I've found it.

Shaking, I pick it up and stare at it.

One match. It only took one match.

Fish Might Fly

I'm staring at the flying fish when the police come to get me.

They're frozen for ever in flight, but still sort of beautiful; even if they'll never shoot up into the air; never bounce over the waves.

So I'm in the Natural History Gallery when Bill the guide taps me on the shoulder.

'Sorry, love,' he says.

I know what he means because there's two police officers standing right behind him, looking serious.

'That her?' asks one. She's short and dumpy, and has a Scottish accent. The hairs on her upper lip are pale where she's bleached them.

Bill nods.

I'm cornered, here at the top of the gallery, surrounded by fish and fossils. For an insane moment I think about launching myself over the balcony; perhaps I'll land on the back of the giant walrus's neck and slide all the way down his back to land by the ostriches. Then it's a quick dash out the exit and through the gardens to grab the next bus to Brixton.

Yeah, right.

I lift my chin to face them and turn myself into stone.

'Are you Frances Eileen Stanton of 19A Plover House, Tulse Hill, Brixton?'

Freeze.

'I'll say it again. Is your name Frances Eileen Stanton?'

Freeze.

Sigh. 'You'll be better off if you cooperate. We have reason to believe that, at two fifteen today, you committed a serious act of arson...'

I tune her right out, this policewoman with her Scottish accent, and make myself hover over the centre of the room instead. It's a nice room, a white curved ceiling and with a gallery that runs all the way round the top.

Skeletons leer at me as they march my body down the stairs and past the frozen birds and animals.

People stare. I watch myself stare back and see them flinch away. Watch the schoolgirl who's struggling and smirking in her handcuffs.

I am a rock. I am an island. I am a monster.

Embers

I can't make fire.

I need to make fire.

I remember being in a vodka haze, out in the life raft. Laughing, crying, striking the matches one after another. Trying to scratch the memories away.

Shaking, I place the match back inside its little plastic bag.

Then take it out again.

I make a little pile of dry seaweed in the sand, and strike the match. Lean low and drop in the flickering flame. The seaweed curls and crisps till it's nothing but black glowing edges, flecks that break off and blow in the sand.

I put on some sticks, dry ones I've collected from the beach. Smoke billows, but the fire's not catching the sticks; there's a breeze coming in from the sea.

I swallow as I think of red sparks shooting up from the flare. Matches waving in the dark. The seaweed withers to an ember that burns bright in the sand.

And then goes out.

The fire's not catching.

I lean forward and blow and blow because that's what you're supposed to do, but it's too late; the sparks have all shrivelled and died and there's just smoke.

Two matches left.

This time I build a wall with stones from the beach. I get big ones and stagger with them over to One Tree, where I bury them on their sides till there's a sort of curved wind-break between my fire and the sea.

I wipe my forehead. Sun's going down fast now; there'll soon be no light because when it gets dark on this island, it gets very dark.

And then I'll be alone again with the shadows and the night noises.

So I take some more seaweed; place the smallest twigs around it like a wigwam; take the second match.

Flare.

Bus

'So,' says Sally, the school counsellor, 'what is your greatest fear?'

Wayne-and-extra-strength-lager-and-bruises-and-school-and-what-happens-after-Year-Eleven-and-the-rest-of-my-life-and-Cassie-dying-and-Social-Services-and-empty-fridges-and-after-one-a.m.-on-a-Wednesday-and-Johnny-being-taken-away-and—

What a stupid question.

'I'm not scared of anything,' I say. 'What are you scared of?'

She smiles. 'This isn't about me, Frances. It's about you.'

I want to wipe that smile off her smug face.

'Got any ciggies?' I ask.

Sally pretends not to hear. I hate that.

'Imagine this bus is your life, Frances.'

She's actually waving a toy bus at me which she's taken out of her desk drawer. She must have all sorts of stuff in there. Dolls, probably, for kids to show where they've been touched by paedos. Puppets. Sweeties, to bribe kiddies to tell her their deepest darkest thoughts. She's sick. I vow to take a look in that drawer one of these days.

74

The bus is yellow. A nice, happy colour.

'Imagine this bus is your life and it's full of all the significant people in your life. Now, who is driving the bus, Frances? Who is driving your bus of life?'

Oh for frick's sake.

I give her my widest smile.

'I am,' I say.

She looks grateful for that. 'Good, Frances. So you're in the driving seat. That means you're in control of your life. Now…'

She holds the toy bus out to me and looks serious. She even opens its tiny door.

'If you're in charge of your bus, Frances, who would you like to get off it?'

I take the bus from her; imagine a tiny Wayne and Cassie sitting inside. Think of squeezing Wayne between my fingers till he pops like a bug.

But really there's only one person I want to get off my bus right now, and she's sitting in her classroom grateful as anything that I'm missing English; that I'm not there messing up her precious lesson.

Here's Frances. Let's put her near the teacher's desk. Let's sit her with someone nice. Let's talktalktalk to her and touch her arm to say, well done, you star, and put smiley faces on her report card and let's benicebenicebenice.

Let's tease her out with words,
fake smiles, fake words, fake promises,
so that she will trust me with her rawest, secretest self.
And then I can pull out her heart like a long piece of silly string.
Bitch.

Fizz

It's burning; it's burning nicely.

I'm leaning forward on my elbows and blowing slow and steady and there's no wind because the stone wall I built is keeping the fire safe and protected.

I'm thinking of the warm Spaghetti 'n' Meat I'm going to have for dinner. In the morning I'll find that pool again but take my plastic bottle this time. And I'll find something to heat it up in on the fire because I'm pretty sure that Steve said that any water's safe to drink if you boil it first.

The fire goes out.

Shaking, I put the last waterproof match back in its little packet and place it in the zip-up inner section of the Red Nylon Bag. I keep patting it to check it's still there.

One match.

Oh God.

I want to laugh. I want to scream.

Fran Stanton who can't make fires. The girl who –

Don't go there. No, don't go there –

couldn't pass a bin, a park, a roof without lighting a fire.

Well, do you know what? She can't light a frickin fire on a beach. Not to save her life, she can't!

And do you know what's so frickin funny? The funniest thing of all?

Well, listen to this:

She. Has. Only. One. Match. Left.

There. Told you it was funny.

I eat cold Spaghetti 'n' Meat made with could-be nut water and wrap myself round and round inside what's left of the life raft. I put my hoodie on and wrap my Nike T-shirt around my legs to keep warm. It gets cold here at night.

So there's nothing to do but to try to sleep.

I try not to think about the shrinking size of the torch beam beside me.

I'm watching a beetle creep across the sand when the light fizzes and goes out altogether.

A Walk in the Park

If you take the main path through the park and keep on going, you come to the lido and that hurts, because it's where I used to take my brother all the time.

It's cheap and clean and little kids love that sort of thing. It was me that taught him to steal and it was me that taught him to swim.

Today the lido is open because it's a bank holiday and half-term so you'd think it'd be heaving and the kids would be out in droves, swimming and splashing around. But it's not and they're not because it's raining, raining, raining.

I only realise how heavy it's coming down as I near the row of kebab shops and restaurants that is Herne Hill. I only just remembered to grab my black parka as I left the flat and it's just as well because my jeans are soaked already and water drips off my hood and off my nose. The park pounds with the usual runners, all dead serious with their armbands and step counters and strap-on water bottles. Everyone's running and no one knows where they're going.

It's early and Cassie won't be up for hours yet. She's sleeping off all the late nights and she's got a few appointments later – Darren 2 p.m., Leroy 4 p.m. – so it's better that I'm out of the flat and out of her hair.

Only a fiver in her purse today. She'll not miss it. I wish she'd miss it.

I carry on past the station, then change my mind and cross back over the road towards Brixton. I walk down avenues of posh houses, gloss-painted front doors in smart navy and green and plum.

Each Peach Pear Plum.

That was the name of Johnny's favourite book. Together we knew all the words, only I'd pretend not to remember and he loved that; he'd shout the end-rhymes and get it right every time.

Little white Fiats are parked on the tarmacked drives; first cars for teenage kids. Inside the sash windows are wooden blinds to stop people like me staring in. A couple of builders sit on some steps, dragging on fags in the rain. They watch me as I walk past and I switch on my Medusa stare.

I am a rock.

Dead Pigeons Don't Cry

I decide to eat before heading back.

Everyone's packed in here because of the rain; the only table free is mine and Johnny's.

Tinny pop music and lime and orange walls. I sit on a brown fake-leather stool with my quarter-pounder-no-cheese.

I want to die because all the kids remind me of Johnny.

That little boy with the buzzed hair who gazes at me with

treacle eyes. He trails his hand across my table as he passes. He's sitting next to his mum now, kicking the bench with his white Velcro trainers. Has a chicken burger the size of his head but he's still making good work of it. He tilts his head to one side in concentration as he licks mayo from his mouth and his mum reaches over and nicks a chip.

I stare out of the window.

My burger tasted so good I could eat three more, but I only have pennies left. I can make a large Coke last hours.

There's Lambeth Town Hall.

I once saw a wedding through this window. A white couple, the girl in a short cream dress, him in brown polished shoes that shone like conkers. And a little crowd of friends, all young, happy and laughing. Two women had sandwich bags filled with rose petals and were throwing, throwing, and snapping, snapping with their cameras. And the groom stooped and grimaced but you could tell he loved it really and he and his new wife clutched each other for all eternity in those photos.

My little brother, busy playing The A-Team *on my smartphone.*

'When can we go home, Frannie?'

'Not yet,' I say.

A dad, his dreads tucked up tight under a black beret, is asleep sitting up; his head sways and nods as he sits with his kids, a girl who stares out the window, and a boy with his orange juice and his iPad. This kid is chubby, cheeks fat as pumpkins.

I sit alone, jeans clinging cold to my thighs.

I am a rock. I am an alien.

Outside, red buses reflect in glassy puddles.

Walking back up Brixton Hill, the rain still falls.

Glassy pavement. Glass-eyed people. By a wall, a crow pecks at a puddle of vomit.

Outside our flat, on the pavement, I see a dead pigeon.
A woman is pulling her kid away from it.
'Why's it got no head, Mum?'
I check the time on my phone: 4.30 p.m.
Cassie should be done by now.

Animal

So today I bleed.

A lot.

Blood drips, over my cupped hands, through my fingers, into the sea.

I watch it drip down the inside of my legs. *My legs are hairy*, I think. Hairy and blistered and tanned as a conker.

The first day's always heavy.

I'm squatting in the shallows, and the water's flowering pink with my blood and the sun's scouring the back of my neck and I'm naked and I'm bleeding and I don't care.

At first it felt strange and raw to be naked; I felt watched by the beach, the whispering trees by the edge of the forest.

But there's no one to bother about. There's no one to see.

My belly throbs. To ease it, I swim, pulling at the water, smoothing out my pain. It helps.

Later, I wash out my bikini bottoms and SpongeBob's still winking. I hang them on a rock and take the tampons from the Hello Kitty bag.

I take one out, just because I don't want to spend the whole day leaking like hell in the sea. But something makes me stop. It feels wrong to be chucking these in the sea when

80

I'm done. And do I bury them? I have no fire to burn them. And there are only twenty in the pack. What then?

Using my knife and my teeth, I tear two strips from the bottom of my leggings. Roll one up into a pad. One to wash. One to wear. They'll dry instantly in this sun.

I feel kind of wild and free.

Blood, hair, teeth.

I am all animal.

Berries

Shall I?

The nail file hovers over one of the blisters on my legs. It's fat and squishy and as big as a small jellyfish. But what if it gets infected or something? I once read a horror story where a man's legs got gangrene and he had to chop them off himself.

I use the nail file to try to sharpen my safety knife instead. Then I punch holes in three could-be nuts and gulp down the water. I'm getting to like it very much; it's warm and clean and slightly sour.

But I need to be careful because there's not many left on the ground and what if the wind doesn't shake any more down? There's no footholds on those palms, like on the mulberry tree in Brockwell Park.

I decide to smear the pulpy stuff from the could-be nuts all over my legs. I don't know if it'll do any good but it feels cool and soothing on my blisters.

Then I pull on Joker's red T-shirt and smear on some of

the lip balm.

Made with petroleum jelly, the little tin says on the side.

For a moment, something flickers in my mind.

I lick my lips and almost, but not quite, taste cocoa. Lip balms are always like that: smell so good but never taste like the smell.

Next I have to sort out my shoes. I can't just use T-shirt sleeves again; my feet are still cut up and sore from my last trek in the forest. I end up tearing what's left of my leggings into strips and levering the cardboard base out of the rucksack. When I've hacked at it with my knife, it's in two sections, which I use as soles. I place them on my feet and wind the legging strips around tight as I can.

The bag's too scratchy on my bare shoulders so I turn my hoodie into a makeshift sling and stick a could-be nut and my empty water bottle into it. Then I push the knife down the side of my SpongeBob bikini bottoms.

There. Don't I look the part?

Creaking a little in my new shoes, once more I enter the sweating forest.

If the knife was sharper, I could maybe make some progress. But it seems to be getting blunt with all the work it's been doing. I have to tear branches and creepers away after hacking at them for what seems like hours and I kick at quite a few trees in rage.

Soon I'm too sweaty to be angry. It's like I'm in a bathroom and the hot taps and shower are turned on full, and then someone turns on the heater and closes the doors and windows.

Or I've just climbed inside a hot oven.

And if I thought I'd have the energy to just open a could-be nut and swig from it while I was in the jungle, I must've been mad. The swilling nut in my sling tortures me.

But don't throw it away 'cause you don't know when you might find another.

It seems easy at first because all I do is follow the broken and kicked-at-in-rage creepers. But then I realise that it's not so easy to see my path: already the trees are netting themselves together again, criss-crossing themselves in crazy lines.

What if I get lost like last time?

And I have no torch; not any more.

I squat and pee.

Around me, the forest simmers.

Distant creatures howl; a large grey ant on the leaf beside me cleans the air with its feelers.

There are loads of palm trees here; fat ones that look like giant pineapples, skinny ones with strange brown flowers. None with could-be nuts on them though; those seem to only grow along the beach.

Reaching up, I tie a knot in the huge leaf of the palm nearest to me. I decide to do this to each one as I pass; that way I'll know the way back.

Once my path is barred by a monstrous, storm-toppled tree, old as time, bound and choked by hundreds of snaking vines. Saplings thin as fingers shoot out from its ancient branches, bunching together to reach the sky.

I clamber through in my cardboard shoes; crawl over this sleeping dinosaur with its many knotted eyes.

After days or hours or minutes, I reach the pool.

Something has eaten the dead rat; only its bones remain. Above the water's surface a thousand tiny flies flicker.

I wade in to where the water seems cleaner and fill the bottle. When I hold it to the light, the water inside looks lovely: brown and cloudy and floaty.

Mmmmm-mmm.

Later, I think, I'll have to use the last match to boil this water and make it drinkable. And I have to find more containers; I can't keep trekking all this way for one bottle.

It's when I'm screwing the lid back on and placing it in my sling that I see the bush.

Its drooping branches kiss the pool; a pretty bush with striking glossy leaves. But it's not these that I'm staring at. Because it's hanging – literally hanging – with bright red berries.

I wade in closer. They look like a cross between a blackberry and a redcurrant.

I pick one and squeeze it. Purplish flesh squishes out, full of tiny black pips. I think of blackberries from the park and strawberries from the market and the blueberries we'd nick from Brixton Marks & Spencers.

It looks all right. It feels all right.

Surely it wouldn't do any harm if I tasted just one? I could spit it out straight away if anything happened.

Slowly, I raise it to my mouth; put it in.

Oh dear me, oh dear me, wails the bird.

It tastes slightly sour and prickly but most of all it's *juicy* and my stomach is gurgling because it's been so long, *so long*, since I've eaten fruit.

I eat another.

After several minutes, I stop and stuff the rest of the berries in my sling.

When I catch a glimpse of my reflection in the murky pond, my chin and teeth are dripping red like Bella frickin Swan after she's eaten a woodchuck.

I have food and water and a knife swinging at my hip, and for the first time on this stupid island I start to feel different: sort of capable and free and even happy.

Almost.

Stupid me.

84

Fever

Kick sand over the mess I've made.

A thin reek rises.

Stagger back, stagger back.

Crawling on hands and knees.

It's cold and hot and cold.

Wrap myself up in everything I own.

Mustn't drink the water.

The sea's all black now and the forest bawls. The creatures come crawling.

Need to go again. Stumble out of my shelter, stumble through the dark sand, cool as salt through my fingers.

Cover it up, cover it up.

Must

Sun scours me awake.

Sometime or other, the fever stops.

I am better. I am not better.

I wait, huddled under my rubber shelter, for the night to creep in again, for the sun to drip from its melting sky into the waiting sea. There's Fang Rock, cut out in black paper and pressed against the wet paint of the ocean.

I wipe the crusted sick from my mouth. Panting, I bring the could-be nut down on the rock, bring it to my mouth. Lie on the sand, let the liquid in, turn my head, am sick again.

Must keep on, keep on drinking myself
    alive.

Do Dreams Have Wet Noses?

The stars shudder when I wake.

I'm wrapped up inside my hoodie and lie gasping, mouth dry as sand. It's warm in my bed because I seem to have a hot-water bottle pressed behind my knees.

Hot-water bottle?

Slowly, I reach my hand down and feel something soft and firm and warm.

When I listen, it pants.

There it is again.

Oh my God.

I lift the covers slowly and something is curled up behind my legs. Something that is staring at me with gleaming eyes.

I snatch my legs away and wriggle into a sitting position.

'Oh my God, oh my God,' I whimper.

When my eyes get used to the dark, I see:

Two eyes, blinking.

Two ears, pricked.

One head, tilted.

If it's a dream, it's better than the last one, but I'm waiting for this –

    dog, it's a dog –

to turn into a giant rat or maybe a dripping-haired girl –

    don't go there, don't go there –

86

with pearls for eyes.

But it doesn't.

The dream just sits there, head tilted, panting gently.

Then it butts my arm with its nose.

Do dreams have wet noses?

'Good dog,' I say.

The dog yawns out smelly breath, warm as sewers. Then it settles again by my side and wriggles down into the hoodie blanket.

I sit frozen for a moment next to my stinky-breathed dream. Then I curl up on to my side and close my eyes and dream-dog sighs and sneaks in behind my knees and I slide back to sleep to the whiskery tickle of its breath on my skin.

Hushabye

We have a secret, Johnny and me.

Because never does he stay in Cassie's room at night.

Ever.

The minute I hear him cry, I'm out of bed and stepping over the boxes in the hallway.

'Shh-shh, Monkey.'

He's standing, holding the bars and shuddering, little fists all slimy hot with tears. Face all hot and wet and streaming. I lean forward and help him climb out. He's too old for his cot really.

Cassie sighs and turns over in her sleep.

I'm twelve years old and strong as a giant.

Better

In the morning the dream-dog is gone.

As I lie there remembering its little body pressed against mine, the warm-stink of its breath, I realise that I had no bad dreams last night. For the first time since coming here, I slept well.

I take out the Eezi-Meals and line them up on the sand. There are thirteen. When they've gone, I don't know how long I can last on just could-be nuts.

But my head, my stomach, are no longer spinning. I'm able to split and pierce my first could-be nut without shaking. I think I might be better.

I stand up, go into the sea to wash. I peel off my filthy bikini and wash my body carefully as if I'm a baby. I scoop up water and let it trickle over my arms, my shoulders, my still-sore belly. I scrub my bikini as clean as I can and chuck it back on to the beach and then I float back in the water and close my eyes. The sun dapples my eyelids with shifting patterns as it kisses my cheeks, my nose, my eyes. I let myself drift in the shallows, let the warm waves take me where they will, bumping and nudging gently.

Reluctantly I get out, my toes sinking in the sucking sand. But the sun is tender as it dries me; shrinks the water-beads on my naked skin.

Slowly, I dress. My boobs and bum are London-white against the nut-brown of the rest of my body. It's like I'm one big stencil which the sun has peeled pieces off. I put on SpongeBob and he's already dry. Next, I wrap my red T-shirt around my head to keep the sun off. My hair is ragged and full of sand and salt but I twist it into a knot and shove it under my makeshift hat.

I stuff the fishing line from the Red Nylon Bag into my rucksack and also the washbag; there'll be things in there that will be useful. Finally, I get my Ray-Bans and knife.

Holding my bag up high over my head, I wade into the water and climb on to Fang Rock. I'm going to have a go at fishing.

Even though Fang Rock isn't so big, the effort of climbing up out of the water tires me out; I must still be weak after my bout of sickness. I get myself comfy on a ledge and wonder how many days and nights I lost to the berries. I wish I knew how long I've been on this island. Will I live out the end of my days here? Is this it then? Is this what happens to monsters?

Even though my hands are shaky, I manage to pierce the top of a could-be nut after only a few attempts. I must have learnt a lot already, since being on this island. I drink deep till I feel my strength coming back.

So, how to fish? There are limpet things on the rock, which I suppose I can bash off with my knife and use as bait. I stand up, grabbing at a ledge to steady myself when I feel myself swaying. Taking my time, I collect a small pile and peer underneath one of them. It's fat and orange and frilly, and when I poke at it with my finger it shrinks right back inside. I take my nail file and prise the creature from its shell; then I jab a hook in.

I'm not bothered by the slimy squelch of strange frilly things that live inside the shells. All I care about is hooking a fish. There are six hooks on the line so I bait them up, one after the other.

Then I unravel the line and cast it out, far as I can. I sit up high on my rock, and I let my line down and I fish and I think about my dream and how it feels to be held. I remember a warm body and warm breath, and hands that hold tight to mine. I remember the huff of sweet breath on my cheek.

I'm sitting up high and alone when I see.

Something white is nosing about my camp.

Eyes Like Treacle

I squint through my sunglasses and there it is again: small and busy and running in and out of the forest. It must be some kind of bird. I've seen big white ones on the beach that look like the pelicans in St James's Park. I took Johnny there once to watch them getting fed their fish. He got tired though; it's a lot further than the Horniman. These birds tend to huddle together at the far end of the beach and when I approach they rise into the air slowly with a great *whup-whup-whupp*-ing sound.

But pelicans don't wag their tails.

I leave my fishing line wedged in a crevice and scramble down the rock into the sea. Then I half swim, half wade to the beach and wait behind One Tree, panting.

Nothing at first, then –

it must be a dream, it must be a dream –

a little dog, tongue lolling, trots out of the forest and noses busily into my bedding, pushing and tugging the clothes and raft rubber around till it feels it's comfortable. Then buries under my hoodie and settles down so that all you can see is its black nose.

I stare and stare and blink.

'Um. Dog?' I say.

I move slowly from behind the tree so that I don't startle it.

But it doesn't even move when I crouch down next to it and lift back my hoodie. Just gives me a hot little lick on my hand and sighs.

So I squat there and stroke its ears and it's the first time I've touched anything living –

anyone –

for about a million years –

well, since Johnny –

and it feels nice, just crouching there, stroking its warm little head.

'Where the frick have you come from?' I say, and this time it doesn't feel mad and lonely to be speaking out loud; it feels sort of OK.

'Where have you come from, little dog? Huh?'

My voice needs oiling but I can't help smiling as he?/she? gives a stretch and its legs stick out stiff and straight from my bedding. I notice that it's a little boy dog. He has the shortest legs and can't possibly be comfy like that, but he falls asleep there, huffing gently.

'Did you come from the plane? Is that it? Are you the pilot's little dog?'

I remember the dog in its travel bag; a freckled arm reaching over me to stroke it.

'What's your name, eh?'

I search on his neck but of course he has no collar. He's been through the wars, this little dog, just like me; his ears and neck are covered in cuts and scratches. But he doesn't look too thin, and he's obviously found water to drink.

This thought excites me till I realise it's probably just the same muddy pool I use. Dog must find plenty of rats to eat in the forest.

In the end that's what I call him: just Dog.

He's mostly terrier, with short stocky legs and ginger patches on his back and both ears; looks a bit like a Jack Russell. He has eyes like black treacle and stinky breath, which I don't mind until he wakes up and pounces on me, licking my ears and neck as thorough as anything.

Which he does a lot.

When I go back to my fishing rock, it seems like Dog has brought me good luck because there's something caught on the end of the line. When I reel it in I find a crab, legs circling like clockwork, and I don't even think twice about bashing through its brains with my knife.

Because I've got two to feed now.

Burn, Baby, Burn

'So you see,' I tell Dog, 'we have to make a fire so that we can boil water because once all the could-be nuts are gone, we've only got the dirty pond, and without water we'll die.'

Dog sits with his head tilted, listening carefully.

'!' he says.

'Three days,' Steve liked to say. 'That's all it takes.'

So we make our preparations, spend hours hacking away in the forest, bringing back dry wood and piling it neatly on the beach.

It's good to be active, but really I'm delaying time; I'm terrified to start, to strike that last match.

This time I remember to tie knots in the palm leaves, like Hansel and Gretel, so that we can find our way back from the jungle. Not that I need to now: Dog is my guide, a small white shape always ahead, always looking back to check if I'm following.

We find some real coconuts, the normal brown ones, and carry armfuls back to One Tree Beach. I hack off the hairy husks and pull them apart to form dry bundles.

There are sticks strewn on the beach, and lots of prickly-looking seaweed that is bone-dry. But the best find of all is a giant piece of driftwood that makes me pant and swear as I lug it across the soft sand like it's a dead body through sugar.

We make piles of the seaweed and tiny twigs I've collected. And I set out my tools: my lip balm, a cardboard box, a handful of coconut hair. With shaking fingers, I place my very last match on a flat stone.

Coconut hair, cardboard, twigs: surely one of these will burn?

But what if they don't? What if the fire goes out again like last time? And the time before?

I push the thoughts away and, with Dog beside me, I build a low wall, one stone at a time. The cardboard box is the one containing tampons and I pour them out on the sand and rip the box into tiny strips. These I place next to the pile of coconut hair.

'We can do this,' I tell Dog.

His tail twitches in agreement.

Now for the lip balm.

'Cause if it's made from petroleum jelly, then surely that's like petrol — surely that burns?

I stare at the lip balm in my hand; take a strip of cardboard and smear it on.

On an impulse I take a tampon out of its plastic.

Dry cotton.

There's a much better use for this now.

I pull the tampon apart till it's no longer bullet-shaped; it's fluffy and drydrydry. Then I smear lip balm all over that too.

Burn, baby, burn.

I pile all my kindling in the middle of my stone wall.

'So you think we should go for it?' I ask Dog. 'Use the last match?'

Dog gives me a hot little lick and settles down to watch. He trusts me. 'Course I can do it.

So I take a breath. And strike.

The beach breathes heavily over my shoulder, watching, waiting.

The flame –

my last flame –

flickers.

Leaning forward, I place the flame against the fluffed-up cotton. I blow, nice and slow. I wait.

And *whoosh.*

It bursts into flames, just like that.

On goes the coconut hair, a little at a time. Careful now – I don't want to knock out the fire. It's still at its baby stage and I must slowly breathe it into life (but inside I'm screaming, *yesyesyes*).

I breathe into it, steady and slow. The island is with me now, breathing and smiling.

All the world has shrunk to this moment.

And it grows. My little flame grows.

Add dry sticks and then some more.

I almost forgot the shredded cardboard but do I need it?

I toss it on and the fire likes it and licks it clean. It loves the seaweed; sucks it up like Cassie with a bag of crisps.

I seize the sticks and the driftwood; throw them on.

When the fire's burning strongly, I drag on the huge log. The fingers of flame explore it delicately and I watch as it blackens.

I just need to find something to put pool water in – maybe there'll be cans or tins cast ashore by the sea – and then I can boil water at last. It won't matter that the could-be nuts are running out. And we can cook our food. No more raw crabmeat, which takes a million years to get out of the claws.

Whatever I do, I must make sure that the fire's kept going.
'Cause if that goes out, there's no matches,
   no matches left,
   and then where will we be?
The fire can't ever go out.
I'm not going to die out here.

I used to love burning things. I used to love fire.

It's like you stare into the flames and you see all the colours of the universe there. And you get sucked into the very heart of the fire and you're dancing, fighting, and it's OK to spit and snarl and crackle; it's OK to feel pain, to scream, to roar.

I used to be able to stare at a fire for hours.

Look Away Now

Even though I try so hard to blot it out, to turn myself into stone, I still see her face.

Miss, with her fake smiles and writer's notebooks and let's pretend –

   let's pretend –

   to be interested in what Fran Stanton's got to say because then maybe she won't play up in class and then maybe she'll achieve her targets and then we'll all be happy.

'You've got talent,' smiles Miss Bright. She's new; she's shiny-new. She digs around in a big cardboard box. 'A writer's notebook, for your first novel.' She calls it my magnum opus, don't ask me why.

'How's your magnum opus?' she always says.

One day I leave it on the desk for her to read.

It was that simple, and I was that stupid.

The flames lick and spit and I have to turn away. I don't want to see what I am 'cause looking into the heart of those flames – it's like looking into my stinking, rotten soul.

I get up then; walk away from the flames, and then I'm running, running, over the sand, down towards the sea, trying to get the pictures out of my head. If I had vodka I would drown it all out, but I don't. So there's only running, and yelling and dancingdancingdancing and Dog barks and runs and dances too; we're wild things, we scream and kick sand and we don't cry.

When I'm finished I'm shaky and sick. Big mistake to dance in the sun. I throw another log on to the fire. Then I lie down with my T-shirt over my head and listen to my heart running races with the sea.

Let's Pretend

Miss Bright is beaming. Her hair's wisping out of her ponytail and she looks about twelve years old. Eyes outlined prettily in purple shimmer.

'So here's a writer's notebook. Bring it to my after-school club, if you like.'

The notebook's in my hands. It's a dusky red colour and the cover's nicely textured, with a sort of weave. I like it, but am careful to shrug and shove it in my bag without looking like I'm looking.

'Have you signed my report card?' I ask.

'What? Oh yes, here it is.' Miss takes it from a pile of sheets on her desk and scribbles something into Monday, unit five.

'Well done, Fran. Fab lesson today,' she says.

She's always saying stuff like 'fab' and 'coolio' and 'super'.

She hands the report card back to me and later I see that she's done a smiley face, with two pigtails coming out of its head. Fab lesson.

'So just do an ink waster, let it all flow. Don't worry about punctuation, don't think too deeply about it. Just write.'

Miss is perched at the back of the classroom, legs swinging, face smiling. She's always doing that – sitting unobtrusively. She's not one of those teachers who stalks about, swinging their arms and talkstalkstalks at you all lesson till your eye-balls pop with boredom.

She's new – an NQT, which means Newly Qualified Teacher, which means let's all piss about in her lesson 'cause she won't be able to control us.

But it's not like that in Miss's lessons.

She's quiet and soft but she gets even the bad lads at the back to hang on to her every word.

She says 'thank you' a lot.

'Thank you, Sam, for that comment,' she says, when Sam-the-big-man sniggers and says something under his breath that probably doesn't bear repeating.

'Thank you, class, for how you entered the classroom to-day.' Seeming not to notice all the fightingpushingshoving but smiling at the only two kids who've sat straight down.

'Thank you for cheering us all up this Monday afternoon, Shasta.' Shasta, who's just farted and fallen accidentally-on-purpose off his chair.

I stare at Miss's pen. I don't have my own, 'course I don't. Girls like me don't bring their own pens into school. My tiny bag's crammed with my fags, lighter, spare inhaler, Monkey's drawing of Anakin Skywalker and a clutter of lip balms that I swiped from Superdrug on the way to school.

I can't write anything. It's all crap. Everyone's scribbling away, even Tyra, even Jaheem with his headphones on.

The starting line on the whiteboard is: *Once on my way to the bus stop…*

I start to write.

"Cave Girl"
by Fran Stanton

*Once on my way to the bus stop, a girl rose like a wraith
to greet me, all streaming mascara and waving arms and
acid-jaggy teeth.*

*'My boyfriend – he's beaten me up – I need help. Please.'
Her eyes flit to my bag.*

*'I need money for my bus fare – to go to my mum.'
Yeah, right.*

'Please,' she repeats, giving me a ghastly grin.

*She's no older than me, probably. Looks about sixty
though.*

*She stares as I open my purse. Hungry eyes. She has
badly dyed hair with the roots showing, and her arms and
bare legs are silver-scaled.*

*'The bus fare's seven fifty,' she informs me. And all the
time her eyes are flitting round, perhaps for her pimp
boyfriend, perhaps for her dealer.*

*I give her a couple of quid and she melts away, back into
her hole.*

All day I think about her.

All day I worry for her.

'And three, two, one, pens down.'

Everyone stops writing and sighs.

Miss goes round, and I sit cringing in case she gets me to
read mine out.

But she doesn't.

When she passes me, she murmurs, 'Very strong', and

nudges my arm a little.

I'm not going to write in her stupid notebook.

'Course I'm not.

Rooftops

I take a swig of my cider and light a new fag from the old one.

In front of me, there's the Gherkin, and to the left of that, the London Eye. Everything's sort of misty and hazy.

I've got a pile of blankets and an old mattress that I've found up here, and cushions. I've made myself a nest from vintage scarves. I've brought candles and matches and my notebook because this is where I'm going to do my writing.

I chew Miss's pen, which I never gave back.

Below me, I can hear children playing in the park.

'*Write a fairy tale,*' she said. '*A story for children. Just let yourself go.*'

Once upon…

Once upon a time…

Once upon a time there was…

To get up here, I have to wait for Albert to start his litter-picking, then drag the broken old ladder from the empty balcony downstairs and take it all the way up to the top floor. There's an iron ladder that hangs from the ceiling for maintenance work. Albert is supposed to lock it with a padlock but he never does because he's up and down the flats all day; it's too much bother. Basically, anyone can get up on the roofs if they want to.

I look down and see a large lady with Sainsbury's carrier bags waddle to the ground floor. Never seen her before, but then no one sees anybody round here. I hear her footsteps go up the steps. There are no lifts in these flats because they're only three storeys high. She'll be a while.

I blow a smoke ring and think of Johnny, down in the flat. He'll be playing games on my phone, eating the packet of biscuits I gave him. I made sure he did his spellings first though 'cause I don't want him to be a loser like his big sister.

No one's supposed to be on these roofs except for repair work, but I can see it's been used before. There's this mattress I'm sitting on, and a row of dried-out plastic pots. Cannabis plants, dried up and dead. I know because Cassie tried to grow them once; we couldn't use our bathroom for months because of all the special lighting and plastic sheeting she'd rigged up. She's more into Tennent's Extra Strength nowadays.

I rearrange my cushions and settle into the evening.

Evening noises over Brockwell Park include:

Kids playing on the swings and chattering away in Portuguese or Spanish.

The *thwack thwack* of tennis balls, even though the courts are miles away.

Planes from Heathrow.

A pipe. Someone on their balcony is playing a pipe, like one of those hollow things from the African room in the museum.

It feels good to write, sort of freeing.

I tuck the blankets more tightly round my legs and take another handful of crisps. It's getting cold but it's OK; the late sun's still slanting over my face and arms.

I've run out of fags now but I hardly care. Can't stop can't stop scribbling.

Wayne won't be back for a while.

It's March or April and the day melts into night like the cider on my tongue.

"Our House by the Sea" by Fran Stanton

Once upon a time there was a little girl and she had a brother. Their daddies had left and their mother had gone far, far away.

But that didn't matter because the little girl knew that when she grew up, she'd live in a house by the sea and she'd have all the time in the world to look after her brother. She'd cook and she'd clean and she'd fix the roof when it leaked and make a garden full of flowers and shells.

There'd always be cold wine in the fridge and vodka in the cupboard and lots of books on the bookshelves, which she'd make out of boxes that she'd paint in bright colours: yellow and orange, and blue like the sky.

Outside there'd be a little garden, small as a pocket, but it wouldn't matter because it'd be big enough for the two of them. Each evening after all the chores were done, the girl and her brother would cuddle up in the last of the sun on a bench specially put there amongst the flowers. The girl would drink wine out of a vintage glass and the boy would drink milk, which gave him a big white moustache. And they'd watch the sea as it endlessly patterned and unpatterned under the bluer-than-blue sky.

Let's Be Partners

Next day, I go into school early so that I can leave the notebook on Miss's desk. Then I leave to hang around town a bit because who wants to be on time for registration?

English is unit four, and all morning I'm waiting for her to notice.

I'm waiting for her to read it.

Miss reads it and is delighted, 'course she is. Her blonde wavy hair is up in a messy knot today. She wears vintagey clothes. There's always a button missing or a tiny hole in her cardigan. She doesn't look like she tries too hard.

'Let's be critique partners,' she says.

She knows and I know that she's playing it cool. Doesn't want to scare off the difficult girl.

But then she leans forward and starts to give me feedback, and it's careful and precise and she's really read it, you can tell. She's even placed Post-its in the pages with scribbled comments. She really cares about this memory, these words.

I can feel them turning into a story.

'So, try to develop your characters a little more,' she says.

And she puts the notebook back on my desk. Turns to write on the board.

I snatch it up and put it in my bag, and it's like a prize, this book. All day I think about it, lying there at the bottom like a dragon's egg.

Once upon a Time

In my story, I have a character called Carrie and there's this girl called Anna and her little brother Jake. A nasty bloke called Aaron moves in and once he shoves Jake so hard when he's whining that Jake falls against the table and gets a massive bruise on his face. Anna and Jake are always hungry and Carrie is always asleep.

There isn't a bedroom for Jake or Carrie because all the rooms except for the lounge and Anna's room are filled with junk, so Jake has to sleep in Anna's bedroom with her. Anna doesn't mind. She once spent a whole night reading Jake *The Magic Faraway Tree*.

My story's a good one.

I really get into it once I'm past chapter seven, and I start describing this crazy dream Anna and Jake have:

'So we're living together in my house, and I've got a little job. I'm an artist. I paint the sea, and always there's this view of the sea, like when we went to Weymouth that time, do you remember?'

Anna snuggled closer to Jake and smelled the shampoo and warm scalp smell of his little head. She'd washed his hair that night, because it was Sunday and she didn't want him to get bullied at school for being a 'gyppo'.

His soft hand squeezed hers.

'More, Annie,' he whispered. 'Tell me more about the house.'

'Well,' she said quietly, 'it's in Weymouth, just on the seafront, and it's only a little house, just a terrace really, but it's the best one on the row.'

'Why is it the best one, Annie?'
'Because it has a bright painted door – yellow because it's a happy colour – and it has the best front garden. Only tiny, but it's paved in shells that we've collected from the beach, and this is where you do your homework, Jake, and I sit sipping Pinot and watching the sea.'
'What's Pinot, Annie?'
'It's nice white wine, Jake, which is what I'll be drinking when we're there.'

I've stopped the conversation there because Miss said it's not a good idea to make dialogue go on too long.
'You've got to weave in some action,' she said.
So.

Just as Anna was describing the tiny bedrooms up in the loft, the white walls and smell of clean, fresh paint, and Jake was snuggling in close, his warm breath huffing on her cheek, the door burst open.
'Get that boy to his own bed,' bellowed Aaron, his pig eyes glinting in the half-light.
He leaned lower, his mean breath beer-sour.
'He'd better not have bleeding well wet the bed again.'

The Could-be Pile

The sun beats down as I saw into the plastic with my safety knife. Dog and I have decided to cut up the life raft because it's definitely punctured and there's no chance of us sailing away on it like *The Owl and the* frickin *Pussy-cat*. No way. So we might as well put it to good use. It's good work; if I get our new shelter finished today, we'll sleep well tonight.

It's on the fringe of the forest but I don't mind because Dog is with me now and he'll chase any monsters away.

The tin cans are wedged in our fire, the water inside them bubbling away. Whatever happens, I make sure that the fire's always going.

It's the last thing me and Dog do before we snuggle down for the night: make sure that we shove another couple of logs on, so that we're warm and safe and our water's always boiled.

Sometimes we get it wrong and the driftwood must be too wet or something because the smoke billows into our faces and sets Dog wheezing and me coughing, but still it's better than the alternative.

The fire can't ever go out.

We have a could-be pile, Dog and me; it's where we store things that might be useful some day: bits of rope and broken plastic crates and lifebuoys and oil drums and even a rubber duck we found caught up in some roots. Our could-be pile is growing day by day with all the stuff we bring back from our foraging trips to the swamp.

We're making the roof of the raft into a hammock. I use a sharp rock to pierce it at opposite ends and then thread blue nylon rope through it. I pull the rope tight and then tie the edges to each tree so that it's secure.

Dog waits in the shade as I use one of the life-raft pieces as a sheet to help me drag a big piece of driftwood over the beach. He wags his tail when he sees me, his little rump wriggling in the sand. I lie down to take a break from the sun and Dog jumps on me and headbutts me with licks till I roll away, laughing.

'Oh my God, Dog – leave off, won't you?'

He sits nicely then, grinning like hell.

It's a good spot we've chosen, Dog and me; sunlight plays around the edge of the palms and scribbles crazy patterns on the soft sand. We're not close enough so that we get could-be nuts hurled on our heads but I can still watch the palm leaves sharpened by the sun.

From here I can see:

One Tree Beach.

Fang Rock.

And, right at the other end of the beach, the little cluster of rocks that hide the swamp.

Squinting at it reminds me that we need more plastic bottles for water. And while we're at it –

'Coming to check for fishies, Dog?'

His little tail wags so hard I swear it'll whizz away.

Dog's fish-trap is the best; it's basically his own travel bag but with stones weighing it down inside. When it got washed up by the sea, we set it in the shallows at the start of low tide with its door propped open; then all we had to do was to go away and come back again. When we came back that first time, a squid and two fish were waiting for us. The fish are so stupid they get washed inside and when the tide drags back they can't find a way out again.

Today there are three big blue fish and one that kills me, it's so beautiful; when I hold it up it shimmers pink and coral mother-of-pearl and its fins spread like delicate lacy fans.

I toss a blue fish to Dog and he swallows it whole. Beautiful or not, we've got to eat.

'Didn't even taste that, did you? Pig.'

He grins at me, tail whirling, and I decide to leave collecting the other fish until later.

If you climb over the rocks at the far end of One Tree

Beach and wade right out, even further than Fang Rock, you can just see the white flash of another beach, tucked up tight in its cliffs. Except it's deceptive 'cause when you finally get there (after swim-wading for hours), it's not sand but swamp, and it's crawling with weird, twisted roots with leafy tops like trees. I think they might be mangroves, like they have in Florida.

This swamp is the best place for foraging.

I'm wearing my new shoes. I've made them by cutting up my bra and using the cups as the front section and the straps around my heels. Pity they're only 34B but it's a lot better than using a T-shirt or leggings. At least they don't come off all the time.

We wade further into the swamp; well, I wade and Dog swims hard as he can. Dog immediately climbs up on a root-bank 'cause he's knackered after swimming so far; he can't paddle for long with those short legs.

A bright light glints, down by my foot. I bend down and tug and it's a pink plastic mirror, with most of its glass missing. There's an arrow-shaped shard left and I peer into it curiously.

A stranger looks back at me; I see a wide green eye, a triangle of dirty brown skin, a straggle of tangled hair. I turn the mirror this way and that and see hollows under those eyes, the sharp edge of a cheekbone.

Dog is bored; he gives a very small whine and looks at me hopefully.

'?' he says.

I put the mirror carefully into my bag.

'Want Frannie to pick you up?'

I'm about to take him when I see a small movement in the water. I thrust the jam jar in, quick as thinking; hold it up to the light.

Inside, a sea horse floats like a ghost.

I tilt the jar and stare.

It's a perfect thing, transparent, all its pulsing life on show.

If I wanted I could turn it to stone. I could freeze its furling fins, its unblinking eye, its coiling tail. Turn it to ice.

It floats and trusts in my hands. I am a giant.

I set it free, watch it slide like a sigh into the folding water. I watch for a long time.

Shark Swamp

Dog waits on the bank as I climb down to inspect the roots.

Today there's good pickings. So much that I have to leave some of it behind for later. Tucked up between the twisted stems I find:

>   3 large tin cans, labels scratched off by the sea
>   2 broken flip-flops, different sizes
>   1 big, empty white tub with *MARINA BAIT* on its side
>   1 glass jar with a label that says it once contained gherkins
>   3 empty fizzy-drinks bottles: Fanta, Sprite and Dr Pepper

I'm glad that I've found more tins; they'll be useful for cooking. I've been thinking of making fish stew with could-be nut water. I don't want to leave the drinks bottles because they're so useful for storing the water I've boiled on our fire, but then I remember that the pool's been looking a bit low lately and think that maybe we don't need so many after all.

What about when the water runs out? a sneaking voice says, but I shove the thought out of my head and get back to my task.

We pile everything carefully between two gnarly could-be mangroves that look like they're having an arm-wrestle and I stuff what I can into my bag. I can't imagine chucking any old crap into this beautiful sea, but then I remember my drunken rage on the life raft. I suppose it's good for me and Dog that fishermen are such tossers.

I tug yet another plastic bottle from the white roots. This time it's a Pepsi Max bottle, still with its lid on and some brown liquid in it. I sniff it and slug it and it's warm and wonderful, such a magic-chemical taste after coconut water.

It's when I'm shoving the bottles into my rucksack and other ideas of how I could use them are buzzing round my head –

great for catching rain and maybe even small fish if I weight one down on its side, and what about gutters? –

that I see it.

A fin, yellow-grey and smooth as a smile, is knifing through the water.

Shark.

Fin

Now I'm splashing, dropping all my things – backpack, knife, bottles – scrambling up on to the root-bank.

'Dog. *Dog* – stay where you are,' I pant.

For a horrible moment I think he's going to jump back into the shallows; his little feet are skittering on the roots as he peers down.

We huddle on the bank, watching the shark as it coasts,

leaving an oily trail in its wake. From above we can see it quite clearly; it's about as long as my leg, freckled on its back like a pebble. It's ultra confident, I can see that; knows these waters well. I wonder if the scratches on my legs and feet have left blood-traces. Maybe it's tasting me as we watch.

We shrink back when it reaches our bank.

It's definitely man-eating, I think. Will it rear up? Will it rear up like a crocodile?

It's only when it changes course and starts heading back to the open sea that I start breathing again.

'*Stay*,' I tell Dog.

He whimpers, tail quivering.

Keeping the dark hook of the fin in sight, I slide back into the water and retrieve my stuff, every minute expecting to feel a jaw clamp down on my ankle.

There could be more. These waters could be infested with sharks.

Dog whines.

'All right, Frannie's here.'

I stoop to pick up my knife, drifting in the water with its string unfurling. I'll need to reattach the tin-lid blade. I made the knife by inserting a tin lid into a piece of driftwood, then binding rags and string round and round the handle. It's a lot sharper than the safety knife – if you don't mind the risk of losing your fingers.

The fin is a distant speck now, far out to sea. I start to relax.

Till something touches me on my leg and I scream.

Ghost

It's only a fishing net, wrapped around my leg.

I unravel it and follow it like that hero with the ball of wool in the Minotaur's maze. It's all twined around the roots like a giant web.

I'm excited; this is a Real Fishing Net which is going to double our food if I can mend it. I unsnag it from the roots, quick as my fumbling fingers will let me, and my heart's skidding because Dog doesn't seem at all happy up there on the bank, and I'm trying not to think of the shark nosing round like it owns the island.

'Frannie's nearly finished, Monkey,' I say.

Did I really say that?

I stare into Dog's trusting eyes as my fingers workwork-work to undo those knots.

'!' he shouts.

And it's back.

The water is cut in two as it slices straight towards us.

I yank the net and then I'm grappling at twisted roots, fingers sliding through mud, feet slipping and sucking.

'Oh God, oh my frickin God –'

And all the time Dog's barkingbarkingbarking like he's ready to take on five sharks, if only I'd let him.

I see a flash of its skin, freckled and pale; it leers, opens its jagged mouth, and tears at the section of net that's still trailing in the water. I whimper, breath ragged. Claw myself up on to the roots.

Dog's vanished; then I see him on another tree island. He's looking around, darting back and forward. That's when I notice that the sea has come in; we're surrounded by water and Dog's little tree island is shrinking fast. He'll get cut off.

Only the leafy tops of the mangrove-trees are showing now, their scrubby roots snaking over the water. There's barely any bank left; his tiny island has all but disappeared.

'Dog, go home,' I shout. '*Go home!*'

Dog barks at me, his little feet scrabbling. And then he's gone; he's scrambled through the remaining root-banks back to One Tree Beach, in the next cove.

But I'll have to swim back. I have no choice but to get back in the water.

Smile

Nearly there.

My backpack's hitched high on my shoulders, bra-shoes, bottles and what remains of the knife and net shoved safely inside. I'm swimming with nice long strokes and so far nothing's happened. To calm myself down, I make myself think about how we can leave the net in the sea overnight, weighted down with bottles. I try to decide how this would actually work; where I'd need to tie them.

And Fang Rock is right in front of me, I'm really close now; I can see the late sun glinting on its seaweedy back. My arm-strokes are soothing. I can see lit-up pearls of water on my dark skin.

Then the monster rises.

For an instant I see:

An eye, black and evil.

A lemon-grey flank, satin smooth.

A mouth like an upside-down smile.

I pull myself through the water, lungs screaming, checking back every so often to see if the shark's following me.

It is.

It's like a wasp, but casual. It's not flapping around, this one. Just waits for me to become a piece of drift-meat.

I'll not go without a fight though.

I'll kick it. Punch it between the eyes.

I tread water as its fin carves out an arc in the water, straight towards me.

Then two things happen:

The first is that three humps appear with fins like sickles, and the shark leaves, fast as a knife through grease.

The second is that I feel the bump of sand beneath my feet.

I'm home, but there's no Dog on the beach to greet me.

Cardboard and Parakeets

Cassie's put cardboard at all the windows in the lounge again. Only good thing about our flat and she covers it up.

'Can't sleep with all that light,' she moans, cringing from sunlight like Edward frickin Cullen.

I rip it away like I always do. There's tidemarks of old tape criss-crossed all over the glass.

'Ow, ow,' whimpers Cassie.

I chuck a pillow at her and she pulls it over her face.

She's in her usual nest on the settee. Eats, shags and sleeps on a pile of grubby blankets. Around her, the fug of flat lager, old bedding and stale skunk. The stink of being Frickin Useless.

A handful of crisp tenners is sticking out of her grotty bag. I whip two for myself and tuck the rest away in her purse in case she loses them when Wayne comes calling.

Still raining, but the sun is out.

We have a balcony – not that you could call it that really. It's more a dumping ground for old crap. I swing open the door and breathe in rain and sun and mown grass. Then I step over all the carrier bags of empty bottles and beer cans; the old pushchair that was Johnny's; the dead runner beans that Cassie tried to grow from a free seed packet on a magazine. I step over and lean on the railing overlooking the park. Mouldering clothes hang forgotten on a sodden washing line. I push a pair of Cassie's huge leggings aside and watch a bird fly out of one treetop into another. It's bright green, the colour of McDonald's walls.

It's a parakeet; the trees are screaming with them.

Lime-green birds in a wet, grey London park. Do they remember? Do they…

Staccato

…remember

that there were once so many shades of green?

Green as gold, and green as blue and white-green, black-green, dancing-green.

Layers and layers of leaves and sky and song.

Up close, a creature creeps forward on a leaf, feeling its way with wavy legs. It flies, light as air, then *swoosh*, lands on a blue flower and sucks greedily.

Thirsty work, flying.

There's the clackaclack bird with his gunfire call; close behind the *trillatrillatrilla* of all those little birds jostling for space.

Cuhcuhcuhcuhcuhcuhcuhcuh, goes their mate. *Yo, brothers, come round some time*, he's saying. *You know where I live.*

Plink plink plink plink plink. The plink plink bird makes staccato notes in the forest.

The trees twist themselves in knots trying to reach the sky.

Grand Designs

I haven't seen Dog since the shark came.

I called and called his name.

I searched the beach, the forest. Even returned to Shark Swamp once the tide went back out.

It's been three nights, three days.

To keep myself busy, I work on our shelter. Home Camp. Except it's not a home without Dog.

I've sawn the plastic bottles in two and shoved the top parts inside the bottom halves upside-down. I've lined these with my cut-up leggings to filter out all the gross bits from the water before boiling it.

So I did remember something from *Hi I'm Steve!* after all.

The bottle filters are constantly dripping with my new drinking water. If you let it settle before boiling, it's kind of OK. Not that the pool will last for ever, not without a rainfall. Not much chance of that now: the sky's a cruel blue today.

I slump down against a tree to take a break.

Here the sea sparkles white-blue between my legs and the palm leaves shiver and the heat beats time with my breathing, which is slow as a sigh.

Overhead, trees tall as tower blocks cast their shadows. It's like the birch trees in Brockwell Park. A place where we'd hide out, me and Johnny, watching all the winos and druggies drift in like ghosts.

I have my shelter now, almost made. I've killed myself over the last few days, rebuilding, shifting, sawing. I've even started making a palm roof over our hammock; half-plaited leaves lie in the sand.

The fire is the centre of Home Camp, of course. Beside it, the log pile's kept well stacked, and next to that is my toolkit. I've got three knives for different purposes: my blunt safety knife for coconut-opening; a sharp flint-stone for the quick killing of crabs; and my tin-lid knife for cutting and filleting fish. The prettiest shells line the entrance of my home. And there's even a beach-garden feature made with coloured glass-bottle fragments, blurred into gemstones by the sea.

Look at it, a home any girl would be proud of.

But it's not enough.

Sighing, I pick myself up and go to check the bottle-net.

It's out by the rocks, under the mountain I tried to climb, that very first day I arrived.

Wading in, I reach out and start to drag the net in.

And that's when I hear it.

Limpet

'!'

A bark, high and thin.

Surely that was Dog, coming from inside the mountain?

I drop the bottle-net and wade through the water to the rocks. All the fish we've caught are making me stronger. I don't pant now when I run for my morning swim or when I drag branches over to the camp to keep the fire going.

My foot slips even before I've begun to climb.

I gasp and ignore a throb of panic.

Imagine breaking a leg here. Imagine.

I begin to climb the rocks at the base of the cliffs. It's the only way to get to the other side of the island. They may be sharp, they may be slimy, but I'll do it.

'Dog,' I shout. 'Dog!'

It's hard to grasp the rocks because they're all green with some sort of lethal seaweed, worse than any ice rink. It takes about ten years just to edge a metre or so into the sea.

I keep going.

And my fingers and toes are gripping white-tight now; the sea's swirling below me. I crawl to the very furthest tip of the outcrop, right to where it juts out to the infinite ocean. If I fall now, I'll be dashed to pieces of meat by the waves. The current's strongest here.

I crane my head, desperately trying to glimpse the other side of the mountain, to hear Dog again. But there's nothing. It's impossible to hear over the ledges 'cause they're filled with jostling birds.

'Dog? Where are you?'

Again and again I shout, at the wind, the screaming gulls.

The cliff is straight and high and impossible. There is no way past these bastard stinking mountains.

Pebbles

My hands are cut from the rocks, but it doesn't stop me from making a spear.

I spend ages choosing the exact right sapling from the trees that fringe the forest. It must be the straightest, the supplest. And in my head I'm hearing Dog's bark, high and shrill.

Was he hurt? Was he calling me?

It was the shark that made me lose him.

All day I saw at my chosen sapling.

All day I think about the shark.

I think of its mean, flat eyes and its downward smile.

I saw harder, till there are hard blisters at the top of my palms, and three times I break my knife and have to mend it. There are plenty of tins on the could-be pile.

I use a piece of smashed rock as a tip. It looks like flint and it's sharp enough to spike a could-be nut with a single blow from my rock-mallet. I wrap string round and round so that it's nice and tight. Then I hurl it across the beach in one great arc.

It's a good, strong spear.

I pile up pebbles and practise knocking the stacks down, over and over again.

'What do you think, Dog? Is my aim getting better?'

'!'

'Well, thanks for that. I'm not that bad.'

To make up for it, he gives me a little lick on my leg. I hand him
a pebble and he takes it solemnly in his mouth; trots off to place it on
the sand. Then he rolls on it, scratching the top of his back.

'Weirdo,' I say.

Dog rolls and I throw.

The rock pile topples.

Then and now, the sun dies. Melts like marshmallow in
the burning skies.

Shark

This time I'm ready.

I have my spear and some rope and I'm full of fury.

Let me at it.

It takes ages to die.

It's lemony-grey, smooth as a pebble, and it's thrashing,
thrashing as I stick it.

I'm mad. A wild thing.

I stab it again and again with my home-made spear. The
monster grins and thrashes its broken-glass teeth as the waters
stain pink around us.

Hot-metal blood in the hot sun.

Once, its teeth rake my leg and its jaw clings on even in
death.

This man-eating monster is only small after all, as long as
my leg.

I pant as I swivel my spear down into its brain.

There.

I've come prepared. Wrapped around my waist I have the

anchor rope left over from the life raft. Quickly I tie up the fish and drag it on to the sand.

I try to move it back to camp. It won't budge.

Already the ants are interested. I stare into the eye of the shark and it stares back at me. Its eye is flat and evil, like a child has drawn it with a felt-tip pen.

Wayne's eyes.

I'm going to have to carve it up right here.

The sun is at its fullest, sick and white. My neck is burning even through my T-shirt. I can feel the prickly heat on my chest, my legs, my feet. But I can't leave the shark for the rats to find.

I take my tin-lid knife from my bikini bottoms. My fingers tighten around the handle. It could break in two and the string could snap. If it slips, I might be eating Fran's Finger Fajitas instead.

Ha!

I turn away from the shark's staring eye and start sawing into its flesh.

I Spy

It's as I'm lying on my back, arms paddling, that I see the smoke.

It's thick and white and it's rising in a spiral, wavering a bit to the right in the breeze.

Now that it's safe to go into the sea, I've started doing lengths up and down the beach, but not too many, in case I use up valuable water. The pool's getting low.

We made a good signal, Dog and me; you can see it for miles. Maybe someone will see it from another island. Or a ship or a plane.

But something's definitely wrong.

When I realise what it is, I lurch, swallow water.

I cough and retch and take breaths till I calm down. The water sloshes over my chin as I strain my eyes to see.

There's the mountain, looming up behind the cliff. Impossible to reach; impossible to get to.

And there it is again; a thin column of smoke, wavering only slightly.

But it's not coming from our beach.

It's not our fire.

All at Sea

There's someone else on the island.

My heart trips. Smoke means people. Smoke means survivors.

I need to get to the other side of the island.

The smoke is quivering, torturing me. I lift heavy arms and try to crawl across the swell, moving like a snail towards the rocks. If I could swim round them, I could reach the other side of the island, find Dog and find people, and be sitting round that fire.

People.

I don't care if they're savages; don't care if they're going to kill me and eat me; don't care if they're bird hunters with big feathered headdresses. I imagine them whooping and dancing around their fire, turning the spit; a skewered pig, maybe, or –

drift-meat —
something worse.

Maybe they eat people. Children.

Maybe they eat little white dogs.

But then the smoke is gone. And now I'm not even sure if I imagined it.

'Nooooooo!' I moan.

Don't let it be gone.

I tread water, staring. I'm no further to the rocks or the other side of the island. In fact, when I turn back towards One Tree Beach, I realise that I'm miles out.

Fang Rock is the size of a nail-clipping and I've drifted far out to sea.

Drift-meat

I swim towards the white curl that is the shore but it's not long before I realise I'm not getting anywhere. I'm swimming as strong as I can but I may as well be swimming through treacle for all the progress I'm making.

That's when I start to panic.

I'm going to die, I think. *I'm going to die.*

And in that moment I know, with absolute clarity, that there's no way I want to die.

Not like this. Not ever.

Not when the sun's screaming-bright and the cliff's sharp-edged and blue-shadowed and the seabirds are whirling above me and every colour seems to be brighter and stronger than it's possible to be.

Not like this.

So I tread water and take deep breaths; try to think.

The water's calm. It's not like a roller's going to submerge me. I'm warm, sort of. Won't die of hypothermia just yet.

So relax.

I fix my eyes on the distant shoreline. If I focus on one point, I'll know if I'm drifting further out.

I focus on One Tree.

Whatever I do, I'm going to get there again. I just need to rest a while longer.

I am a dot rising and falling on the waves. I am nothing.

I have never been more alone.

I swim, trying to keep my head over the bigger waves, trying to rise up so that I can see. Each time the wave swells, I think I see it, a thin column of smoke trembling. Each time the sea falls, I lose sight of it and panic.

I reach with my arms, drag the water and it's like a dream where you move in slow motion. Time slows. I can't get there, can't reach those rocks that guard the cliff like jagged teeth. Each time I push, the sea muscles in, keeping me in my place.

I'm going to die out here, and now I would give anything – anything – for there to be somebody else here, for me not to be alone.

Anyone from TeamSkill would do – even Trish, even Joker.

Kieran. That was his real name. Not Joker.

I kick with my legs. I'm tired; I can't keep this up much longer.

Or let it be Coral or Tiny, who was called Paul.

But then I remember that they all died, didn't they?

Coral's hair swirling like smoke, blind fingers tapping at my legs.

Joker was first. Then Trish. Both broken on the floor, they

124

couldn't have made it out of the plane.

My voice is thin as wire. And the wind picks it up and tears it to shreds.

A wave hits me full in the face, drowning my voice, making me choke.

Don't let me die like this, not all alone.

I might as well be a piece of flotsam. Driftwood.

Drift-meat.

I might as well be dead.

!

Something nudges my attention.

Something is barking, quick short barks.

Dog!

I can just see him, a tiny white dot on the shore.

I won't leave you.

The sky's turning violet, which means the sun's about to set. With a lurch I realise that if I ever get back again our fire may have gone out; this is the time we'd be dragging more wood, stoking it.

I shiver and focus on One Tree again. I've drifted further to the left, and the waves are getting bigger, like they always do in the evening.

If I ride with the waves, I think, I can let them take me as far forward as they can; then I'll swim for it. I'll swim for that shoreline like it's a magnet.

I check behind me; wait.

The next wave's a big one; it swells like a breathing monster and I keep my head up out of the water as I rise too, let myself bob like a cork on top, fix my eyes on the lone tree on the beach.

The wave carries me forward and the tree gets a little nearer; and then:

Take a breath.

Swim.

Fix.

Pull.

Breathe.

Fix...

...Till I can't swim any more, but I've refused to let the wave drag me back and now I'm being carried forward again in an almighty *whoosh*.

And it's the same thing again:

swim, breathe, fix on tree –

and One Tree's getting closer, it really is –

and I've forgotten all about the plume of smoke –

because there's

Dog.

He's there –

he's there on the beach, waiting for me

and barking, barking.

I can hear his sharp little yaps as I swim.

'Coming, Monkey,' I gasp

as I pull,

dragging the water

with throbbing arms,

and I can do this,

I'm nearly there.

So close now.

Oh, Dog.

Oh, Monkey.

The hard sand rises up to greet me as I collapse.

I'm going to be licked to death at this rate.

It's only then that I realise what's different about him.

Someone

Dog is wearing a collar.

He sits grinning as I reach out to it; touch it like it's hot.

Neatly tied. Plaited. A perfectly-made collar placed around his damp neck.

I stroke it in wonder; trail my finger over its nubs and bumps. A beautiful thing, made with precision out of some sort of stem or reed. I glance at my half-finished palm roof, messy and a little bit crap.

Then Dog wriggles away and goes to his favourite spot in the shade, half buries himself into my hoodie blanket.

It could be a tribesperson, I think. It's like those beaded things in the display at the Horniman. Me and Johnny used to look at them; I'd make him choose his favourite.

'How about that blue one, Monkey? The one with all those feathers and bones. It's a sort of necklace.'

'Nah.' He shakes his head. 'I like that one.' He points to a red beaded headdress with a million beads sewn on.

'Amazing,' I agree. 'We so need to get you one of those.'

'Will you make me one?'

After I've made dinner and cleared a space to eat and done my coursework and tomorrow it's rubbish day and Johnny's got to do his spellings and we need more washing powder and while I'm at it I might as well sweep the sky.

"Course I will, Monkey.'

I snap back to the present. Hug my knees.

It could be a survivor like me.

Derek-the-co-pilot or *Hi I'm Rufus!* or Tiny-whose-real-name-is-Paul or the pilot. Would any of them have taken the time to make a perfectly-woven dog collar? If it's bird hunters, they'd know things. Like how to make boats and how to kill pigs and –

how to eat little dogs.

Would they make a collar?

But what's the point of there being anyone else if you can't frickin reach them?

I look over at Dog and he's exhausted. Gives a little stretch and a sigh and then he's sound asleep, the sort of sleep that lasts till morning.

Dear Whoever

Where the frick is it?

I rummage through my Hello Kitty bag, cursing.

Out goes the nail polish, lip balm, tampons and, finally, the eyeliner. The nail file is with my other tools, useful for undoing knots and smoothing the edge of my tin-lid knife.

I take the eyeliner and pull off its lid. It's a little melty from the sun, but it'll have to do.

I have a piece of paper-thin curly bark which I've noticed peeling off certain trees in the forest.

What should I write?

What do you say to:

a) A bird hunter cannibal?

b) Some psycho damaged kid who's gone half-mad from being alone on a desert island for far too long? *Like me, for instance.*

c) A calm, knowledgeable, practical type, preferably the pilot or co-pilot, who happens to be a total expert in survival skills, and not only knows how to persuade the biggest crabs to reveal where they're hiding, and can swiftly and humanely catch and kill a pig and roast it in some cool dug-out firepit so it's ready just in time for dinner; but can also get water from rocks and tree trunks and, heck, can even make it rain?

Someone like Hi I'm Steve! for example.

d) All three? They've made a camp together and are having a frickin party.

'Remember your audience and purpose, folks!'

Miss's voice, confident in our abilities.

All of us in her writing group are scribbling away, up for the challenge.

We have mugs of hot chocolate and biscuits, 'cause Miss has sneaked them out of the English staffroom on a tray. She got me to help her make them, even though students aren't allowed in there.

'Hurry,' she laughs, 'teachers get very possessive over their mugs. Better not use Mr Hale's – it's got a photo of his cat on it.'

So, remember my audience and purpose.

In the end, I write:

HELLO.
MY NAME IS FRAN. THIS IS MY DOG. THANK YOU FOR
HIS COLLAR. WE LIVE ON ONE TREE BEACH ON THE
OTHER SIDE OF THE MOUNTAIN.
HOW CAN I REACH YOU?

I wonder if Whoever can read English, or can read at all.

Do bird hunters need to read? So I draw a crude picture of the mountains and my beach, showing my location. The eyeliner is totally blunt down to the wood, so I sharpen it with my knife, but then the point breaks so I end up drawing One Tree with turquoise nail polish. I add an arrow just to show where we are.

It looks crap, but it'll have to do. I roll it up tight and slip it between the weave of Dog's collar. He's still asleep, whistling with each out-breath. His toes twitch.

I curl up around him, and close my eyes too.

I may have written a message, but there's no way I want Dog to run off and leave me on my own again.

No frickin way.

Blue as Periwinkle

We hang the fish next to the strips of shark meat on to a washing line that's hooked in the sun between One Tree and our camp. Well, I do; Dog watches.

It's a bit fishy-smelling but better than leaving it all for the pelicans to snatch. They'll eat anything.

Dog is fat as a flea on his fish diet. His breath still stinks though.

'Love you more than Snickers bars,' I tell him. 'Well, almost.'

Dog pants, tail twitching away the flies.

The washing line is made from the same twine that I used to tie the shark. And we have a gutter now: it's made from loads and loads of plastic water bottles, cut in half and stacked inside each other so that they're overlapping.

Except it never rains here, does it?

We both stare up at the unblinking sky and it's bluer than blue, as always; not a cloud, not a whisper of grey that might mean rain.

'We need a better roof, Dog,' I tell him.

I dampen a stick in seawater then spear two of our fish with it. Gutting's easy. Basically, all I do is hack the heads off on my chopping-stone and open the bellies to pull all the guts out.

'!' says Dog. He loves fish-gutting.

He watches me as I thread the fish on to the sharpened stick and skewer it into the sand over the fire. Not too close because it needs to cook gently.

I stare at the smoke from our fire as it billows and rises, sprinkling little flecks of ash into the sky.

I keep seeing a different smoke plume.

Below the cliffs, I stare across the sea, straining my eyes. Perhaps I can see it again if I look hard enough. I might be able to see it, rising up behind the mountain.

I can't. But I keep thinking about it, and it's weird how something like that can make your eyes prickle.

While we're waiting for the fish to cook, I make tea by boiling pond water in a coffee can and adding two lime leaves. The lime trees live by the poison-berry tree by the pool – *which is drying up, it's drying up, it's drying up.*

There'll be no need for my filtration system when the pool has gone.

I try not to think of it. Dog doesn't like could-be nut water. Time slows. And all the time I'm thinking of that pool with its few centimetres of water and buzzing flies. I imagine the sky darkening and splats of rain big as my hand slapping into the upturned coconut shells, running along the gutter-

131

ing into the *MARINA BAIT* tub.

I sit down on our bed and Dog jumps up and curls at my feet. We still need to finish the roof. And maybe make a better stove, out of an oil drum.

I look up at the sky through the rustling palms. Listen to Dog breathing and the trees creaking as the sea sighs.

After dinner, I let Dog lick my fingers, then wash the fish-gutting knife in seawater. Then I sit Dog down so he's giving me his full attention.

'Listen, Dog,' I say.

He pants stinky fish-breath and darts a lick at me.

'You need to leave Mummy and deliver that message,' I tell him.

His tail twitches.

I point to the mountain. 'Go,' I say. Then, more firmly: '*Go.*'

Dog hurls himself on his back, wriggling his hips backwards and forwards. He wants his tummy tickled.

I sigh, and lie back on my bed. I think about weaving more palm leaves together to finish our roof.

Plaiting palm is like braiding hair. I used to braid Johnny's hair when it was longer. I used to get absorbed in the rhythm of plaiting, of keeping track of all the separate sections in my fingers.

'Tell me the story again, Frannie?'

'One day, Monkey, we'll live together, you and me. We'll have a bay window and that's where we'll have breakfast every morning. We'll sit at our table and we'll look out over all that wide blue sea, and we'll eat our toast and watch the seagulls.'

'What about Mum?' he asks. 'Will she be with us?'

'Of course,' I say.

'And what colour will the sea be?'

'It'll be blue as cornflowers, blue as periwinkle.'

Johnny would wriggle and squirm and in the end that's why we got him the buzz cut.

Palm leaves are definitely easier.

I get off the hammock and pull two leaves towards me. Over, under. Over, under. By the time the sky melts, I've woven together three pieces, which makes a tiny section of roof.

But it's no good. I can't settle, not with that smoke spiral sneaking and pushing into my mind. Smoke does that. You can close all the doors you like, but sooner or later it will get you, snaking in and around like a bad memory.

The taste of guilt.

Uh-oh

Miss seems different today.

She's absent-minded as she checks through the register, adding behaviour points and putting in lates.

'Won't be a minute, Frances,' she says.

I can see my notebook, there on her desk, on top of her filing tray.

The door's propped open but it feels hot in here. Nothing feels right. And yet I still think — *stupid me* — that Miss is going to critique my work, that we're going to have a cool discussion about my story, the one that's growing by the minute; the one about Anna and Jake.

I look around at all the posters on her wall. It's like Miss really cares about writing, it's not just for exams. Like, with her, it's all real.

The road to hell is paved with misused apostrophes.

133

If there is a book locked deep within you, you have to set it free.
Writing is easy. You just stare at a blank page and weep.

But there's something wrong. I can sense it, sure as if I'm a dog smelling a fox.

I get up and wander about Miss's classroom. I'm always doing this, wandering. I'm the sort of student who gets up in the middle of the lesson; rearranges the dictionaries, picks up the teacher's board marker.

Miss is quiet, tapping away on her screen, but I can tell she's watching me. I move closer to her desk, and that's when I see it: my story, photocopied, slipped under her class list.

Why has she got a photocopy?

And I want to snatch it back, right there, right now. I don't want to stay here, in this stuffy classroom.

'So is the writing club still on?' I ask.

I still don't frickin get it.

Miss doesn't answer. Instead she does something she hasn't done before. She takes a chair and drags it over to her desk; places it next to hers so that there's no barrier between us.

She keeps my red notebook in her hands. There are no Post-its sticking out of it today. This time my story is like an unexploded bomb.

I want to snatch them all back, all of those words.

'So is writing club not on then, Miss?' I repeat.

'Frances, is there anything you'd like to tell me?' she says.

'Why have you photocopied it?'

She sees me looking, slides the sheet under her teacher planner.

'I thought your story was…very good,' she says.

All of my hackles are up. I flit my eyes, looking for an escape route.

'I think I'll go now, Miss.'

But her eyes are all wrong too. And the noise of the pages

in my notebook as she turns them is way too loud.

I want to snatch it back, take all the words back and lock them safe inside me.

'Is there something you'd like to talk to me about?'

Miss seems hesitant, like she doesn't know the words to this script yet. I want to help her out. She's only new after all.

'If there's anything going on at home…'

I stand up. 'There's nothing,' I gabble. 'Everything's fine.' It's hard to breathe in here. I snatch my book back.

But she doesn't need it any more, 'course she doesn't. She's got a photocopy.

The minute I look in her eyes, I know what she's gone and done. Her eyes slide past my shoulder to the door and, just like that, my world crumples.

There stands Mr Pearson, Head of Safeguarding and Pupil Welfare, his face all careful concern.

I pick up my bag.

'Think I'll be going now, Miss,' I say.

I push past them both and hurry out of English Block.

Double-crossing bitch.

Flies

The pool is almost dry.

It's half the original depth now and buzzing with flies.

But that doesn't stop Dog from lapping thirstily.

'Move over, Dog,' I say.

I crouch down and push the Pepsi Max bottle under the water. Muddy bubbles rise as it fills.

The pool's starting to smell a bit nasty. The dead rat's mostly gone now though; only its little skull remains. I'll have to make sure this water's well and truly boiled.

Dog pants at me, tail wagging. He's happy; he's had his fill.

I put the filled bottles into my rucksack. Lick my lips with my dry tongue.

Only three today.

There's no choice but to push on through the thickest part of the jungle in search of water.

Dog runs on ahead; he keeps any bird hunters away from me and reminds me to tie knots in the leaves as we go.

And all the time the sun's getting hotter and harder.

Blind

It's dark in this little bay, overshadowed by the monstrous trees. Only the sea glistens. Here, the trees end in gnarly tangles and a miserable stretch of sand that you can't really call a beach.

There are cliffs, and there are caves. The mean little beach soon runs out, so I pick my way over the rocks, hoping my bra-shoes won't unwind. Below, the water shimmers blueblueblue, the sea settling and unsettling.

Dog runs ahead, jumping from rock to rock. Sometimes he slips, his little feet scrabbling, but he never minds; just picks himself up and carries on.

I've tried to avoid the green rocks to be safe, but it's no good. My hip hurts because I've slammed it hard so many times by falling on to skating-rink slime and my bruises are going to turn all the colours of the sunset.

There are fish in these rock pools: bright flitting things that shiver and vanish as soon as you put your hands in their warm world. We could catch crabs here, Dog and me.

'!' says Dog.

He's found something.

A dolphin, cast up on to the rocks, its sides bristling with sandflies.

I touch it with my foot and a sweet stench rises, thick and cloying. Its skin is hard as rock and there's a gaping hole in its side where things live now. All day that smell will follow me.

'Ugh. Leave it, Dog!'

Its flesh is dry as old bones, dry as my tongue.

When I turn to call Dog, he's disappeared.

And then I hear him.

His bark sounds smothered and faraway. It's coming from deep inside the rock face.

I edge myself around the cliffs, but there's nothing; only more rocks. And all the time, the water swirls blue-as-chlorine, blue-as-plastic, blue-as-daylight.

Where the frick is he?

I stand, bottle in hand, squinting in the sun.

'Dog?'

The tide is still out but it's on the turn, little licks and flicks around the tiny beach.

Tucking my bottle in my sling, I strain to hear him.

'!' repeats Dog.

The crusted walls scratch my hands as I push on further. All at once something cold and wet touches my leg and I scream.

'Jesus, Dog, you nearly frickin killed me.'

He disappears again and I curse. Don't want to be stuck here at high tide, not when there's the fire to keep going and the dark descends sudden as a hand scribbling over the sun.

Twice I slither and twice I cut my hands on the rocky wall. But then I see the crack in the rocks. And that's where his bark's coming from.

I clamber up and stick my head inside and you have to squeeze through the gap in those pressing rocks in order to get inside. Maybe there's a cave on the other side. Maybe it's just a never-ending tunnel. I wriggle my shoulders through and am met by solid darkness.

I feel like I cannot go back and I cannot go forward. Like I'm frozen in this dark space. And all the time I'm tortured by that sound, that *trickling* –

It could be water. You know it could be water –

but I can't climb into that cave.

I can't. It's just too dark. And silent, apart from the dripping.

Suddenly I'm desperate to get out, desperate to see daylight.

I can't hear Dog any more.

He's left me again.

Sunken

Dog still hasn't come back.

He went into the darkness and hasn't returned. Last night, for the first time in ages, I slept alone. There was no warm body curled into mine, no panting breath hot against my leg.

He went into the cave like he knew it was there.

He left me.

138

So I lay listening to the heaving sea but all the time I was listening for

the

thunk

of could-be nuts falling to the sand.

But there's been no wind. Everything is warm and still, as if the island is holding its breath, waiting.

Waiting to die.

I spent hours just calling him. Even pushed through to the back of the crevice where it starts to twist, but I couldn't go further; couldn't bear the darkness, those pushing rocks. The way my voice echoed back, mocking me.

Maybe Dog's found a way to the other side of the mountains.

Maybe he's gone back to Whoever. Will they see my message? Will they tell me how to reach them?

I thirst.

Sometimes I stare into my mirror for hours at a time, just gazing. The girl inside stares back at me through sunken eyes.

I spend hours watching her.

And all the time, through the shimmering smoke of our fire, the sky burns cruel and blue.

Candyfloss

I squat and pee in the sand.

My urine drips dark. I haven't had any fluids for two days, and three —

three is the magic number —

means death. Everyone knows this.

I know I should be getting could-be nuts down from the trees but when I look upward they are a million miles away, clutched up high in the spindly palms. I reach for them with my finger and touch them, one by one. Then spread my hand and blot them out.

All my thoughts are confused like candyfloss in my head, like clouds –

except there are no clouds.

Once I get a stick; it's the longest, thinnest one and it even has a fork at the end which would be perfect to hook round those nuts if only I could stand for long enough and if only my head didn't swim like all the water that's trapped inside them is sloshing round my brain.

I did try, before.

Dog and me, we used to spend hours trying to get those nuts down. My hands stripped raw from climbing the palm trees, Dog barking below. Like, why would you make a tree with no branches?

No.

- No. of could-be nuts left: 0
- No. of filled water bottles left: 0
- Pond water left: 0
- No. of clouds in the sky: 0

Knock, Knock. Who's There?

'Cassie,' I hiss. 'Get up.'

'Course, she can't. There's stuff all over: sliding piles of magazines and receipts and bills and cans, cans, cans.

I clear the cans away and open the window.

'There's someone knocking. Shall I let them in?'

'Leave me alone,' she whines. She's flicking through the telly guide with the remote, trying to find a black-and-white film she hasn't watched.

The rapping again.

'Hellooo?'

Bits of a face peek through where the chain is: an eye, a cheek, a nose stud.

'Hello, my name's Angela Cockerton and I work for Lambeth Care Services?' she says.

I say nothing. Wait.

'It's just a friendly visit. Nothing to worry about. We've had your family referred to us by the school?'

She has an accent. First, I think it's South African, then I realise she's Aussie or maybe from New Zealand. Her voice goes up at the end.

'Right,' I say. I'm trying to stay calm because alarm bells are going off inside my head and it's difficult to think straight.

We've been visited by a social worker before, when Johnny was a baby and Cassie wasn't coping well, but that was before she started drinking, and that was before our flat was such a state. Johnny's dad was still with us and he was a personal trainer with massive OCD, which was about the only thing good about living with him. Bleached our work-tops to within an inch of their lives, and everything in its place like we were in the frickin army.

'So...can I come in?' She's still smiling.

'Wait there. I think I've left the grill on —' is all I can think of to say, and I leave Angela-the-social-worker dangling on the chain and dash back to the lounge.

OhGodohGodohGod.

And in my head: *So she's done it. Miss has done this.*

'Cassie,' I hiss, shoving her duvet back over her and sweeping all the crap into more carrier bags. 'Say you're ill, OK? You're ill.'

She nods. 'I know, love, I know. Would you just pass...?'

I shake my head as she nods towards the stack of Tennent's.

'Chewing gum,' I say.

She gapes like a chick in its nest and takes the gum I offer her. At least her breath won't stink like a brewer's.

All the rubbish goes in the kitchen cupboards. That's the good thing about them always being bare. More storage.

I open the window wider, take a breath, put the kettle on.

Then I unhook the chain and let the social worker in.

Angela is small and smiling and has dimples. She has a satchel bigger than she is over one shoulder. It's covered in festival stickers.

She's still smiling as she comes into our lounge, but her eyes are darting about like sparrows.

She holds out her hand to Cassie.

'Hi, I'm Angela? You must be Mrs Bailey?'

Cassie looks up at her blearily. Takes the offered hand with a confused look on her face.

'Mum's sick,' I say.

They both look at me.

'I feel awful,' agrees Cassie.

'Got one of your migraines, haven't you, Mum? She can't

142

see anyone when she's like this,' I add pointedly.

Cassie moans a little and closes her eyes.

'Oh, I am sorry to hear that,' says Angela. She looks round for a place to sit and finally perches on the end of Cassie's settee.

She rummages inside her satchel. 'This won't take long?' she says. Draws out a ton of papers. 'We have to take each referral seriously, as I'm sure you're aware? Just got to follow procedure...ask a few questions about your son Johnny —'

I freeze. 'What about Johnny?' I say. My heart's going *thudthudthud* now.

And all the time I'm thinking, *what has she said? What has Miss said about my story?*

Bitch. *Bitch.*

She's been blabbing off to Mr Pearson and social workers and God knows who else. All that crap about critique partners and up on the roof and the red notebook and magnum opus.

I want to kill. I want to scream.

Angela scans through one of her sheets. 'Well, I'd really like to talk to him. Is he here?'

'He's at the park,' I say. 'What do you want to know? He's playing with his friends. He's got lots of friends.'

I'm gabbling. I stop.

Angela nods kindly. 'I'm sure he has too? I just want to check that your mum is coping OK? To find out some basic information and to see what strengths and difficulties your family may have? Whether there's any more support we can offer —'

'We don't need your support,' I blurt out.

There's a snore from the settee. Cassie has gone to sleep.

I swallow. 'Would you like some Turkish coffee?' I ask.

I go into the kitchen, trembling. Wayne has left his

Marmite jar of skunk out on the worktop so I shove it in a saucepan of congealed baked beans and hide it with a plate.

It's Miss. She's done this. She's put them up to it.

My hands shake as I measure out two scoops of coffee into my special pot. I found the Turkish coffee pot on Camden Market and it's beautiful: tiny and made of battered copper. I add a cup of cold water to the coffee and whisk it up with a fork.

It needs to heat slowly so I put on my music so that I don't hear Cassie snoring and Angela thinking *what?what?what?* as she assesses the state of our lives. Ella croons that she has a cosy little flat in what is known as Manhattan and the coffee grinds settle slowly into soft mud as the pot rattles and simmers over the gas flame.

To do it properly, you're supposed to place a couple of cubes of marshmallow on a tiny saucer but we have nothing like that. The closest thing we've got is half a packet of Haribos.

I decide to leave it.

Angela is calling.

I unplug Ella. 'Just coming,' I say.

I feel calmer now I've made coffee. Coffee is the real me. Not the one talking to social workers in this pigsty of a flat.

'Ooh, lovely,' she says. 'Turkish coffee, my favourite?'

We sip in silence.

Cassie farts.

'Um, while your mum is taking a nap, shall I start with you, Frances? You are Frances Stanton?'

I nod.

'So apart from your coffee-making skills – and this is lovely coffee by the way – what do you like to do when you're not at school?'

Outside, dogs are barking.

Someone is shouting from the street, 'Yeah? Yeah? You're the big man. Think you're the big man?'

'Frances?'

'I dunno. I do my homework and revision,' I say. 'And make the tea to help Mum.'

'Do you help Mum a lot? What sorts of things do you do to help her?'

'Oh no.' I smile. 'Mum's only like this when she gets a migraine. They're very debilitating, you know. Most of the time she's looking after us and going shopping for food and making lovely meals. Our favourite is Mum's home made moussaka. That's Greek, you know.'

'Yum – delicious. Can you show me round the flat, Frances? Shall we start with your kitchen?'

Shit.

Angela's crouched on the floor, peering into our cupboards.

'It's shopping day tomorrow,' I say.

'What are you going to eat today, Frances?' Angela stands up and her shoes make a tacky noise where they're unsticking from the lino.

'Oh, today's our takeaway day,' I say airily. 'We get pizzas from Herne Hill, as a treat.'

'And for breakfast?' Angela is running her hands under the tap. She looks around for a tea towel and wipes her hands on her trousers.

'Um. We get croissants from…'

'From the bakery in Herne Hill?'

I nod and Angela sighs.

'Frances, will you show me your bedroom?'

And so it goes on: Where do you do your schoolwork? Where does your brother sleep? Who gets Johnny from school? Who makes sure you both go to school? How often does Cassie have migraines? Are there any other regular visitors? Who cooks in this household? Does your mum's partner or either of your fathers ever visit?

I'm showing her the books I read to Johnny when she notices his mattress.

'Ooh, lovely. *Each Peach Pear Plum*, *The Little Boat* – they're from the Bookstart pack, aren't they? I can see the bag under the bed.'

We're sitting on the floor because there's not a lot of furniture in mine and Johnny's room. In fact, it's pretty empty when you consider how jam-packed with junk the rest of the flat is.

Angela stops looking through the books and wrinkles her nose.

'Frances, does your brother wet his bed?'

I frown. 'Sometimes, when he's got to sleep alone. He's fine when he's with me though.'

I haven't got round to changing his sheets yet. I mean, he's hardly ever in his own bed anyway so what's the point?

Outside, birds are shrilling.

Doors are slamming.

Then: screaming, screaming, screaming.

I leap up, books flying.

'Johnny,' I say.

Wet

Turns out I'm good at dying.

Fran Stanton. Spat out. Died on a rock. The end.

I'm doing a great job of it; have even curled up on my side so that, when it happens, I've made it easy. Like I'm asleep.

Lie there staring at the fire 'cause those flames, they don't let you forget, do they? Let's burn all those memories back, just in case you'd forgotten them.

Ha.

The fire's getting low. There's only a settling of ash; a blacked-out log, which would shiver into dust if I touched it.

Half a day left to die.

I feel the flies tickling as they land. They know, 'course they do. They're rubbing their little feelers together, waiting. Dead dolphin, prickling with sandflies.

Dead wood. Drift-meat.

'!'

My fingers grip the sand as I try to turn. Dying is forgotten.

'!'

It can't be. Can it be?

And there he is in a shiver of sand, all butting nose and hot licks, and his little hard head ducks away from my groping hand and he's –

all wet.

I press my finger to his fur and lick it.

It's fresh. A tiny, tiny burst of coolness in my parched mouth. A shiver of water sprays me cool as he shakes. Dog is wet and tired from the cave. His fur holds a million drops of water and I bury my face in his warm, breathing flank and suck. It is fresh, not salty. Dog sighs as I try not to waste a single drop.

It's only after I'm wiping fur and sand from my mouth that I see it. See something

so strange, so miraculous

that it's all I can do to
remember to
breathe.

Virgil will Deliver

The message is tied securely to the front of Dog's collar with fishing wire. It hangs, a little folded square, tied like a parcel.

With trembling fingers I untie it, Dog watching me solemnly. He knows this is a momentous occasion.

I curse. There's no way I can undo all those tiny knots. I make Dog wait while I get my knife.

'Sit still. Don't want to hurt you.'

Dog knows not to move.

I finally cut through the fishing wire, and stare at the little note-parcel in my hand. Its edges are neat and precise. One more cut with the knife, and I'm through.

I start to unfold it. It's made from a weird sort of shiny paper, like it's waterproof. For a moment I wonder where I've seen this sort of paper before, and then I remember the water-resistant notebook from the Red Nylon Bag. I have a vague memory of ripping pages out and watching them soar into the gull-filled, wave-tossed sky a million years ago.

It's been folded loads of times, like Whoever was aiming for a Guinness World Record in paper-folding. Eventually I get to the final layer, and open it to reveal the message. It's in tiny, neat, cramped writing, in a sharp pencil, on a tiny piece of paper, as if Whoever is reluctant to waste even a scrap of vital resources.

I blink, then reread. Then I start to get angry.

Like, what the frick does that even mean? Who the hell's Virgil? What's the point in writing in code, when it may be your only chance to give vital information?

On wobbly legs, I reach over to the wood pile and chuck a couple of could-be nut husks and some sticks on to the fire. Watch it whoosh as it lives again. I feel like hurling the stupid message into the flames too, to make those crabbed numbers crinkle and shrink.

But 'course I don't.

Instead I sit on my hammock and stroke my finger over the paper. Stare at the message, like it'll start to speak.

Probably not a bird hunter then, not with a water-resistant survival notebook.

Maybe it's the pilot. Of all the people it could be, please make it be the pilot. I can't even remember his name –

the co-pilot's name was Derek –

but the last thing I remember him shouting was,

'BRACE!' and everyone's screaming now, everything's tilting...

I lie down with Dog, and prop the note up on a rock so that I can see it. Tomorrow I'll write back. Maybe in some random code, or Elvish or something.

Ha.

The sky feels different today, sort of bruised and angry. There's an edge to it. And, settling over the mountains, something I've not seen since I've been here.

Clouds.

149

Weymouth

I swoop Johnny up into a hug and we both run into the sea. Cassie's just behind us, free and happy with her shoes off. She's enjoying the feeling of the cold water on her swollen feet because it's a hot day, hotter than any we've had this summer.

Everyone's in families but we're a family too.

Like that mum with her two boys, all three of them in wetsuits and gleaming like seals while their dad takes a picture.

'Smile,' he's saying. 'Smile.'

Like that pair of old ladies sitting in their camping chairs, sharing a packet of Doritos with their sudoku on their laps. They're sisters, I suppose, and they come here all the time, to hear the seagulls, to nod in the sun.

Like that teenage girl sitting on the bench on the edge of the beach. She's with her little dog and he's up on the bench beside her, head cocked. He's hoping for one of her chips but her dad gets in there first. She pushes him off, pouting. He laughs and gives her a cuddle.

A pair of hands grabs my face then. Johnny's on my hip and pulling my face towards him, so that I'm looking just into his eyes.

A woman who's paddling turns to us and laughs.

'Wants to look at his sister, don't he!'

But it makes me sad, that Johnny needs to do that, at two years old. That it's the only way to get a whole person to himself. I am his whole world.

We're in Weymouth and it's the first and last time Cassie's taken us to the seaside.

We stare into each other's faces, Johnny and me, and around us the wind flaps, and dark spots are on the beach; dark spots that blur and bleed and everyone's laughing and rushing under their beach-tents and pulling plastic bags over their heads, and Cassie's tugging us and we're laughing and running, running over that churning sand before we get
wet.

Storm

The splats of rain darken the sand like ink blots. More and more of them, till I sit up and crawl forward on my hands and knees. Feel them splash on my hands, cheeks, forehead.

Dog leaps up and I fall forward and lift up my face and open my mouth.

Let me at it, let me at it, let me at it.

Sweetest, warmest, fattest rain ever.

Filling my mouth. Plumping out my fat, thick tongue.

It began with a warm shiver that lasted all day. Me and Dog felt it as we plaited more palm leaves; dragged driftwood for the fire. When we waded in deep to pull in our bottle-net, even the fish seemed to bristle with some sort of knowing energy. Their eyes fixed the sky as their mouths gaped and ungaped.

Dog doesn't like it.

When we've drunk our fill, he sits and mopes on our bed, front paws burying his nose. His eyes follow me as I heave boulders and rocks to weight down what remains of the life raft.

Then the sky seems to heave as it crackles and unzips itself.

I leave the log I'm pulling and go and sit by Dog.

'!' he says, but in a small voice.

'Oh my God.'

Already our camp is soaked. Dog pants and presses against me whilst I stuff all my treasures into my bag: broken shells, my Ray-Bans, fishing line, all the pebbles that Dog has brought me.

The fish that's hanging on the washing line is swaying and getting pulpy; I hope it won't waste.

The sky howls, and cracks its jagged teeth. Me and Dog sit shivering. We watch the palm trees bend double and hiss, their fronds flapping wildly like a crazy wino's hands. The sea is bruised and blue; its waves bash the shore, breakers big as juggernauts.

All at once One Tree cracks and sails across the beach in slow motion. It lands metres away from our shelter.

'We can't stay here,' I shout. 'Come on, Dog, we can't stay.'

I gather up our stuff any old how, in a panic, Dog running loops around my feet.

Shoes, I need my bra-shoes. And where the frick's my knife?

The storm snatches branches and leaves and shelter poles and flings them into the sky. As me and Dog race to grab our cooking tins and bottle-net, a branch soars over and crashes in front of us, missing Dog by millimetres.

'Run, Dog. Run!'

I'm screaming and shouting but my voice goes nowhere; it's caught and tattered by the wind.

A gust scoops me up like a pulsing hand and throws me sideways. I land on my hands and knees in the sand, terrified for Dog.

'Dog. *Dog!* Where are you, for frick's sake?'

I pick myself up and the sea's hurling itself against the shore; behind it, the sky is purplish and bruised like a horrid flower. The storm spins the sea; spins the sky; wobbles its way towards our camp and I watch in horror as it shrieks and shreds Home Camp to pieces; bits of palm roof whirl.

There is no sign of Dog.

And I'm running, running, back towards camp, back into the forest. I have no idea if it's safe to be near all these trees in a raging storm but all I know is –

oh God, oh God –

I've got to find Dog because

I can't be alone, can't be alone,

not on a night like this.

The rain smokes and sighs. In front of me a tree snaps, barring my way, and I scrabble over its fallen log, sobbing now.

'Dog? *Dog,*' I scream. 'Oh, please come back.'

I break through into the Poison Pool clearing and it lights up white-sudden, a stage full of screaming trees. Splash through its muddy waters, claw my way over branches. Trees are crashing

    – snapping like a fistful of twigs –

    hissing, steaming rain,

    twigs and thorns stabbing my hands, face,

    tearing my legs.

I twist round because there's only one place he'll have gone, only one place that he'll be safe in this storm, and that is the place that I hate most of all –

it's dark, it's dark, it's dark –

and somehow I'll have to squeeze through that craggy tunnel into whatever's on the other side.

But I have no torch.

Oh God.

There is a knotted palm leaf, and another; through my rain-blinded eyes I see them and follow.

Monkey

Johnny is wailing outside the front door and when I let him in his head is covered in blood.

'Ow, ow, ow,' he screams.

'Oh Jesus, ohmyGod. Johnny, what happened? What happened?'

Angela is hovering, white-faced.

'Get a towel,' I hiss.

'It's all right, Johnny. It's all right.'

I hug him to me and he's heaving and there's blood everywhere, on my top and on my hands and in his tears and eventually we get him to sit down on the kitchen stool and he calms down enough to talk to us. There's a nasty gash on the side of his face and I'm glad there's a towel pressed against it because *Idon'twanttolookIdon'twanttolook*.

'Monkey?'

'What happened, love?'

Johnny buries his face into my chest and I kiss his head and stroke his hair.

'Tried to jump off the swing,' he mumbles.

'Oh, Monkey.'

'Think there was some glass on the floor. It hurts, Frannie, it *hurts*.'

'I think he'll need to go to A and E with that,' says Angela. 'Would you like me to drive you both?'

I nod numbly. Johnny is calmer now, his little shoulders shuddering.

Angela clears her throat.

'Do you think one of us should wake your mum?'

Flash

The sea spits and lashes over the rocks as I climb.

Once, twice, the sky splits.

Once, twice, I slide off the rocks' slimed shoulders and have to swim, choking and gasping in the churning water. It's difficult to climb back up then. I cling to drenched ledges, face pressed into shivering stone. And my legs are liquid and the sky shudders again as if it's taking a photo of itself.

Flash. There's Fran on the rocks. Flash. There she is in the black water; can you see her dark head bobbing?

The crack in the rocks is there, where it's always been. This time its walls are slimed by rain. Eyes tight against the rain, fingers slipping and grasping, I squeeze through. And this time I push further. A faint light now, green ghost-mist. I climb through into the cave that lies beyond, with its dripping, sighing walls.

And there is Dog waiting for me, nose in paws, shivering.

'?' he says.

I laugh and cry and hughughug him.

We cling together, Dog and me, in that dripping cave of sighs.

Stars

Johnny is leaning so close his breath is warm on my ear. We're reading his favourite picture book, *The Little Boat*.

I turn the page and now Johnny is almost asleep; his head sinks heavy on my shoulder.

We're sleepy, Monkey and me; the lull of the words rocks us.

So at first we don't hear the car outside or the footsteps on the stairs or the rap of the letter box. We are with the boy and his boat as he plays by the side of the water.

I turn the page but we never get to the end because then the rap comes loud and clear.

'Wait there, Johnny. I'll see who it is.'

I settle him on my bed and go to answer the door.

When I peer through the chain I see Angela, but her smile looks all bendy today.

'Can we come in, Fran?' she says.

When I open the door, I see that Angela has brought a tall man, who looks like another social worker, and two police officers.

'Can we sit down?'

There's nowhere to sit so Angela perches in her usual spot next to Cassie's feet on the settee and the rest of us remain standing. After a while, one of the police officers draws the stool in from the kitchen.

'This is my colleague, Lee Jackson,' says Angela.

Lee nods. He's got dreads tied back in a headband and his eyes don't meet my face.

'Fran, is your brother here?'

I nod, and Angela gestures to her colleague.

'Would you wake your mum for us please? And then would you go and fetch your brother?'

'He's asleep,' I say.

Something about her face, about all of their faces, is scaring me.

I push Cassie's shoulder.

'Cassie – wake up. There's people here.'

'Mmmm?' mumbles Cassie.

I shove her hard and she gasps and opens her eyes.

Angela takes a deep breath. 'Mrs Bailey, we're here because we have some concerns about the welfare of your son, Johnny. We believe…that his safety might be compromised whilst he remains living here…'

Even Cassie's listening now.

'…and that it is difficult in your current situation for you to meet his care needs. So I'm afraid that we're going to have to take him away, just for a few weeks while we make some assessments –'

'You're not taking my brother,' I say.

The room is swimming and the light through the window seems to be pounding white-spears into my eyes. Somewhere I think I hear seabirds scream.

'You can't take Johnny.'

Angela is leaning towards me; she's taking my hands in hers and it's her fault, it's all Miss's fault.

'Where's he going?' Cassie is saying. 'Where are they taking my baby?'

A female police officer is holding her.

'You said you'd help us,' I say.

Her eyes are shiny but I make mine like stone.

'You're just like all the others,' I say.

She turns away then. 'Will you come with me to get

Johnny?' is all she says.

He's tight asleep in my bed. *The Little Boat* is splayed next to him as he dream-breathes.

'You're not taking him,' I say.

Angela takes a deep breath. 'Frances, you knew it was on the cards. Your mum isn't keeping to the terms of the care protection plan. She didn't attend the pre-proceedings meeting. She hasn't answered our letters.'

'I look after him. I've always looked after him,' I say.

'I don't doubt it, Frances. You're a very capable girl, and it's obvious that the two of you are incredibly close.'

We both look down at Johnny as he sleeps.

'I want to go with him.'

Angela closes her eyes for a second. When she speaks, her voice is low and calm. 'It's your brother I'm concerned about. You know they found bruises, at the hospital. You must know that it's for the best.'

I shake my head; I don't want to hear this. I don't want her to make me think that she's right. She's been trained to do this, I realise. It's all part of her training.

Below me, Johnny sighs in his sleep as Angela's words drift in and around me. I am Other Fran, floating over the scene and looking down.

'Sixteen years old…it's not fair that you're his carer…take the pressure off you…exam year at school…regular access visits…'

I snap back to myself.

'What if I don't let you take him?'

Angela sighs. 'Frances, the police are here to support me in taking Johnny to his foster care. If you protest, you'll make things even more upsetting for him.'

I stare at her. I think that even her voice has changed. It's not rising at the end into questions now; she sounds firm and definite about killing me inside.

I stare till her eyes flicker away, and then I crouch beside my little brother.

'Monkey?' I say. 'Monkey, wake up.'

He stirs. I touch his sleep-dampened cheek.

'You need to wake up now, Monkey. There's people to see you...'

Angela crouches down then.

'Hi there, Johnny,' she says.

'Hi, Angela.'

I get his school bag, the one with Spider-Man on it that I got him for Christmas. I empty all his pencils and spelling books and football cards out of it. Look around for some clean socks and pants.

Angela is talking to him quietly. I shut my ears because I'm stone, I'm stone, I'm stone.

Get his inhaler, check there's a refill; his little glasses from the side of his bed. The Doctor Who T-shirt he wears for pyjamas.

I stare at the page we got up to; the little boy with his sun hat and his boat.

Then I close it and put it in his bag with the rest of his books.

'Noooo,' Johnny wails.

'Johnny, it's just for a little while,' Angela is saying.

Johnny runs to me and flings himself around my waist. 'I'm not going away. I'm not, I'm not, I'm not –'

I lift him up and put him on my hip. I can still lift him, even though he's heavy now.

'Shhh, Monkey,' I say. 'It's not for long. It's like...it's like a little holiday.'

But he's howling now, and he's still howling when we go

159

back into the lounge.

Cassie starts wailing too when she sees us.

'You're not taking my kids away, not my kids. Tell them, Frannie, tell them –'

Lee is squatting down in front of her. 'It's only your son. Just until you're better able to take care of him, Miss Stanton. So that both you and your son can get the support you need.'

'Noooo,' wails Cassie. She reaches out to me, to Johnny. Her fingers touch me, damp and teary. She tries to pull me into her misery, but I flinch away.

Johnny is gasping into my neck.

Both the police officers' faces are carefully blank.

Angela doesn't make eye contact with me. 'Frances is sixteen,' she says to Cassie. 'She's a very capable girl. We try to avoid taking children into the system if at all possible, but we don't feel that the current situation is a suitable environment for Johnny.'

The female officer coughs. 'Now, if you could just sign here, Mrs Bailey, just to say that you are in agreement that you have handed over responsibility of your child to the care services.'

Beside me, Cassie moans and shakes her head as they try to give her the pen.

I hear Angela's voice; she's crouching down to speak to her, and her voice is low and calm.

I kiss Johnny's head; breathe in the smell of him, like an ache.

'I'll come to see you soon, promise,' I say. 'Love you, Monkey.'

This sets him off howling again.

In the end they have to peel him off me, an arm and a leg at a time.

I follow his eyes following me all the way out of the flat,

all the way down the stairs, all the way to the police car.

His little hands reaching out like stars.

Dead Man's Bay

There are jellyfish in the trees.

They shiver, shiny and surprised.

Me and Dog blink at them as we emerge, stumbling, from the forest, and it is these that are taking our attention, not the dark bundles lying here and there on the beach.

So we don't see the things the sea has spat out. Not at first.

Our shelter is gone.

I swallow as I take in the space where our camp used to be. Our little attempts to make a home, all vanished. The storm has torn up our roof like tissue.

Here and there, shreds of cooking pots, curls of palm roof, scraps of plastic lie twisted.

I look across the beach. One Tree has been torn out of the sand and thrown across the bay. It looks like a bent elbow, broken and pointing.

I touch a jellyfish. Already it has crisped in the sun.

Dog barks and barks from across the beach as I search for our stuff.

I find a few scraps of our kitchen: the giant clam shell we used to serve food; the sharpened twig we'd use for snail kebabs. The *MARINA BAIT* tub is bobbing near the rocks, near our broken fish-trap.

161

'Quiet, Dog,' I shout. 'For frick's sake.'

He won't stop yapping and yapping.

I can't see any sign of the fishing net. Our canopy, which took so long to make: hours and hours of gnawing at the trees with sharp rocks and my safety knife, jumping and swinging off the branches till they finally groaned and gave; hours and hours of dragging tree trunks through the forest, gasping in the pulsing heat. All for nothing.

And then I see the fire. Dead. The sodden log blackened and no embers, no heat, no life.

No matches.

That's when I want to howl and howl, because I really don't think I can take any more of this; don't have it in me to drag myself from this wet sand and get myself standing and start all over again.

Because I can't do it. Not on my own, not even with Dog.

There are things on the beach.

I start to gather them in my sling, not caring, not seeing:

A trainer, half-buried in the sand.

A set of headphones, the kind that lock you in so no one hears or sees you. They have a skull sticker on them, half-scratched away by the sea.

A piece of metal, twisted by a madman. It's white and silver and looks vaguely familiar.

Dog's really going for it now, hopping back and forth, sniffing at one of those dark bundles and then leaping back as if he's been stung.

No matches, I think. *No fire, no matches, no way to boil water.*

I make my way up to Dog slowly 'cause it's difficult to walk when your legs feel like stone. It still doesn't register, not even when I see the pelicans swoop, *whup-whup-whup-*ing across the sea. Not even when I see the sandflies fizzing and jostling like they're at a circus.

Not even when I see what's all over Dog's nose.

He grins at me, tail wagging.

'What's that, Dog? What have you been —'

And then I see what he's been looking at
and I stop
and drop my sling
and just scream and scream.

Soft as Sugar; Sweet as Meat

Coral's face is half-eaten away and there are sandflies in her eye sockets and in her mouth. She has no tongue. Instead, meaty shreds hang from her jawbone, where gulls have been tugging.

The sand is soft as sugar between my toes.

And there's something crawling out of her mouth: the crab's pale arms wave blindly.

The sweet stench of her rises like fug; then the sun heaps it on, more and more.

She's all chewed up and spat out.

I turn round; make myself look at the others. Because it's better to know, better to see, than to imagine. Even though the sight of Tiny's torn-away arm; of Trish's top, still with its smiling TeamSkill logo; the whitebonegapemouthemptyeye-bristlemeatsweetstink makes me sob and splatter-retch on to the sugared sand.

But this is better than the dreams I would have if I didn't see.

I kneel by the water's edge and splash my face. Breathe deep. Stare at the sea ruffling and unruffling.

Then I walk over to the thing that was Coral and gently untie her shoes. They're red canvas pumps and come off easily. A fly lands on my arm and I brush it away; trying not to breathe till I am well away from her.

Hi I'm Trish! is no longer smiling –

'cause she has nofacenofacenoface –

but she still has her clothes and still has her badge with her name inside its rainbow logo. She is lying very close to Tiny, and I wonder whether she was with him at the end, when the final wave washed over them and filled their lungs. Then I remember the snapping sound of her ankle. She would've been trapped inside the cabin; maybe Tiny too.

I hope they were together.

Wiping my eyes, I wonder if I can force myself to tug off her sodden jeans. Jeans burn well.

I can't.

And I have no matches.

Chunks of metal that must be plane wreckage are scattered by the far rocks. There's no sign of the pilots or Joker. A glass bottle half full of clear liquid has been flung by Tiny's feet and I pick it up.

I make myself put Coral's shoes on. It's agony at first because my feet are all cut up from the rocks but I take the laces out and that feels better; Coral's feet are a size bigger than mine. The laces go into the bag too.

I take a swig from the bottle and start to giggle.

It's Trish's vodka.

Once I start giggling I can't stop.

Seating Plan

I stand up.

'Frances?'

Pick up my things.

'What are you doing?'

Place the chair under, ever so carefully.

'Don't like it here, Miss.'

'Go back to your seat.'

'Stinks, Miss.'

'Frances, there is a seating plan.'

'Stinks of lies and promises and *crap*, Miss.'

'Fran–'

'Think the stink is coming from *you*, Miss. So, if you don't mind, I'll just sit at the back.'

'Frances Stanton, I need you to move back to your allocated place.'

'Miss Bright, I need you to move back to your desk, away from me because I'm not being funny or anything but your breath really stinks.'

Titters from the classroom. Everyone's listening; I can feel them drawing all the air out of the room because they're listening so closely.

Sigh. 'Well, it's your decision, Frances.'

Then she gets down and crouches by me; it's that stupid thing they all do – get down to the level of the kid who's playing up so they're not threatened. I can read her better than all those books she likes to read us.

'You have a choice, Fran: you can either comply with my reasonable request of moving back to your seat, or, if you insist on continuing to disrupt my lesson, then I'm afraid I'm going to have to reroute you.'

Rerouting is this thing where you have to go and sit at the back of a Year Seven or a Sixth-Form class with a great fat boring textbook and everyone ignores you. It's stupid 'cause they're never going to be able to make me leave this classroom.

Ever.

Miss turns her back to me and prepares to write the date on the board but I'm not having that.

I'm. Not. Having. That.

'Fuck you,' I say.

My voice could shatter glass.

Miss's back freezes.

And everyone's listening so hard they're going to spontaneously combust.

'OK, Frances,' she says – and I'll give her credit, her voice is only a little bit shaky. 'It appears that you have made your choice. Please take this book and make your way to room E6.'

She thrusts a tatty textbook at me. It's open at a page on similes. Happy cartoon bubbles telling me that:

Her face is as white as snow.

The sky is as black as a witch's cloak.

I am so angry I could burst.

'You can stuff your stupid book,' I scream, and hurl it across the room.

I leap up out of my chair and slam my desk over. I kick it.

Everyone stares. Everyone waits.

A million hours pass.

Miss swallows. 'OK, everyone,' she says. 'It seems that Frances needs…um…a little while to calm down. Please pack up your things and follow me. It's a lovely day so we'll work outside.'

And I have to watch as they all troop after her.

I am alone, in this stupid classroom with this stupid book.

I grab Miss's marker pen and scrawl in big black letters all over her desk:

TRAITOR

Shrinking

The red cover is hardest to tear but I manage it, hands shaking. All those pages, all those stories, all the words, words, words. I scatter the pieces over the piles of magazines, all the books I could find, anything that could burn, newspapers, junk mail, unpaid bills.

Picture books.

I hear the ducks from the lake, still splashing even though it's late. The park's locked up. I had to climb over the railing by dragging up the old trampoline that's been at the bottom of the flats since for ever. Around me, the dark shapes of the kiddies' climbing frame and wooden tunnels in the playground. Below me, the coolness of the sandpit.

The smoke smells good; it reminds me of bonfires and Grandad on his allotment, chucking all the bad weeds on top of the pile. And all the time the smoke from his pipe curling, curling, a million years ago, before Johnny was born.

My notebook flickers. I've torn the pages out and scrumpled them up into little balls on the sand. They light easily and I watch the words wrinkle.

I've made one last entry in my red notebook, especially for her, for Miss.

And I've even done it as an ink waster so, Miss, if you ever read it in hell, I hope you really like it.

Dear Miss

You're a snake. A smiling snake.
I want to rip out your ponytail and spit in your face and scratch out your eyes and rip the vintage buttons off your stupid frickin cardigan and pull out your hair and slash through that smile.
No more stories, Miss. Are you listening? Can you still hear me?
I hope you frickin can. You lying, treacherous bitch.
Made you look so good, didn't it?
'Write me a story, Fran' and 'Why don't you set it all down?' and 'Let's do an ink waster, an ink waster, an ink waster — maybe it'll turn into something.'
You've been waiting for me to come out,
prising me out
like a crab out of its shell. And you've taken the innermost secret part of me, the bit that I've hidden and covered up and protected, and I let you read my dreams and all

the time you've been waiting.
Maybe it will make me
open myself up like a blank page
and, while you're at it, why don't you scour lines through
my words and scribble deep gouges in my heart and rip
out my heart and tear it up, tear it up
into little fleshy shreds.
Because that's what you did
when you told.

I screw up more pages because the first ones are going out already.

The words wither to embers that flash and die in the sand. My rage burns.

And I watch the words wrinkle till they burn into an idea.

Clean as Forgetting

I don't know how long I sit in our tattered camp under the trees.

I clean my bleeding feet with seawater from a bottle and my torn-up leggings. From out of my Hello Kitty washbag I take:

    1 black eyeliner
    1 turquoise nail varnish
    1 broken mirror.

And between swigs of vodka, I outline my eyes precisely with the eyeliner, taking great care with the flicks. My eyes stare back at me, glassy and huge. There are fragments of dirty brown skin and flashes of wet cheek and red peeling fore-head, but they belong to a stranger.

I concentrate only on making perfect flicks.

When I'm done, I replace the cap on the eyeliner and put it back in the bag.

Another swig of vodka, clean as forgetting.

Off comes the lid of the turquoise polish. I stretch my legs out in front of me and they are long and brown and grubby. Old scabs and new scabs cluster from rock scratches and sandfly bites. But this doesn't matter.

What matters is applying my nail varnish, carefully, breath-ing in the fumes. The polish gleams like a blue teardrop on each grimy toe. I do my hands next, holding them to the sun to dry. My hands are black shadows like palm leaves; through my frond fingers the sun shivers.

I blow on them to make sure they're dry and put my Ray-Bans on.

Vodka.

Lie back now.

Because vodka tears are the sweetest.

Cave of Tears

We can't stay here, Dog and me, that is certain.

One Tree Beach, our little camp, our home, they're all gone; all smashed and broken. One Tree Beach has become Dead Man's Bay.

I think of the weeping cave and its sucking tunnels and

look at Dog.

'There's got to be a way through to the other side of the island,' I tell him. 'We've got to be brave, Dog.'

He wags his tail solemnly. Watches me as I refill the vodka bottle with rainwater and place it into my rucksack along with the Hello Kitty bag.

So we leave the broken-backed forest with its smashed-up trees, its tumbled logs and branches. We leave Dead Man's Bay with its flies and flesh and pelicans.

Dog leads and I follow.

A bark, high and shrill; it comes from the back of the cavern.

I push against the darkness, one step at a time.

'Wait for me,' I say again.

His bark bounces off the unseen walls and mocks me. I follow and grope my way further in.

One foot. One foot at a time. It's like pushing against a force field. I breathe hard and focus on reaching the back wall where Dog waits for me.

Then, moth-soft, a breath on my cheek.

I scream and scream and scream, loud as bells, loud as gulls.

And Dog joins in, yipping and yawling. He's here with me; I can feel his wet fur pressing against my legs.

'Oh God, oh God,' I say. 'What was that? What the frick was that?'

As if in answer, two bats flit up and out of the cave, squealing. I can just see them, like scraps of cinder with my unblinding eyes.

'Keep going, Dog,' I say. 'Frannie's all right now.'

But I am so not all right.

The back of the cave doesn't stop; it is an endless passage, a nightmare thing. Here, the dark is rock solid. I reach forward with my hands.

'Wait for me,' I say.

My fingers shrink from touch. Eyes wide and stretched and unseeing.

Dog is fast. I pant as I try to catch him up, Coral's too-big shoes squelching and slipping – here is wet slime, there's a rockfall. But Dog is always there, waiting; my little white guide.

Deeper and deeper we go, till the tunnel twists round and there is the ghost-light –

light at the end of the tunnel –

which I saw the first time I came. It's a weird light, sort of blue-green, all shimmering and glowing like a misty pool.

The rocky floor begins to descend and I gulp –

Oh God, not deeper down –

and Dog's claws tick-tack on the stone as he leads the way.

When we climb through the window in the rocks, I stare and stare.

We Are Rock

We're in a cavern the size of St Paul's Cathedral and it's both beautiful and terrible.

'Careful, Dog,' I say, but this time it's only a whisper.

This is the sort of place that makes you shiver because it doesn't care about you; you're nothing and it's been here for millions of years, sighing, weeping.

Glistening shapes squat in the middle of the rocky island like little hunched monkeys. *Stalagmites*. I remember from school. They're huddled in groups, these stone gargoyles. Crocodile-shaped stalactites cluster around the roof. They're prehistoric claws, ugly, grasping; hanging like twisted turds.

Inside this huge stone chamber, I feel small and soft and raw –

but I am a rock.

'*We are rock and you are flesh,*' they say.

There is a *splash* and Dog's swimming round and round a wide pool, his little face held up, tongue licking the water every now and then.

I shout a warning and the cave takes my voice and bounces it from wall to wall.

Carefulcarefulcarefulcareful.

I look up and there's a sun–hole shining over this shimmering pool. It's beautiful and misty and high up like a promise.

'That's where we're going, Dog – to the other side of the island.'

It's like, I don't know, something unlocks inside me and I want to let everything, everything in: all this fear and beauty and wonder and promise – I want to strip myself raw and throw myself at it; soak up the light to kill all the shadows.

I take a deep breath.

Then I strip off my T-shirt and jump in.

The water slaps me *coldcoldcoldcold.*

I whoosh upward, gasping.

'Oh. My. God.'

And the chamber takes my voice and throws it around, turning it into something sweet and beautiful, like choir music or something.

OhmyGod God God God Go-o-o-o-o-ddd.

I swim around with tiny strokes because it's too cold to stretch your arms and the water freezes my chest so I can't breathe.

Dog has climbed out, and is waiting for me, on the other side of the pool. I can feel him shiver from here.

I soak up just one more moment of this bathing light; I'm on stage and the spotlight is on me, alone in this strange cave theatre. I turn my face up to the light and close my eyes and inside my head I say a little prayer, just one, because it's that sort of place.

Dog waits like a ghost in the shadows. He knows where he's going.

Shivering, I follow.

Black Water

Here in this passage, the dark is solid as a punch and my eyes strain on blind stalks. It's like my eyes are never going to get used to this dead-weight blackness.

Dog's bark is always ahead. I turn round, and the glow of light from the cavern has shrunk to a thumbnail.

'Dog,' I shout again, and my voice echoes, high and tight and anxious.

I go forward. Think of the torch that I no longer have.

We're in a thin sort of passageway that's slimy with sea-water. A passage that goes up and up.

After hours or minutes, we break through into a watery tunnel, which must be at the edge of the coast 'cause the sea's coming through, closer and closer each time. There's a dim light in this passage, revealing another chamber. Here it's like entering the jaws of some prehistoric creature. All veined belly, cruel mouth. Below, swirling water. In front, the glistening rock has tapered to a bridge. We'll have to get across somehow, even though it's a narrow ledge. I'll just have to crawl, shuffle.

Beneath me, the water sucks. There's not much time before the water comes in and cuts us off. We'll be trapped between the sea and the other side of the island. Trapped inside this mountain, in the heart of hell.

I start to shuffle across the bridge.

Dog is already over on the other side. He pants, watching, but I'm hugging this rock because any minute now the tide's going to come in and when it does I'll be beaten and battered like a rag doll. Rocks slip beneath my sliding fingers. I hold on, gritting my teeth as the wave-swell bashes into me, my fingers clawing so hard that I must have lost at least three fingernails.

I hold on – just.

Then sigh with relief as the water sucks back out.

Muscles shaking with the effort, I claw my way over the water, along the slippery rock. My knees burn and my hands throb with pain and I sit and get my breath back, and listen to the suck and glop of the seawater as it, too, rests.

'?' says Dog.

'Not much further,' I say. 'Wait for me, Dog.'

I look across the chasm. Halfway there.

Through the greenish light I can see the rocky passage up ahead. It's definitely going up and I feel a flip of excitement in my belly. Soon, soon, we'll be on the other side of the island, Dog and me, away from the dead things, away from the rats, the things that sneak in the forest. There'll be fresh water and a new shelter to build; a new little-house-by-the-sea.

Below me, the water gulps and ploshes.

'Wait there, Dog,' I say. 'Don't go without me.'

But he seems uneasy; his little feet dig into the ledge, as he

175

watches something behind me. I twist around.

The tide must be coming right in now; I can make out the roll of it, surging into our dark cavern.

'Dog, you've got to hurry!' I yell.

I'm frightened now. The next swell of water will cover up the tunnel. He'll be drowned; swept off his ledge in the tide-surge.

'Please, Dog. Please go. Off you go, Monkey.'

But he won't budge. His little claws are clinging on to that rock and his eyes are watching me. He watches me, tail twitching just a little, those treacle eyes never leaving my sight.

Then he cocks his head, and he's gone, through the tunnel.

There's a hissing roar, and seawater swells and crashes over me. I throw myself forward and grip on to the bridge, pressing my cheek against its stone surface and gasping as the icy water hits me.

A sucking sound and it pulls back, ready for round two.

'Dog,' I shriek. 'Dog.'

Dog's gone and I'm here alone, in this secret, sighing cave.

My cries echo round me like a flock of bats, and once they start, they don't stop. It's like something's been unleashed and I'm a blind thing inside a cave and I'm whispering, whispering for someone to find me.

This is how I will die. Shivering in a cave, in the dark, because this is how monsters live and how they die. They don't die on beaches. They die inside rocks.

Hand over hand, I shuffle over the bridge to the other side.

I know why I'm cursed, 'course I do.

I've always known.

London's Burning

Today is Sports Day. See how thoughtful I am?

I may be fucked up but I'm not a killer.

I only want to burn down every brick, every book, every lie –

> *'cause books are lies and Miss is a liar.*

Mr Sparrey, the caretaker, turns and says, 'All right, love? Shouldn't you be outside?'

Out in the sun, everyone's choosing teams and doing stretches and getting ice creams, and the teachers are all relaxed and they've got their sun cream on and their bad fashion shades on, and some will have even got their legs out.

The PE staff are on the loudspeaker.

The Head's picking litter and pretend-smiling.

The coast is clear.

A carrier bag clinking with bottles.

Heart *boomboomboom* angry.

I hate.

It's so easy to get inside English Block. No one's bothered locking it.

There's no one on the landing. Usually there'd be a cluster of Year Sevens messing about doing drama, but not today.

So I head straight for the stock cupboard next to Miss's room. It's that easy.

Shut the door. Here are piles of exercise books (old and new), old coursework, controlled assessments, sugar paper filled with students' scrawl, books, papers, sliding piles of essays.

More importantly, there are all the books Miss loves so much.

So let's destroy!

What will it be first?

How about a heap of textbooks? I rip the plasticky covers off and shove the paper middles on to the floor.

Next, the Shakespeare plays. Off with the plastic jackets. Off with their heads. On to the pile they go. I splash the vodka around and the smell of it is sharp and sweet.

Slosh.

I sweep all of the books off the shelves and there are hundreds of them; all those stories; all the words Miss likes. I want her to realise why I've done it.

Slosh.

Bitch. Behind that smug, I-really-care-about-the-kids exterior, behind the nods and the shoulder-taps and the winks and the smiley faces, she's no better than the rest of them.

She's worse 'cause she pretends to care; she prised open my soul and she saw what was inside.

I take a long gulp of vodka.

It's her fault, all of it. That Johnny's gone –

his little hands reaching out like stars.

And if she knew – if she only knew – what her interfering, double-crossing actions would lead to.

Looking after Johnny made me *me*.

So who am I now?

I am nothing and no one

without him.

Keep waking up and he's not there. The sound of his breathing is missing; the warm huff on my cheek.

Slosh.

Vodka doesn't burn. It's not enough.

I know what will be enough.

Shiver

The science labs are below the English rooms and now I know how to make the pain go away.

I start to float, right out of my body, right above myself. I drift, bumping against the ceiling, and watch myself turn all the Bunsen burners on and close all the windows except one.

A fly is trapped inside one of the strip-light fittings. As it crawls, it feels everything gently.

Patpatpat, checking, checking.

Other Fran walks out of the lab and closes the door. I know she is walking around the side of the building, reaching into her bag.

Everyone is outside, on the field. Teachers are chatting in the sun. All the students are stretching and racing and lazing.

Other Fran slides the matchbox, takes a match.

Whirr, goes the fly.

The flame shivers a little.

Then it is flung through the half-open window.

WWWHHHHUUUMMMPPPPP, goes the science lab.

And the girl that is me feels nothing.

Where the Rocks Weep

The walls weep.

I have changed to a crawling creature; I lick the cave walls with my fat shining tongue. My shoes are gone, drowned in the water. My rucksack too, lost in the swell when I tried to get out my drinks bottle. I have only my Hello Kitty bag, which I clutch dog-like in my teeth.

About me is only darkness now; these breathing, weeping walls.

Time trickles and drips; for centuries I climb, hand over hand.

And the dark creeps behind me on slithering elbows.

Water Like Diamonds

My throat has a thousand flies buzzing in it, waiting for me to unhinge my jaw and let them out, a swarm to block out the

whitelightwhitelightwhitelight.

And always that insect sound of endless hissing: *churra-churra.*

There's a break in the rocks. And a slimy ledge, and the rocks are different here; they're smooth and wet and furred. They're covered in *moss* and that means, that means –

Water.

And behind the moss is splintering light, endlessly patterning.

Moaning, I break out of my cave and there's a curtain, a tower: endless, deafening, hurling, hissing water, bright as diamonds, fast as bullets.

Churra-churra churra-churra.

It could be insects but I don't think it's insects.

I'm behind a waterfall.

I try to touch it and it's hard as stone; they'll snap my fingers off, those water-swords.

I crawl, slither, fall over the mossy rocks, downdown-down, and I'm aware of the endless roaring beside me and the terrible glare of sun that blinds me, strips me raw.

I fall, into water burning-cold; into sun that unpeels my eyes.

Falling Light

The water's hailing down now, stabbing the darkness away. I drink and drink like a dog, and all the time water tumbles over me, cuts me like shards of glass.

When I'm done, I collapse into the pool, lie back with my face staring at the sky.

I could die now, in this sun, in this burning water.

As I sink lower, the water weeds stroke me and I drown.

I'm sorry, I'm so sorry.

Lie back, lie back, give in to all this brightness.

Turn my face up to the sun and let it melt me. Blister my stony flesh in slow splashes around me.

I didn't mean to do it, didn't mean to hurt anyone.

Let the waterweeds stroke my hair.

There's nothing for me now, there's only the sun that unpeels and the water that burns.

So let it end here, in this moment. The last thing that I will see is that leaf with its diamond beads of water. And behind the leaf, that pile of stones. Stone placed over stone with perfect precision. Five stones in total, all carefully balanced, neat as you like –

I blink my gritty eyes. Think.

Stones don't balance themselves.

Something about the neatness, the precision, reminds me of

reminds me of

tiny cramped numbers scratched in sharp pencil.

I have time to register that the mountain's spat me out on the other side of the island; I've been spat out right where Whoever lives –

the bird hunter, the smoke-maker, the dog-catcher, the –

Be careful what you wish for.

And then there's a splashing noise, and movement, and two hands grasp me under the arms.

A voice, hoarse and panting.

'Oh fuck,' it says.

Feet

The voice is not what I expected in heaven. And it's too posh for hell.

There's splashing and gasping and someone pulling at me, dragging me out, but I'm too busy dying.

I don't come easy. It's nice, being dead. I try to beat them away.

'Getoffgetoffgetoff,' I say, but my voice comes out all wrong. That can't be me, that ragged howling. Sounds like a beast that's been dragged from the shadows.

When I'm out of the pool –

can't be Poison Pool 'cause it's far too clean and there's no waterfall there, 'course there isn't –

there's that voice again.

'Christ, oh shit. I can't believe it, I don't believe it.'

A hoarse voice that's not been used in a long, long time. Cracked, but posh as plums.

Through drowned hair I see:

Two perfectly plaited flip-flops containing

Two peeling freckled feet.

Then my stomach twists with pain and I cough and gasp and retch up water all over them.

Face

A face, hovering.

Disappears and appears again.

Is it an angel? Do angels have matted red hair and ginger beards?

'Go away,' I tell the face. 'Leave me alone. I want to die.'

I curl up tight as pain.

The face comes back again and again. The face says things like 'Who are you?' and 'I think you need to drink this' and 'Were you on the plane?'

It's a face that's blistered and peeling and hollow-eyed.

I close my eyes and ignore it till it goes away.

But it keeps coming back. It gives me water in a tin cup. It tries to feed me.

I'm hollowed out.

Someone has taken a spoon and scooped out all of my flesh, the stone, and left me just this tired old skin.

I sleep. I try to watch, to grasp on to the face that hovers.

It comes a lot, mostly just to stare.

I wish it would go away.

I wish it would come back.

Breathing

'You can go in now.'

The nurse is nodding and smiling. Her voice is happy-jolly, like it's the best thing in the world to be lying in bed surrounded by sucking machines.

I take a deep breath and step inside.

It's the sound that gets me first of all, then the smell.

The noise is a mechanical clamping and sucking; regular, monotonous, like wind being forced through a tube.

I hate it.

I see a bed and curtains pulled back and a cabinet full of bottles and boxes and tubes. The air is antiseptic, sharp and bitter. The breathing machine sucks and resucks.

I feel hot in my mask.

I need to get out of this room of sickness.

But I look at her face.

At first I'm relieved. Miss is sitting up in bed, putting on make-up. She's smiling into a mirror, outlining her eyes in purple shimmer. When she sees me, she waves to me with a bandaged hand.

'How's your magnum opus?' she asks, and I see that she's dropped her eyeshadow pencil.

Because she only has stumps in those bandages. There are no fingers to hold it.

'Oops, silly me,' she says.

Something is happening to her voice. It's getting higher and higher and now it's ringing.

Now I'm close, I realise that a plastic mask presses her poor molten flesh back to keep it in place. As I watch, her face starts to melt like a wax crayon, like a Barbie doll.

Hot fat.

It's splashing on to the bed sheets.

Drip drip.

'Let's do an ink waster,' says Miss, and her voice is high and jarring; it's turned into a fire bell.

Her bandaged hand reaches out to touch me.

Feathers

'It's only a dream. You're dreaming.'

That voice again.

It's buzzing round me like a fly. I want to bat it away and sink into darkness.

I'm lying on something that crackles, but can't make myself care enough to look.

I feel the space where Dog used to sleep, like an ache. Dog will be drowned now, swirled away or trapped for ever in those hell-caves. I curl up, tight on my side.

I lose everything I touch. I'm cursed. I destroy all those

who look at me.

I think of Dog, those treacle eyes.

A hand, reaching out like stars.

A face pressed behind its plastic mask.

And I think of Cassie, rising from the settee.

Love you more than the sun and stars and planets.

A feathered headdress floats in front of my eyes. I squeeze them shut. A bird hunter, I think. But I can't make myself care and I can't make it go away.

'Um, I really think you should eat something now.'

Something cold and wet is pressed against my lips. I lick it. Sweet and cold.

Turn away to my pain.

A sigh.

'Well, I'll leave it here and you can take some when you're ready.'

The voice goes away.

Good.

I lie alone, sweet juice still cold on my lips.

After

They told me afterwards that the caretaker had saved both their lives.

Turns out she was still in the classroom. She was mentoring a kid in her room; she wasn't at Sports Day with the rest.

She won't need to spend time doing her hair in those pretty styles again because most of it's crisped off. It'll be quite a while before she puts purple shimmery eyeshadow on again.

Miss and her student didn't know anything was wrong till the fire bell went off, but that classroom door had always stuck – it never locked properly – and they panicked and couldn't get out.

The caretaker dragged them out; risked his life to get them both out of English Block before the fire service took over.

Miss made the student get out first so she ended up with burns over most of her body. Lost the skin on both hands.

'They've brought her out of her coma now,' Angela says. 'Do you want to go inside?'

We're standing in the hospital corridor. There's a glass window into Miss's room.

'Ant-bac,' says a nurse. In silence we squirt gel on to our hands, rub it in till it vanishes in a whiff of ice.

'She wants to see you,' says Angela. 'She's been asking for you, once she knew what happened.'

'Wear this,' says the nurse.

She passes a protective gown to me. It rustles as I put it on. I don't want to go inside that room.

When I was a little girl, I was taken to see my grandad before he died.

I was eight or nine and he was almost unrecognisable, lying under the hospital sheets.

His hands weren't the ones I remembered, lighting his fags with the blue glass lighter that was always on the sideboard, holding my hand tightly to cross the road to the sweetie shop.

These hands were fluttering birds, nipping and un-nipping at the sheets.

Grandad was fretful. At one point he tried to climb out of bed to go and find my nanna. I remember I was shocked 'cause they hadn't dressed him properly; his pyjamas were too big and they gaped.

My mum tried to push him back into bed but it was no good; we had to call the nurse in the end. My grandad died soon after, followed by my nanna, who wasn't interested in a world without her beloved Frank.

Cassie always liked a drink, but she started drinking a lot more after that. It was good in a way though, 'cause that's when we had lots of TV and movie cuddles. Sometimes all day.

I force myself to move closer and look through the glass at the person that lies at the centre of all the tangle of tubes and wires.

Miss's body seems tiny, a small mound below the spotless sheets.

She's bundled in bandages: her head and arms and hands.

'She was lucky,' says the nurse. 'They're only second-degree burns. She'll need skin grafts of course, but...' She smiles at me. 'Is she your teacher? How lovely, to have one of her pupils come to visit her.'

My face hovers in the glass.

If I stare long enough, my snake hair will wake and coil into S shapes, ready to strike and hiss. My fang teeth will lengthen. My eyes will shrink into empty pockets of hellfire, tiny white-hot pebbles, ready to petrify. Ready to burn.

I tear off my gown. Angela hurries after me.

'I really think you should go and see her, Frances.'

'No.'

'It'll help you with the sleeplessness, with the dreams.'

'No.'

'Do you want to talk about it?'

Keep away from me 'cause I bite, I freeze, I burn.

'Frances?'

Fat as Moons

There's that smell again. It's fruity, wet and sweet. It's killing me.

At first I think I'm in Grandad's allotment, up on the park. I imagine I see his tomatoes, fat as moons, hanging above me. There's even the unmistakable *green* smell of them, like when I'd help him pick them and that scent would be on my fingers. It's the smell of being seven.

But there's a face like a green football, bobbing and nodding with its zigzag teeth and wet pink smiles. I rub my eyes and blink. It's a melon on a post, carved like a pumpkin. Its grass skirt rustles.

I shift around and wonder why I'm lying under a neatly-plaited palm canopy on a sturdy bed laced with fresh leaves. The mattress is squeaky. I reach down and realise it's been made with plastic bottles.

But there it is again. A waft in the warm air. I turn round.

Placed next to me on an upturned tin drum is a clam shell. And on the clam shell, sliced into fat chunks, are pieces of watermelon, fat and pink and spitting pips.

I grab a piece and cram it whole into my mouth.

OhmyGod ohmyGod sugarsweet sugarfizz tastes like sugar on my tongue.

I slurp and suck and burp till I've cleared the plate and

juice drips down my face and neck.

'Good. I'm glad you're eating.'

I spin round, chin dripping.

Boy

A boy.

Tall, skinny–but–not–too–skinny, he's wearing what seems to be a cloth over his head and shoulders, Arab style. There are feathers poking out of the headband of different sizes and shapes – I recognise pelican and gull and the oh–dear–me bird. Freckles peep through a scrubby beard. Behind all the feathers and freckles, a pair of sharp blue eyes.

The boy is holding a home-made machete in one hand and a melon in the other. The melon is as fat as a football and I can't take my eyes off it.

'We've got a real glut. This rain seems to have swollen them into beach balls.' His voice is all rusty, like he hasn't used it in a long, long time.

I stare at him, juice still dripping from my chin. Become aware of my lack of clothes, my filthy bikini, and shrink back into bed, under the palm-leaf blanket. Where is my red T-shirt? My shoulder stings; I have bandages on it.

'You cut yourself on the rocks by the waterfall. You were in a real state. I cleaned your wounds. The top you were wearing is drying – I washed it for you.'

I can't speak, can't say thank you. I cringe back on this boy's bed, just staring.

I don't know how to feel, how to react. I've not spoken to

another human for a million years – since I've been on this rock, and for another million years before that.

'Here.'

His voice is cracked like it needs oiling. He throws me something that once upon a time used to be yellow.

A TeamSkill polo, bleached by the sun.

'Hi, I'm Rufus,' he says, and the boy holds out his hand.

Pleased to Meet You

I have a wild urge to laugh and laugh.

Hi I'm Rufus! It's Hi I'm frickin Rufus!

His hand is still out and I take it as if in a dream. It's hot and sticky and real.

I want to let it go. I do not want to let it go.

'I can't believe you're here,' he says.

He scratches at a nasty outcrop of sandfly bites on his neck.

'I mean, you just appeared, from behind the waterfall.' He gives a shaky laugh. 'Thought you were some sort of demon or something. All matted and wild and filthy. It was like something out of one of those Japanese horror films. You know, like *The Ring*.'

His voice is still posh but much huskier than I remember.

'I mean, you're that girl from the plane, aren't you? Not Coral. The other one.'

He leans forward eagerly. 'Are there any more? Survivors, I mean?'

When I shake my head, I see the flicker of disappointment.

191

'Bugger. When I saw the smoke signal I thought that there would be more. That's why I sent the coordinates. I already knew, more or less, the position of the island we were heading for – I'm interested in that sort of thing – and I thought maybe you were with the pilot or someone.' He pauses. 'So it's just you and me then?'

Yes, I think, *you've got a raw deal there. Thought there might be a whole party of us, did you? Hoping for both the pilots or Trish or even Joker? Instead you've ended up with me.*

Broken, filthy, burnt out. The girl who destroys all that she touches.

Lucky you.

'I'm sorry,' he says. 'I'm not used to speaking to people; it's been so long. Eighty-one days, in fact.'

I don't ask him how he knows. Probably keeps a tally on a tree somewhere. I wonder why I didn't think of doing that, and then I'm drowsy.

Close my eyes. Just close them now.

When I awake, he's still hovering.

I curl up on my side again.

He sighs. He does that a lot.

He melts away.

Skin

When I think Rufus can't see me, I study him.

I think he does that to me too. Sometimes his eyes dart away and he flushes. He flushes easily, even through all those

192

nasty sandfly bites and his sunburn.

He's got the worst skin for being marooned on a desert island. It's skin that would be happiest in a darkened room with all the blinds down. Cassie's lounge, in fact. His skin would love all that cardboard.

There are bites on his face and neck and on the back of his hands. There are bites on bites on bites.

'You're Frances, right? You sat behind me on the plane. And I remember you at TeamSkill.'

I sabotaged your team games. That's me.

'I mean, you were right actually, to not like planes. After what happened. I was lucky enough to have held on to some flotsam – a couple of plastic containers – and I had on my life jacket of course. I estimated that I drifted approximately two hundred kilometres from the SOA, seeing as my raft had no anchor. And I had to guess, really, about the wind, weather, the direction of swells, times of sunrise and sunset and whatnot. I even tried to use celestial navigation to determine my position, but it's practically impossible without a sextant and almanac. Of course, the EPIRB would have transmitted on an emergency frequency the minute the plane went down, so there would have been searchers or a rescue mission. But with the number of islands in these parts, and the distance of the drift, well…I suppose our chances of being found are pretty much non-existent.'

'SOA? EPIRB?' I say dully.

'Scene of Accident and Emergency Position Indicating Radio Beacon. I'm surprised you didn't have one of those in your life raft. I'm sure they come as standard.'

I decide not to mention the radio thing that I chucked into the sea in a rage.

Rufus scratches his head and coughs. 'Well, I'm pleased you're here, Frances. I was wondering if I'd ever speak to another human again.'

'So you knew I was here then?' I manage to say. Like his, my voice is rusty as old tin.

'Well, I guessed there was someone. Like I said, I saw your smoke signal. Jolly clever of you to keep it going with wet leaves like that.'

'Well, I didn't actually. It wasn't…' I nearly tell him that whatever smoke signal I made was definitely not deliberate, but change my mind.

I think of all the times I tried to keep the fire going with damp logs and wet leaves. And of the coughing smoke that would come billowing out and choke Dog and me in our little den.

Dog. I think of his liquid eyes and use my T-shirt to wipe my eyes.

Oh oh oh.

You're the Girl Who…

'Here, don't get upset,' says Rufus awkwardly.

He looks funny, still standing there in his feathered head-dress holding that enormous melon, and I begin to laugh helplessly.

Once I start, I can't seem to stop. I snort and snot into my polo shirt, shoulders heaving. And I'm aware of the boy putting down his melon and patting my shoulder like I'm a little kid.

'Don't cry.'

That does it.

I push my soggy hair out of my eyes. 'I'm not frickin crying. I never cry.'

I wipe my face with the polo and glare at him. 'If you must know, I was laughing.'

'Laughing?'

'At you. At your stupid headdress.'

See the little stab of hurt. *There. I'm glad.*

Rufus shrugs. 'The sun and I aren't friends,' he says.

He's older than he seemed at TeamSkill, maybe nineteen or twenty. Freckles so big the sun's blended them all together, brown blobby islands making a map of the world. The pink skin between them is trying very hard to get brown.

There's an awkward silence.

'So did you see my markers?' he asks at last.

I think of the balanced stone towers and nod.

'I left them in case whoever was on the north side of the island managed to find a way through. Every day, I was hoping…'

He doesn't speak for a moment; scratches at the bites on his hands.

'Anyway, jolly clever of you –'

Jolly??

'– I explored every creek and crevice and the only way through seemed to be a tunnel that of course would be lethal at high tide. I never thought to look behind the waterfall.'

I think of Dog on the rock, trusting eyes watching me, tail wagging, and dig my fingernails into my legs, so as not to feel.

The boy shakes his head. 'So you must have come that way? Crikey. How did you do it?'

I try not to think of the dripping caves, the swallowing darkness. I struggle to sit up; realise that I'm half-dressed – my SpongeBob bikini bottoms wink mockingly from under

195

Rufus's polo shirt.

'Oh, I almost forgot – here.'

He reaches under my bed and pulls something out. 'I made you this – thought it might be a bit more…comfortable.'

It's a skirt like the one he's wearing. Grass tightly strung around a long strip of some sort of plant stem. Precisely and expertly done.

'Thanks,' I say.

It feels strange, talking to someone. Different from when I talked to Dog 'cause with him I never needed to worry about what I was saying. Or what he'd say back. He was always polite and interested. And it's not like I talked to many people anyway, not after the fire.

The skirt ties up at the side and reaches down to my knees. It gapes a bit when I move – as I notice his does – but at least it covers me up a little.

Rufus looks pleased. 'See, it fits well. You were out for ages. Shame all the medicine's back in the hold. You could have done with some doxepin to help you sleep because you seemed to be having the most terrific nightmares. It would've given your body a chance to recover from what it's been through.'

'What are you – some sort of doctor?' I say.

'Well, kind of. I'm a medic. Or I will be. Just got accepted at St Bart's and I'm currently on my gap year.'

He's shaking his head. ''Course, I never planned *quite* such an adventurous year. Was thinking more about doing conservation work in Borneo, or perhaps some work experience in Belize – they have the most amazing jungles and I've always fancied doing Tropical Medicine. And then I heard about the TeamSkill project and it sounded like such a marvellous idea and a real chance to give something back and so I…' His voice trails off as he sees me staring.

'I'm sorry. It's just that I've been here on my own for rather a long time and it gets a bit lonely just talking to one's melons and Virgil.'

I gape at him.

Borneo? Belize? Virgil?

'And you?' he asks. 'What's your story?'

What, apart from burning my school down and nearly burning alive my teacher and a boy who I don't even know, who was probably just trying to get some advice from his form tutor...?

I scowl at him.

'What the frick's it got to do with you? Anyway, you lot all read my notes, didn't you?'

A little pause as the penny drops. He flushes again, all the way up till he's redder than crab claws.

'Ah,' he says. 'You're the girl who...'

I scowl harder and harder; fix him with my Medusa stare. Haven't used it for so long but it'll still work, I'm sure of it.

'Sorry,' he says at last. 'Didn't mean to rub it in.' He laughs and it's not a nasty laugh. 'I guess we've both kind of changed a lot, right?'

My stare must have weakened in its powers.

'At least it's a good skill though?'

'You what?'

'Lighting fires. Best skill for being marooned, I'd say.'

Is *Hi I'm Rufus!* making a joke?

I glare at him till his flush comes back.

New Camp

Rufus has gone to get more wood, even though there's plenty as far as I can see, so I'm left alone at his camp.

It's nothing like mine and Dog's.

I totter round, weak on my wobbly legs, and poke about a bit, trying to explore.

It's like *Through the frickin Keyhole*.

What would Keith Lemon say to this?

Ha.

Neat piles – everywhere. Neat logs, neat tools, neat beds. I had my could-be pile but the things I foraged were all thrown on the heap any old how. Here, everything is ranked in order of size, in order of material. Rufus doesn't have half-finished projects like mine; everything is finished and definite and solid.

His palm shelter is like something straight out of a survival manual.

He has an array of knives. *Array* isn't a word I'd normally think of using, but it's definitely the word to describe those knives.

I poke about his cooking range, his fire.

Stare into the dancing flames; sigh, and chuck on another log.

Inspect his water system.

As well as tin cans with wire handles nestling in the fire –
billycans. They're called billycans –

which I vaguely remember Steve showing us how to make at TeamSkill, he's set up solar stills all around the camp, made from plastic bags.

I take out his chopping boards in different sizes, beautiful pieces of driftwood; it's like he's Jamie Oliver or something.

Wish I'd had that idea.

There's a line strung up with dried fish, just like mine – at least I did something right – and a plastic bucket full of what looks like edible seaweed. Next to it, my Hello Kitty wash-bag. I move it under my bed.

Rufus has several styles of shoe, ranging from foraged flip-flops (I'm liking the mismatched pair in baby pink best, especially the one with the Tinkerbell logo) to beautifully plaited sandals. These are all arranged neatly under his bed.

While I've been sleeping on a raised platform made from bottles, Rufus has been sleeping in his day hammock, which is head and shoulders above mine on One Tree Beach. It's a complicated structure of bamboo poles and grasses and palm leaves, and there's no way I'm jealous.

He's made a pillow out of palm leaves and coconut fibre, and there's something poking out from underneath. I pull it out and it's my own bark message, neatly rolled.

Ha!

It's when I'm tucking it back underneath that something rushes at me, hot and wet and twisting.

And then my heart starts jittering and pounding like it's going to flip out of my mouth and lie gasping on the ground like a fish.

It kills me, over and over.

'Cause it's Dog.

He's come back to me.

His Master's Voice

I squeeze him like I will never, ever let go.

'Oh my God, Dog! You came back. You came back.'

He's real and he's solid and he's overjoyed to see me, I can tell. He's wriggling in my arms as we sink together on the sand and I'm laughing and –

not crying, I'm not crying –

laughing so much.

He's got my ear now, and my neck.

'Ouch, ouch, Dog. Mind my shoulder, you mentalist.'

A whistle.

Dog stops as if shot.

Leaves his hotbreathlicking and

shoots off

somewhere behind me.

When I turn round, Dog is sitting very nicely, very still but tail flicking, gazing up at his master with adoring eyes.

Good as gold. Trained like Crufts. Comes to a whistle.

Rufus bends down to pet him and Dog's tail spins like it's going to fly off.

Rufus laughs when he sees my face. 'I see you've met Virgil.'

Virgil

I hate.

I hate his stupid camp and his stupid headdress and his

stupid melon patch.

Hate his poncy voice.

Rufus crouches down.

'Here, Virgil, come and say hello to Frances.'

Dog stays by his feet, grinning and panting at me.

'Raise a paw, Virgil.'

Rufus makes Dog shakes hands and his little paw is hot and sandy. In all the days we were together, Dog never raised a paw at me.

Rufus whistles and Dog cocks his head instantly.

'I always wonder where he vanishes to, when he goes walkabout. It keeps me occupied, training him up. He's a bright little thing, isn't he?'

I don't know if Dog is bright or not. All I know is that he's the perfect fit behind my knees at night and when he's hot, the bottoms of his feet smell like biscuits.

I decide not to tell Rufus that I knew him first.

'So why d'you call him Virgil?' I say.

'Well, he's obviously named after the ancient Roman poet.'

Obviously.

'We did him in Classics. Of course, Virgil famously guided Dante through the seven circles of hell, and that's what this little chap's been like to me: my guide.'

'Stupid name,' I say. 'I'll call him Dog.'

I click my fingers to get Dog's attention, but he just ignores me.

Traitor.

'Why was your writing so small in your note?' I say suddenly. 'And why did you write in all that code stuff?'

He looks pained. 'I didn't want to waste paper. And I already knew the location we were heading to in the plane, so the rest was just an estimate really. I would have thought that

201

anyone would realise what coordinates were...'

He trails off, blushing.

So he thinks I'm thick, then?

If I had the message with me I'd make a paper aeroplane out of it and sail it across camp, but then I remember I'm not in a classroom now. Even though Rufus treats me like I'm a particularly stupid pupil.

I wish I could fuss Dog, but he's still sitting at his master's feet.

Rufus is hovering, looking at me. 'Well?'

'Well what?'

'Now you've seen around camp, would you like to admire my melons?'

I stare at him. Is he joking again?

But his face is deadpan as he waits for my answer.

I shrug, which makes my shoulder hurt, but follow him anyway.

Dog –

Virgil??? –

trots beside him with barely a glance at me.

Melon City

'Welcome to Melon City,' says Rufus. 'The melons were already growing here half-wild, so I suppose this island must have been inhabited before, but I grew everything else myself.'

I snort, but can't help feeling a bit impressed.

As well as watermelons, Rufus has grown:

Tomatoes

Peppers

Chinese cabbages

Coriander (which tastes of soap).

'The coriander's gone to seed, I'm afraid, but I'm drying it, and you can still use the stems in cooking, although they're kind of woody.'

'What are you – Bear Grylls or something?' I say. I'm thinking that, during all this time on the island, all I've found are a few tiny mangoes and a lime tree but *Hi I'm Rufus!* has grown a whole frickin garden.

'Well, not exactly, although they taught us a lot of survival skills at Gordonstoun. They believe in a holistic curriculum, based on the four pillars of Challenge, Responsibility, Service and Internationalism.' He flushes. 'Sorry, is this boring?'

I smile sweetly. 'No, you carry on. It's, like, really interesting.'

I really want to hear about your stupid posh school with its stupid posh curriculum.

He looks at me warily, but it doesn't stop him going on.

'I was going to grow onions but there's no point really because I've found them growing wild, over by Mosquito Alley, and they're great; small, but strong and sweet.'

It's strange and swimmy here. I wonder if I'll wake up in my own hammock later and this boy with his strange garden will all be a dream.

The insects and dragonflies buzz and chirrup and the green leaves shimmer in the humming sun. Strong stems force themselves over the earth and there are Rufus's tools, all lined up neatly: his home-made spade and hoe, made from sharpened metal and lashed around sturdy sticks; his watering can made from a plastic peanut-butter container with a lid spiked with holes; his leaning scarecrows with their carved watermelon heads and grass skirts. And all the time, there's the *ting ting* of tin cans on bamboo sticks stuck in the ground.

Rufus is droning on again.

I try to catch Dog's attention but he's ignoring me. I want to bury my face in his fur and kiss his warm head.

'I use seaweed fertiliser,' Rufus is saying. 'Brought the seeds with me, of course. I was particularly interested in how Defoe based his character's adventures on Selkirk. Although I thought tomatoes, peppers and chillies more useful to grow than the barley and rice he recommends.'

I blink. 'Defoe? Selkirk?' I say.

Rufus nods patiently. 'As in Robinson Crusoe. Defoe based him on Selkirk, a real-life castaway.'

'I've heard of Crusoe, I'm not stupid,' I snap.

Hi I'm Rufus! flushes. 'Of course, when you're planning an expedition like this, you make mistakes. The cauliflowers and lettuce were a complete disaster – hated the tropical climate. And most of the seeds I'd ordered from specialist catalogues were in my bag in the hold.' He shakes his head. 'But the rest are doing well, as you can see. And as long as I water them three times a day, Bob's your uncle.'

Bob's your frickin uncle?

'Here.'

He passes me a tomato, fat and warm from the sun, and I bite into it greedily. It's hot and juicy and just about the most delicious thing I've ever tasted. I use the TeamSkill polo to rub juice off my chin and think of my own crappy attempts to find food. In fact, hasn't the main fruit I've found been the poison-berries?

Rufus is humming away, fiddling with some string he's tied around his pepper plants.

'By the way, jolly nice bikini you're wearing.'

'You what?'

204

But my gorgon glare seems to have no effect. Rufus is turning his head to flick off an enormous bug, but not before I see him smiling.

A pause.

'I mean, it's kind of making me wish I had some matching trunks, although personally I prefer Squidward or perhaps Mr Krabs…'

I stare at him. 'You're taking the piss, right?'

But he's bending over, squishing bugs or whatever the hell gardeners do. Then he straightens up and passes me something.

'Here – taste that.'

It's a red pepper.

Crunch.

It's hard to be a rock when there's a million taste buds having a party in your mouth.

Bob's Your Uncle

Rufus walks with a swing, slashing stray creepers with his machete while Dog dances at his feet.

Prat. Wanker. Tit.

He's got me working straight away. It's like I'm at his snooty school on one of their stupid army courses.

The minute I'm up on my feet, he makes me:

Water all the veg.

Collect dry sticks.

Help him cut down tree trunks.

Assist him in making another bed for myself to sleep in.

And his *rules*:

'Oh, you need to put your shoes over here,' he says.

'And it's probably best if you don't touch my machete. Best tool we've got – took me ages to make it from one of the plane's fan blades.'

'I like to sort the logs in terms of size, so that it's more efficient regulating the cooking temperature.'

Rules and lists all the time.

The tree-cutting is the worst.

He marches on through his garden and down into the forest which contains the waterfall and the tunnel opening.

I trail behind him, scowling.

All I want is for it to be just me and Dog. We might have been a bit crap sometimes, but we got there, mostly. And there was no one telling me what to do.

I imagine burning holes through Rufus's stupid flapping headdress and his peeling freckled back; taking a match and watching his grass skirt shoot up into flame.

'OK, so you need to press down on this end whilst I bounce up and down on it until it splits. But first of all, I'm going to chop at it to give a dent.'

I fold my arms and deliberately don't look at him as he strikes at the trunk again and again, his headdress swinging. I concentrate on an insect instead; it's moving up a fallen log, front legs feeling the air stiffly, like it's made of clockwork. It's big as my head and would be good to eat. I bash its head quickly with a stone and put it into my Hello Kitty bag, which I've strung from my waist.

I've got a mismatched pair of flip-flops from Rufus's collection and one of his home-made knives tucked into my palm skirt.

I can hear the waterfall from here. Its hiss and rush is lovely but it makes me need to –

I leave my Hello Kitty bag where it is, and find a suitable spot in the trees.

I'm squatting on the forest floor when Rufus's voice makes me jump.

'We're ready to call timber now, Frances.'

'Can't you see I'm busy?' I snap.

Why does he always flush like that? So that the skin around his freckles is stained bright pink?

'Gosh – so sorry. It's just that I need you to –'

'All right, all right, I'm coming.'

I yank up my SpongeBobs and follow him to the tree, glaring.

'These saplings are the best for uprights,' Rufus is saying.

'Yeah right, whatever.'

'So if you would just hold that end down whilst I come and put weight on it...'

I hold the tree trunk where he's pointing and immediately it springs back up, nearly having my eye out.

'For frick's sake.'

'Watch out, won't you? Here, I'll get hold of it again.'

Time and time again, he tells me to hold the tree, but it's stupid and impossible; the tree's too strong and heavy and there's no way I've got the strength to hold it down while he messes around at the other end with his big-man knife.

So I put less and less effort into it each time; I can tell he's getting wound up by the way he takes a deep breath every time he speaks to me. He's got the same sort of tone that Miss had that time I told her I'd eaten my mock paper:

'Right. One more time then.'

'Over there where I told you.'

'Remember you need to press all your weight down, like I said.'

Blah blah blah.

He's lobster red in this heat. Doesn't seem to be able to cope as well in the sun as I can. Somehow this fact gives me great pleasure.

Look at him, with his stupid headdress flapping around like a frickin –

'Christ almighty.'

This is when the sapling whacks him against the head for the fourth time.

I shrug.

Rufus leans against the tree, breathing heavily.

'OK,' he says at last, and I'm surprised he has still kept his temper.

We both look at the half-fallen tree.

'Why don't *you* do it?' he says.

'What?'

'Why don't *you* do it? I'll sit on the branch at the top, and you use the machete to finish the job off. Here.'

And he passes his knife.

I stare at the machete in my hands. It's big and heavy and glint-sharp. Of course, it's totally professional-looking. Unlike my pathetic attempt at a knife, this one could have walked straight off a survival programme.

'Fine,' I say, casually.

Rufus yanks down the top half of the tree and throws all his weight on it, even getting his leg over like he's riding a horse. The tree bounces and creaks.

'OK,' he calls through the branches. 'Ready?'

'Yeah.'

I carefully place the machete against the dent he's made; then lift it back and hack it against the cut. The tree's like iron.

But there's something satisfying about using such a serious knife after all that time with a stick and a tin lid, and I use all my strength for the second whack.

Imagine it's Rufus, with his stupid feathers and bossiness.

Whack.

Here's one for Angela, with her fake concern and rising lies.

Whack.

And a 'specially hard one for Big Wayne.

Whack.

And each time Rufus throws all his weight on to the trunk like he's a WWF wrestler.

Gradually the tree cracks.

When it goes, Rufus leaps off and I snatch back the machete, panting. Trees and twigs rain down on us as the sapling smashes a space in the clearing.

'*Timber,*' Rufus howls, as Dog spins and barks.

I stand beside them and we all stare down at the fallen tree.

I act cool as anything when Rufus high-fives me.

But inside I'm thinking *yesss* and my heart's thudding so hard I swear it's too big for my ribcage.

Barbed Wire

We fell three more trees, sharing a drink of could-be-nut water after each one.

Rufus sharpens a stick with a few slashes of his machete and jabs it down to pierce the top of the could-be-nut. Takes him about three seconds.

He hands me the first one in his ever-so-polite way.

'Peepa?'

'You what?' I say, taking it.

'A young coconut. In some parts of the world islanders call them peepas.'

'Oh.'

I make a mental note of the word. *Peepa.* I like it.

After a quick break, Rufus stands up and claps his hands together. 'OK, um. Now to take them back.'

I stare at the huge pile of trees. 'You *are* joking?'

But he's already at the other end, hacking off the smaller branches.

Swearing under my breath, I gather up the lighter wood into a pile so that we can come back and collect it later for the fire. When Rufus bends to lift the heaviest end, I take the other.

The journey back is torture. The spikes that are all that's left of the branches get caught up in the undergrowth and we have to stop constantly so that Rufus can hack away at the creepers to clear room. And mosquitoes are eating us.

We end up padding our shoulders with my Hello Kitty bag and his shirt. I don't admit it to him but by the end I think that the wood is going to smash straight through to my collarbone.

At one stage I can see the mosquitoes, whizzing around Rufus's head like it's a beacon. He's going to suffer later. But he doesn't complain. Ever. Just picks up the trunk again and resettles it against his shoulder. I close my eyes when he does this, ignoring the fire in my flesh and especially the image that keeps coming into my brain: of barbed wire grinding into raw hamburger.

By the end of the day we have:

Four uprights.

A neatly stacked pile of smaller branches.

And a whole load of throbbing pain.

Rufus rubs his hands together.

'Super work,' he says.

Cliffhanger

'What's up there, Rufus?' I ask him one morning.

We're eating the last of the tomatoes for breakfast. Rufus has been keeping the seeds on his drying shelf and has some baby tomato plants in his melon garden, but it'll be weeks before we can eat them again. Dog is licking fish scales from last night's dinner off a chopping board.

Rufus looks up to where I'm pointing.

'Oh, that's the mountain. Fear Mountain, I call it. I reckon it's the highest point on the island. You can probably see all the way across to the north side where you lived.'

'Have you climbed it?'

He shakes his head.

'Why not?'

'Not much point. It'd just be a waste of energy,' he says, but he doesn't look at me.

'I want to climb it.'

'I don't think that would be a good idea.'

'Why not? I want to see the whole of the island. There may be parts we haven't explored yet. We could find more food, animals…'

Rufus busies himself with the fire, piling on more green palm leaves to keep the smoke going.

'Come on,' I say. 'Let's explore.'

'I really don't think –'

I kick at the log pile sulkily. 'Why is it that you always have to decide what we should and shouldn't do?' I grab his knife. 'Fine. I'll just go by myself.'

I've reached the melon pile when he comes after me.

'You're not going alone,' he snaps.

But the skin between his freckles is pale.

Here, the rock is white like ash.

The rich green of Rufus's garden and the small amount of forest that skirts it falls away to a scrubby blankness, the colour of recycled paper.

It's hard going but I'm determined. I want to prove Rufus wrong; I want to return to camp with loads of stuff or at least a mental map of the island. And I'm desperate to see the rest of the island; to feel light and space and air around me after spending so long in his hot little garden.

I miss One Tree Beach –

Dead Man's Bay –

but mostly, I miss seeing all that sky, all that blue with its endless, careless shimmer.

I don't care that the stones are scattering and getting into my shoes and trickling over the path. I don't care or wonder how far behind Rufus is. I wonder what made this tiny path, whether it's rabbits or goats or whatever else may live on this island as well as us.

'Look – animal tracks,' I call.

There are footprints: pairs of semicircles planted at angles to each other, like a cake with a piece missing. Looks like whatever did them was a lot heavier than a rabbit.

Dog is darting up and down and I smile. It feels like old times, just me and him.

But Rufus is trailing far behind us, holding a sturdy stick

he's plucked from the thicket. Normally he'd be the first to notice. Why the frick is he being so slow?

'I can see our fire from here,' I call. 'The smoke signal's good – look.' I point down to where a steady plume of thick white smoke is rising.

Rufus looks over the edge. I notice that the knuckles around his stick are white-tight.

'You all right?'

'Yes.' His voice is strained.

I shrug and continue upward.

I wonder whether there are goats here.

'Would there be goats?' I call.

I can hear Rufus breathing heavily behind me and get annoyed. Why doesn't he hurry up?

I want someone to share this with me; this feeling of *freedom* as the blueblueblue spreads endless shimmering wings and it's above and around and below me, all this space –

I stumble over a loose stone and steady myself with my hand on the rocky ground.

'Whoops,' I laugh. 'God, it's high up here, isn't it?'

I have to be careful; only a finger's width separates me from this rock and the million miles down below to the ocean. I dislodge a rock and a handful of small stones skitters down the track.

'For Christ's sake, be *careful*.' Rufus's voice is tight and high.

I turn round to look down at him and then I get it.

'So *that's* it: you're scared of heights.'

He's on his hands and knees now, and his face is white-sweat as he grips his stick and holds on to a rock. He's breathing in and out, *hwoo hwoo hwoo*.

'You've got – what d'you call it – *vertigo*.'

'What if I have?' he says through clenched teeth.

'But you don't need to be scared, it's fine. Look.'

And I spin my arms round like Maria from *The Sound of frickin Music*. Just because I can.

'*What are you doing?*' His voice is almost a scream.

'All right, all right.' I steady myself, giggling. I do feel a bit giddy. 'Come on up – I'll give you a hand.'

'*No*. Thank you.'

'Suit yourself.'

I turn away from him and continue to climb. And it really is climbing now; the animal tracks, whatever they were, have long gone. Dog has vanished somewhere, probably looking for rabbits. There's certainly enough animal droppings here.

I leave Rufus clutching his rock and claw my way to a rocky outcrop, right at the top. It's next to a little scrubby tree, clinging with all its strength to the edge of the mountain.

It's tricky, but I manage it.

And the view is

A-frickin-mazing.

What I see is:

One Tree Beach, snaking around to my right like a silver necklace. For the first time I realise how much damage the storm did to my part of the island. I can see lighter patches of crushed trees, as if a giant has punched a fist into them. Rufus's side is untouched; I suppose the mountains must have protected it somehow. It's like the storm chose my beach – my camp – deliberately, to scribble it out.

There are dark blobs on the beach here and there, with seabirds buzzing around them like flies, but I don't think of them.

The jungle, thrown over the island like a fur cloak. It's much bigger than I imagined and I shudder when I think how easy it was to get lost; how easy it would've been to never find a way out.

Our camp, with its rising smoke. That patch there must be the watermelons. And the green fold must be Waterfall Valley with its scrawl of jungle.

Behind me is the cove I could never get to 'cause of the tide. Me and Dog must have passed right under this mountain to get to this side of the island, right through its belly.

I look straight down, holding on to the scraggy little tree for safety. There are rock stacks and frothing currents and inlets with tiny beaches, hot-white and much smaller than One Tree Beach. Beyond them, the ocean stretches far as a dream.

But not empty.

A glimpse of something shiny. As I squint at it, it winks back at me in the sun.

Then it's gone; a cloud passes over and I frown.

'Oh my God,' I shout.

I begin to scramble my way down, slithering, falling on the loose scree.

'Rufus, *Rufus!*'

He's staring up at me, his mouth a black O of terror.

'Frances? What are you doing? What are you –'

He screams as I slide into him and he loses his grip on the rock and we both go slithering down on our backsides –

'*Christ, ouch, shit*' –

till I grab hold of the trunk of a thorn bush and we both lie there, gasping.

Then Rufus unpeels his hands from my legs and sits up.

'Why are you such an absolute shitty bitch?' he bursts out, crimson-faced.

So?

I've been called worse.

I watch Rufus let himself down the rest of the rock face on his bottom, shuffling carefully and taking a million years to find the right places with his hands.

I walk behind him, enjoying the sun on my back, the light and space around me.

Inside, I'm hugging a wonderful secret.

But I won't tell him yet.

Because Rufus can be a right prat sometimes.

Cabbages and Snails

Rufus is strangely quiet when we get back.

He doesn't look at me as he busies himself around camp, laying aside the fishing net he's been trying to mend as he starts to make dinner.

He's laid out the last of the cabbages, and the snails we collected in the Hello Kitty bag this morning and a tiny shrivelled chilli from the ones we have dried.

Without being asked, I pick a pepper and use one of his home-made knives to chop it.

I'm squatting on the ground using one of the driftwood chopping boards and it's kind of nice; this time of day, doing ordinary things, just pottering.

But I know that after dinner we'll have to collect more wood to stock up the log pile, heap green leaves back on the fire and go to check the solar stills and inspect the beds for snakes and bugs and maybe sharpen our tools and there's no rest really; you're never more than one step ahead because you never know – *never* know – when the food's going to run out or you'll get injured or you'll be too ill to forage.

'I like to do it this way.' Rufus takes the knife out of my

hand and starts chopping the pepper into tiny precise pieces.

'Well, I like to do it this way,' I snap.

I hack at it anyhow, just to annoy him.

'Well, I don't think –'

'All done. There. Finished.'

I scrape the peppers into the salvaged coffee can he uses for a cooking pot.

He looks pained. 'I wanted those for the salad.'

I place the snails upside down on the edge of the fire.

'Saw a boat today,' I say, changing the subject. And my heart thuds as I say the words.

He freezes, billycan in hand. 'What did you say?'

'A boat. I saw it flash on the water, really tiny in the distance. I could see it 'cause I was leaning over and hanging on to that tree at the top of Fear Mountain.'

Rufus dumps the cabbage in the seawater and comes to stand opposite me.

'Are you sure? It couldn't have been something else?'

' 'Course I'm sure. I'm not stupid. It was white, maybe a fishing boat. Rufus, this means there might be other islands nearby. We could build a raft and escape!'

He stares. 'But why on earth didn't you tell me? We could have put more damp leaves on the fire – created more smoke!'

Shit.

'I just thought we could make our own raft or…' I see his face, 'maybe it saw us anyway and will come back…I didn't think –'

'That's the problem with you. You never think. Always so stubborn, putting us both at risk by climbing that bloody mountain. And now you might have missed our only chance of rescue.'

He's shaking his head at me and I feel like I want to throw these snails at him, one by one. They're fat and bubbling in their black shells, spitting hot in the fire.

Instead I accept my dish of cabbage and pile on five snails.

'You're always so negative,' I blurt out.

He laughs. 'It's impossible, Fran. Surely you can see that? It's not worth killing ourselves for – we could be dashed to pieces on the rocks just for the vague chance of meeting a fishing boat from an island that might or might not be out there. And where would we head to, just supposing it was seaworthy? We have no means of navigation, no way of knowing if there are any other islands close by –'

'Oh just shut up.' I suck out my snail, scowling.

If I was on my own again I'd have made a raft somehow, I'd have –

'Fran?'

I look up and he's smiling at me. 'I'm right. You know I'm right.'

'You forgot to put chilli on these,' I tell him.

It's cold tonight, but no way am I sleeping near the fire next to him.

No way.

I huddle into my hoodie and try to attract Dog's attention without Rufus noticing. Dog thumps his tail but doesn't come to me; he's enjoying his spot by the fire. I try not to think of Dog's hot whiskery breath and how he'd sneak up just behind my knees to keep us both warm. I try not to think of me and Johnny, cuddled up tight, light still on because he'd want me to read to him, just one more time.

'Maybe we should go spearfishing tomorrow,' says Rufus, from the other side of the fire. Dog has moved to lie at his feet.

Whatever.

Spears Out

Rufus is fully dressed for our fishing trip – of course.

He's wearing:

>His feathered headdress
>A palm skirt, the one that shows his nads
>Plaited flip-flops.

It makes my SpongeBob bikini look tame.

'So what's that you're doing?' I ask.

Try to be nice.

He's smearing himself all over with gloopy stuff from a peanut-butter tub.

'It's mud from the mangrove swamp. I need it for protection from the sun. Want some?'

'No, thanks.'

It's hardening on his face like clay. Makes him look like the Tin Man when he's gone rusty.

'You really ought to, you know. The UV's very powerful in this climate. You may feel your tan offers some protection, but underneath the sun's doing untold damage; the UVA rays penetrate deep into the skin, damaging the dermis –'

'I told you I'm fine. So shall we go then?'

I pick up a spear and make towards the path that looks like it goes to the beach.

'Not that way – over here. And that spear might be a little heavy for you. Try this one.'

Jesus.

This beach is nowhere near as nice as mine, but it's still good to be close to the sea again.

'I call it One Tree Beach, because of that palm over there,'

Rufus says, smiling.

I stare at him.

'What is it?' asks Rufus.

'Nothing, it's just that –'

But I don't tell him.

Instead I pull my grass skirt off and run into the waves, whooping.

There's a curve of shallows and some tall rocks, close enough to swim to.

Rufus is shouting something to me but I ignore him; I'm floating on my back and closing my eyes, feeling the sun invade every cell of my body.

I love, love, love its UV rays. Dermis or no dermis.

Something's moving the water.

I open my eyes and it's Rufus, wading his way over.

'You really ought to move quietly,' he's saying in a stage whisper. 'What I've found is that the fish in these parts respond to the tiniest movement. It could take hours to get them to come back if they've been frightened away.'

What he means is: if *I've* frightened them away.

I raise my eyebrows.

He's stepping towards me with exaggerated slowness.

We'll be here all day at this rate.

'I'll get started then, shall I?' I say.

I stand up and wade well away from him. I have my spear and it's not even true that there's no fish. I can see one now, a fat yellow one, flitting over the white sand past my feet.

I hold my breath and wait. Grip my spear.

Madder than Melons

'Of course, you do know that you need to take account of the refraction from the water's surface, don't you?'

'Chrissake,' I explode. I turn to him, glaring. 'I nearly got that one.'

He looks hurt and wades off, raising his spear high over his head like he's George of the frickin Jungle.

What does he mean, refraction?

The water shimmers as I wait. It's hard to be angry when the sand's silting between your toes and the sea's warm as milk.

The spear's a good one, I'll give him that. He's found a way to secure it tight and firm round that awkward join where the metal meets the sharpened wood. Idly, I wonder what he used to cut the metal with. Where does he forage?

A movement, swift as light.

Stab.

And when I bring my spear up, there's the fish, pinned to its tip, squirming and ready for the pan.

Yesss.

I look around to check that Rufus has noticed and he's looking all red and sweaty. Ha. He hasn't caught anything.

He's nodding at me.

'Well done. Great effort. Did you make allowance for refraction like I said?'

I smile sweetly.

Just imagined it was you, you prat.

'Well, put the fish in the tub over there. Probably best if I check it to make sure it's not poisonous –'

'It's not poisonous,' I scowl. 'I've eaten these before.'

Rufus always thinks he knows everything. I chuck the fish into the tub which he's lined up carefully next to a flat rock for filleting and wade back into the water, deliberately splashing to annoy him.

It's difficult to know if he's blushing or not because he's covered in so much clay.

We start to have a secret spearing contest, me and Rufus. Neither of us will admit it to the other but inside we're trying desperately hard to get the most fish.

I know it and he knows it.

Rufus stabs the next one: it's a beauty, blue and fat as a cushion.

I pretend not to notice.

I'm watching near the rocks. I think the seaweed over here must be teeming with fish, and it turns out I'm right 'cause I go and bag two silver ones just like that. They're only small, more like sprats, but I've decided that it's quantity, not quality.

When Rufus brings over two huge flatfish and slides them carefully off his spear into the tub, I decide I've had enough.

'I'm going into the deeper water,' I say. 'Going to do some underwater diving.'

He frowns. 'Are you sure? I mean, there's the risk we'll lose our spears and there's a dangerous rip round here.'

I scowl. 'What's a rip?'

He's washing his hands in the sea now, checking there's no fishy bits left. Finicky like always. 'It's a rip tide. An underwater current. It can pull you far out to sea if you're not careful.'

'So that's what it was,' I say.

'What's that?'

'I've been caught in one. It was when I saw your smoke signal. I was being chased by a shark,' I say casually. I stab my

222

spear in the sand.

He looks disbelieving. 'Are you sure? I mean, I've seen one or two lemon sharks around, but none that would actually chase you. They're probably a menace to the smaller fish though,' he adds kindly.

'There was a frickin man-eating shark and I killed it and me and Dog *ate* it. And it was a lot bigger than the poxy fish in there.'

I kick the tub.

The tub tips over and our fish slop into the sand.

Rufus looks appalled. 'Hey,' he says. 'Hey, look here!'

I watch him as he scoops the fish back inside. His hands are covered in slime *and* sand. He won't like that.

Rufus stands up and takes a deep breath. He seems to have come to a decision about something.

'Look. I know that you don't like me. You seem very angry about something. But we've got to get on, to survive this island. It was one of the first things they taught us at school when we went on expeditions: the importance of teamwork.' He's squinting at me with his very blue eyes.

My fingers curl.

'I know we've both been alone for an awfully long time. So I get that it's hard. Honestly. But you don't have to be so confrontational about everything. The rip-tide thing – well, crikey. Well done, you. For getting back, I mean…' His voice trails away.

'I don't need you to patronise me!' I shout. 'I've managed fine so far on my own, haven't I? You can't even climb rocks – you're scared of heights!'

I un-stab my spear. Hold it high and aim at the horizon.

We both watch it sail in an arc till it lands on the tallest of the rocks jutting out of the sea.

Rufus speaks first.

223

'What the bloody hell did you do that for?' he says.

His feathers are looking a bit wilty.

I dive into the sea and start swimming away with long slow strokes.

'As I said, I'm going deep-sea fishing,' I call over my shoulder.

Before I absolutely kill him.

I Am a Rock

So, Rufus is swimming out to me, clay-faced above the water.

He's decided to leave his headdress back on the beach.

'Look, I'm sorry,' he calls.

I turn back to face the horizon.

I'm sitting cross-legged on the tallest of the rocks and the spear's still where it landed, wedged in a crevice. I imagine that I'm Medusa, all alone, hideous and feared, on her rocky island, howling at ships, trapping those who come to kill her. Daring them to find her.

She was beautiful, once.

Once, she wasn't a monster.

Once, she loved and was loved. I know 'cause we had to do her in one of the poems for our English exam. It's the only frickin poem I remember.

The sea's lovely from here, blue as heaven and endlessly shimmering. Shame about the boy swimming in it.

I let the sun finish drying me and listen to Rufus thrashing about below.

It took me ages to climb up on to those slippery rocks but

I won't tell him that.

I close my eyes.

He'll be a while yet.

'I did see a boat and I know there are other islands,' I say, when he's finally clambered up.

'I believe you. Honestly.' He's trying to be nice – probably worried for his spear.

'So how about we build that raft I was talking about? We can go on an expedition for materials.'

Expedition. He'll like that.

He flames up. Whoops – the clay's washed off and that neck will burn quick as thinking.

'So what about it?' I say.

I'll need his help. Don't know anything about boats and he's got his *seaman* skills.

'We–ell,' he says.

I grit my teeth. I know he's only pretending to consider. He leans forward earnestly. 'Look, Fran –'

'Frances.'

'Look, Frances. It's just that it's impossible to get to –'

'No it's not.'

'It's too risky. Don't you realise that if one of us gets injured, that's us finished?' He's really flushed now. 'I'm going to train as a doctor –'

'Well, you're not one yet.'

'If I know one thing, it's that any injury, any accident, any disease we contract – we'll be done for, Frances.'

He scratches his head and, for a moment, I almost believe he's sincere and not some overbearing, full-of-himself posh boy who's too chicken to try the one way to get off the island.

'Maybe I'll just swim then,' I say, just to annoy him. But

the rocks beneath the cliff are swirling even on this calm day and I remember the iron grip of the rip current.

Rufus sighs. 'I'm afraid the smoke signal's our only chance.'

I stand up so that he can't see my wet face. Raise my arms to dive back in.

'Haven't you been listening to a word I've been saying? You can't dive here. You could hit your head and –'

His face is white even with his sunburn.

I let my arms fall.

'And hadn't you better retrieve the spear?' he asks tightly.

Hadn't you better retrieve the spear?

'Ooh, yes, silly me,' I say.

I scramble up to the very top of the rock where the spear is.

'Oh dear,' I call. 'It seems to be stuck.'

He swears. If you can call 'oh bugger' swearing.

'I might need some help up here. It's really wedged and I can't…don't want to break it…'

Rufus's head appears over a crag. I wait till he clambers over and is standing beside me. He can barely stand up straight because he keeps wanting to hold on to the rock for support.

'Here,' I say.

He looks at the spear in my hand.

'But it's not –'

And that's when I stumble into him.

'Oops,' I say.

We both go over, dropping like birds into the waiting sea.

One More Time

His little feet are clenched around the edge of the tiles. Half-term holidays and the lido's screaming.

'That's right, Monkey. You can do it.'

'I'm not sure, Frannie.'

'Sit down if you want. I'll catch you.'

'I want to stand like the big kids.'

'Well, I'm here waiting. See?'

I hold out my arms and the pool attendant smiles at us.

'Back again?' he says.

We both watch Johnny.

He raises his arms and tucks in his head. Takes a deep breath and –

The pool man chuckles. 'There he goes.'

'*Well done*, Monkey.'

'Like a bird. Lovely,' he says.

Monkey's in my arms; his little legs are kicking madly as he gasps.

'I did it, Frannie.'

'I know, Monkey.'

I kiss his wet head.

Water War

Everything's bubbles and swirls, a dream-world of whirling hair and kicking legs and the sweet-shock of the water.

Then we whoosh up to the surface, gasping.

I'm laughing; I can't help it. That was the biggest rush ever, and the sky's screaming-blue and my eyes are streaming.

'Oh my God, *oh my God.*'

The rock soars above us, giddy-tall.

Beside me, Rufus is speechless.

Then he isn't.

'You, you – absolute *shit.*'

'You forgot "bitch",' I tell him, treading water.

'Why did you do that? After what I just said about danger and avoiding accidents, you decide, in your wisdom – because you know everything; Frances *frickin* Stanton knows *everything* about how to survive on this bloody island – to *push* me, when you know I don't like heights, and –'

'*I know everything?*' I scream at him.

We're face-to-face now, hair streaming, and Rufus is still clutching the spear, face twisting.

'*I* know everything?' I pant. 'You're so patronising.' Once I've started, I can't stop. 'You've been bossing me around, ordering me about since I came to your part of the island –'

'That's rich. That's rich, coming from you. I've never known such an obstinate, wilful, intractable cow in my life. You're pig-headed –'

'Me, pig-headed?'

'Reckless.'

'Anything else?'

'Impetuous.'

'Why do you always sound as if you've swallowed a dictionary?'

'Cow-bag.'

'Wanker.'

We're spitting words into each other's faces. His blue eyes

228

are splinters and it's like the island's holding its breath, listening to us.

Rufus looks down at his hands, which are empty.

'And now you've made me drop the sodding spear.'

We both look at the spear, which is drifting away from us, peacefully. Every so often it rolls, as if it's basking in the waves.

'I'll get it.'

I dive under before he can stop me and I follow its shape, letting the sea absorb me into its wavering world.

I try my best, I really do. But it's kind of hard to seethe underwater.

Rufus ignores me when I get out of the water.

He's busy gutting the fish and doesn't look up.

Whatever.

I place the spear next to the other one and wonder whether I should go back to camp alone, but I'm not actually sure which path we took; there are several possibilities and I don't want to ask him.

Instead, I wander down to the end of the beach and potter round the rock pools. The sea sparkles teasingly and I wish, I *wish* I could get a boat and sail out, right to the horizon.

There are birds here, picking their way about the rock pools on long, red legs. They make a high piping sound and I know they're oystercatchers; I've seen stuffed ones in the Horniman Museum.

The real thing's better though. I sit watching them, trailing my hand through the palm shadows on the sand.

'Ready?'

You forgot Cow-bag.

I get up and follow him, arms folded.

Follow the shadow of his headdress, which moves across

the sand in long, flickering lines. Rufus is holding his flip-flops. His feet march purposefully along the edge of the sea.

OhmyGod. No.

'*Stop*,' I cry.

He freezes. 'What now?'

'Do. Not. Move.'

I'm running now, heart flipping.

'What is it?'

'*Stay there.*'

He's frowning; thinks I'm playing another one of my tricks.

I shake my head; can't breathe. Make him look down at where I'm pointing.

At the monster in the sand.

Will It Get Us?

I know it's a monster 'cause me and Johnny used to scare each other about it in the Horniman Aquarium. One puncture from one of those spines and you'll never see tomorrow.

'Go on, dare you.'

'No. You do it, Frannie.'

'I think the glass is cracked just there.'

'Will the poison come out and get us?'

'Yikes, I don't know. Shall I test it and see?'

'Yes, yes. Go on, Frannie.'

Huffing his breath against the glass as I place my finger against the crack and pretend to die.

'Hahaha. Again, again.'

Swapsies

'Stonefish,' I pant.

We both look down at where I'm pointing.

Spines like barbs and big as a lobster, it's knuckling into the wet sand, trying not to be seen.

Rufus leaps back, breath hissing.

'Christ. Bloody hell.'

'I know,' I say.

We both peer down at it and Rufus prods it with his spear.

I shiver.

'Well, thanks for, um, telling me.'

'Better put your flip-flops on,' I say.

He nods, white between his freckles.

We walk back together, both inspecting the sand as we go.

The fish smells good.

Rufus does it a different way from me, placing the fillet on a flat stone in the coolest part of the fire. I don't care how it's cooked so long as I get to eat some of it.

My stomach growls.

Rufus clears his throat. 'Listen, about what you did today...'

'Let's forget it,' I say. I'm busy chopping limes. It's a relief to be using a properly made knife after my tin-lid one. I'm not so worried about losing my thumb.

'No. I never thanked you properly.' He coughs. 'I mean, you probably saved my life.'

Well, I did save your life. No 'probably' about it.

'Just forget it.'

The cooking fish hisses as Rufus talks.

'It was my father who made me scared of heights. I was at boarding school…'

He's attacking an onion with the machete and I worry he'll have his hand off if he doesn't watch what he's doing.

'Here – give me that,' I say.

His hand is trembling. I make him swap so he has the smaller knife.

'I was seven or eight – I hadn't been at Gordonstoun long – and the masters took us to North Wales on an outdoor expedition course. We had to do orienteering and part of the route was up Mount Snowdon.'

'Oh yeah?' I say.

'As a treat for being the first ones to finish, we got to use the zip wire. I was last up and as I stood there, looking over the valley, I knew I couldn't do it.'

'Why not?' I ask. I chop a chilli into tiny pieces, sucking in my breath as the fire goes straight into the cuts and sores I always seem to have on my fingers.

'It was like my father all over again, when he used to make me do the monkey ropes –'

'The monkey ropes? Jesus, were you brought up in a zoo or something? Didn't you ever, like, just sit down and watch a bit of telly?'

I think of the days and days doing just that with Cassie.

Rufus ignores me. He's gazing across his melon patch with a tortured look on his face. I take the knife off him.

' "Higher, boy, higher," he'd shout at me. "I'm not having a boy of mine acting like some sort of nancy boy." '

Nancy boy?

For a moment it's like Rufus is seven years old again. I see the gangly kid he must have been, shivering as his father

232

forced him up the tree or whatever the hell it was.

'And the harness,' he blurts out. 'It was so *tight*. I could hardly move my legs to climb, it was so hitched up.'

I look up at him. 'So not only did you get shoved up a pole, you also had a massive wedgie?'

He blinks at me. 'I'm sorry?'

I pass him the chilli and limes. 'Never mind. At least your mum wasn't a dodgy old prossie.'

That makes him blush.

'I'm sorry,' he says. 'I suppose my problems must seem rather petty compared to what you had to put up with.'

'I think the fish is done,' I say.

The fish is incredible.

Every single, limey, chillified, soft, flaky mouthful of deliciousness.

'Unctuous,' Rufus says.

'Definitely,' I agree. I have no idea what he's on about.

Pause.

'So…swapsies?' he says.

'You what?'

'Swapsies. Now I've told you one of my stories about how messed up I am, you could tell me one of yours?'

I stare at him.

'I mean, all I know is that you live with your mum and her boyfriend…' His voice trails off.

'I don't think so,' I say.

I put my tin down and get up to stoke the fire.

Loan Shark

'So what made you want to burn your school down? Didnae like it there or what?'

The Scottish policewoman has brought me a cup of tea. Her name is Christine, but she says to call her Chrissie.

'She's landed herself in a bit of a mess, this one,' she tells Wayne. 'She's not talking to me. I don't know if it's sunk in yet, what she's done.'

Wayne shakes his head. 'I'm shocked – we all are. Don't know how I'm going to tell her mum. This one's always been difficult. You know what teenage girls are like.'

His hand's gripping my shoulder. I can feel his thumb pressing and rubbing.

'What will happen to her?' he says.

Chrissie-the-police-officer looks serious. 'There'll be a court hearing of course and, it being an arson attack, there's a serious chance of Frances being taken to a Young Offenders Institution. But it's her first offence, so...' She shrugs and Wayne makes a face.

'What a mess,' he sighs, and Chrissie nods. I stare at the desk. There's a lipstick mark on Chrissie's mug. There's a plate with plastic packets of biscuits. They start talking about what action the school's taking; when the court hearing will be.

I still smell of smoke.

I wonder if Miss does too.

The police officer told me that Miss is in a coma. That she suffered burns, and did I know what that meant? How did I feel about what I'd done? The policewoman is nice, but her eyes tell me that she's shocked. She'd be appalled to have a daughter like me.

'Well, I think that's all the paperwork done,' she says.

Wayne looks at her.

'Anaïs Anaïs, am I right?'

She stares.

'Sorry, sorry. It's a habit.' He smiles. 'It's just that my old mum used to wear it. Reminds me of her, that's all. My favourite perfume.' Wayne sighs. 'What are you like, eh?' he asks me.

He turns back to the policewoman. Thrusts out his hand. 'Thanks for everything, Chrissie. I'd best be getting this one home now.' He shakes his head. 'I don't know. Teenage girls.'

Christine-who-likes-to-be-called-Chrissie tucks a strand of hair behind her ear.

She's still looking after him as we leave.

And now we're in the car and the traffic's slowing down.

I've still got the biscuits the police officer gave me: a little plastic packet of bourbons. I hate bourbons; they always taste dusty and nothing at all like chocolate.

'Haven't said anything to your mum,' Wayne is saying. 'She's got enough on her plate. So I've had to borrow the money for your bail.'

He presses the horn and swears at the car in front. He reaches over and takes his time pulling a load of home-made CDs out of the glove compartment.

I concentrate on pulling the plastic biscuit packet into tiny strips and ignore him.

Wayne's found his CD, one hand on the bottom of the steering wheel. The other's trying to shove the rest of the cases back.

I edge as close as I can to the window.

A voice starts crooning about stars shining. Wayne's put his own record on. It's from the time he got through to the second stage of *Sing Your Heart Out*, when he thought he'd make it big. Even Cassie stayed awake long enough to watch him perform in front of the live audience. The real Wayne sings along to his gravelly voice, drumming his fingers on the wheel. Thinks he sounds like Frank Sinatra, but he doesn't; Sinatra's voice is smooth as velvet.

'Want to know who sang that? That's The Mamas And The Papas, that is.'

Well, and the rest, I think. I close my eyes and try to smother Wayne's voice with Ella and Louis Armstrong's version. It's not working.

'And now me. It's gonna be my debut single. When they sign me up.'

Yeah right.

The car shakes as Wayne reaches round to the back seat. I dig my nails into my hands; I wish he'd keep his eyes on the road.

'Crisps?'

I shake my head; listen to him opening a bag with his teeth.

He's crunchcrunchcrunching, wagging his head in time to his own voice singing about lingering till dawn.

My nails dig.

The lights change to red.

He's leaning towards me now, voice breathing out a waft of cheese 'n' onion crisps.

We're stationary now.

'So, thought about what I said before?'

Not this again.

'You'd be a great backing singer, love. Get you in a nice little dress up on that stage. Just you an' your Uncle Wayne.'

I turn away from him and stare at a sticker on the dashboard. *Elvis is King. Long live the King*, it says.

'Most girls would give their right arm for an opportunity like that. I'd buy you some nice clothes, make you look pretty. You oughta be more grateful to me.'

There's knives as well as gravel in Wayne's voice now.

'After all I've done for you and your brother: housing you, keeping your mother in work, putting food on the table. You owe me.'

'Yeah, yeah, I know,' I say.

Wayne moves closer, his cheesy breath damping my cheek.

'You just need to be a bit nicer. Smile more. You're lucky to have me looking after things. I just need a bit of appreciation, that's all. It's not everyone who'd have you back after what you've done, is it?'

When I recoil, he laughs.

'All right, all right, I get the message. Think I'm interested in a little freak like you? Your mother shoulda got rid of you long ago. What are you? An arsonist what burns her school down, makes her teacher all disfigured. What if she dies? Have you thought of that? They'll put you away, lock you up for life. You better be nice to your mother and me – you're lucky to have a nice home like this, a monster like you.'

Wayne's on a roll.

I close my eyes. Try so hard to freeze but it's not working.

'Know what that policewoman told me? That she's lucky to be alive, your English teacher. Got her face half-melted away. Your little brother's lucky to be rid of you. He's better off without you.'

Don't tell me things I already know.

Wayne leans closer, eyes bright. 'They won't let you be alone with him, not someone who's done the things you've done. You're a danger – nearly killed a kid, didn't you? Think they'll let you see him unsupervised? Not on your nelly.'

I stare at the dashboard; try and melt it.

Wayne snorts and turns the CD player up. There's a break in the traffic and he throttles up, swerving into a gap in the outside lane.

I listen to him crooning about dreams all the way back to the flat.

At least his hand's back on the steering wheel.

Wayne's World

I brush crisp crumbs off my leg and follow Wayne up the steps to the flat.

'Come on, then. Come see your mother,' he's saying.

We pass the landing where I can get up on to the roof and I wish I was there; wish I was on my mattress with my earphones on.

Wayne unlocks the door.

'Here she is,' he says. 'Here's your little darlin'.'

Seems like Cassie's been on the skunk all day; the room reeks of it: sort of stale garlic mixed with cut grass. When she sees me, she rises up from the depths of the settee like a terrible fish.

'Baby,' she says.

'I've found her. I found the dirty little stop-out,' Wayne says. He smiles at me. 'Go and hug your mum, love. She's been worried sick.'

Cassie smells unwashed. She pulls me into her pain and she's soft and smells of need and hurt and no hope and pathetic, pathetic, she's pathetic, she's –

I wrench myself away. Can't bear her clammy hands

squeezing sohardsohard like it's going to bring me back. Like hugging's going to make it all better.

Cassie sways a moment, all bleary and bloated. Her confused eyes are killing me.

She sinks back down on the settee and Wayne goes and stands by her; caresses her shoulder.

'I'll make some coffee,' I say.

Cassie reaches for him and leans her head against his chest.

I push past them into the kitchen.

As I wait for the kettle to boil, I can hear Wayne fussing over Cassie.

'No, no, don't you get up, love. I'll tell you later what she's been up to. Let me deal with her, don't you worry. Let me light us both a little rollie – there you go. That's right. That's better, isn't it.'

I'm removing plates out of the sink, trying to find a mug, when I'm aware he's standing behind me. I can smell the smoke from his fag.

'You shouldn't treat your mum like that.'

'Like what?' I say.

'It's not fair, not after what you've done.'

I rinse out the mug with cold water.

Wayne doesn't move away. Just stands there, smoking.

'Got a nerve, you have.'

I take my time with the mug.

'What?' I say.

The kettle steam is misting the window. I reach over to open it.

'Coming in here, bold as brass, making coffee.'

'It's my home. I live here.'

I squeeze past him and get the coffee. Spoon it into the pot.

'Coffee?'

'I don't think so, love.'

239

He reaches on top of the fridge for a six-pack.

'I haven't told your mother about you being held in custody. But I won't be able to bail you out next time, sweetheart. You'll be lucky if you get only two years for what you've done.'

I watch his fingers snap a couple of cans out of the plastic.

'What you looking like that for? She needs a drink. We all do, after what you put us through. It's no wonder your mother's the way she is.'

The coffee's bubbling. I take a spoon.

Wayne leans up close so I'm looking straight into his eyes, black and too-small in his smiling face.

'You need to start toeing the line, darlin'.'

Cassie bleats from her nest.

'Wayne?'

'Coming, love,' he says. He takes a family pack of crisps and a bag of doughnuts from the worktop. 'Look what your Waynie's got for you.'

At the door he stops and turns to me.

'Try and be nice, love. Remember you owe your Uncle Wayne.'

He winks and the smoke from his cigarette rises high like a spiral.

Truce

'Sorry,' says Rufus. 'I shouldn't have asked.'

'No, you shouldn't,' I say.

'It's just that – well, I thought…'

'Forget it,' I say.

'Listen here,' Rufus is saying. 'I know you hate me and I guess it's because I annoy you, and I'm always saying the wrong thing. But…I just want to say that I don't hate you, Frances Stanton. So…truce?'

The shivering flames are making me sleepy.

I turn to look at him in surprise. Hate? The word is ugly and weighs like a stone on this island, in this quiet night.

'Truce,' I say.

That's the night I move my bed closer to the fire.

Bottoms

I hold my fist against my mouth to stop myself spluttering.

Rufus bends down as he salutes the sun.

He's stark naked except for his grass skirt and I can see his nads if I'm looking. Which I am.

I've followed him down to his One Tree Beach for once, desperate to know what he does so early each morning.

He's at it again, touching his toes. Then he springs back into a sort of low plank, kissing the sand. Another flash of bottom. He's strong though, I'll give him that.

And very bendy. I watch him arch like a cat and that's when he sees me looking.

'You have a very white bottom,' I remark.

He freezes, but just for moment. Then he carries on, cool as you like.

'I have a very lovely bottom,' he says, upside down.

Is it possible to sound any posher than that?

'You look a right tit,' I say.

'Why, thank you,' he says between his legs.

I watch for a little while longer and then I turn to leave.

'Fran?' he calls, then.

'Yes?'

'Why don't you join me for yoga?'

I stand next to him, giggling. We press our hands together in a sort of prayer shape and stand straight and tall.

'First, a slight backbend,' Rufus calls. He's well into this because he's ordering me about. Which of course he loves.

I do a slight backbend and even this makes me sway. Above us, the sun wobbles high and bright.

'Now forward, all the way down. Straight legs.'

There's no way my legs are going straight. But it's kind of nice, just hanging there and looking down.

Between my legs I can see:

Rufus's flip-flops, perfectly lined up.

A white stone in the shape of an arrow, lying on the sand.

A tiny stick insect crawling over the white stone.

'Now for chaturanga.'

'Chatu-what?'

I attempt to lower myself to the sand on to just my hands and toes and I collapse, panting.

'Cobra. Downward-facing dog.'

This one's easy. I decide I like the ones that are topsy-turvy best. I shuffle myself round till I'm opposite Rufus and we look at each other upside down.

'Hold for five breaths,' he says.

We stare and we stare.

Rufus's eyes aren't pure blue like I first thought; today they have stars in them.

His eyes drop before mine.

Ha. His flush goes all the way up his neck.

Tooth

'Fran?' Rufus looks white. 'Come over here. I need you to look at something for me.'

I leave the melons I'm watering.

He's squinting into his knife-blade with his mouth open.

'What is it?'

'Ay oo.'

'Well, for frick's sake get your hand out of your mouth when you're talking.'

'My tooth,' he says.

He looks worried and that makes me worried.

'Which one is it?'

He points and I take a look.

It's kind of hard to see into someone's mouth when they're flinching and moaning but I do my best.

'Hold still. I'm going to use the knife to see better.'

That stops him. He sits still like a good boy as I check every one of his teeth till I get to –

'Oh God,' I say.

It's on the bottom left: a gruesome molar with half of its enamel missing and wobbly as hell.

'Is it bad?'

'Um.'

'How bad is it?'

I tell him.

Rufus curses. 'That's the one I damaged playing rugby. Had to have root-canal work done on it. I just bit down on a sodding coconut and then…'

We sit face-to-face, looking at each other. I know what he's going to say next.

'Will you…'

'How much daylight's left?' I ask.

After, Rufus lies down on his bed with my polo shirt wrapped round his face. I've soaked it in seawater and wrung it out so it should be nice and cool against his cheek.

I bring him warmed seawater in a coconut shell.

'Take another swig,' I say. 'It'll clean your mouth out, stop any infection.'

'Who's the doctor now?' he says. Well, he doesn't exactly say that 'cause he has a mouth full of tampons, but I understand him.

I leave him and start to tidy up a bit. Try not to look at the rock, the blood-spots on the ground and the string.

As I wash up, my tongue feels each of my teeth in turn: all there, all firm, none loose.

I sigh with relief and continue to scrub blood. The polo shirt might be almost in tatters but it's the only one we've got.

Tooth Fairy

He's sleeping at last.

His face is soft and sweated with sleep and I lean over and kiss him, soft as feathers to not wake him.

Slowly, gently, gently, I reach my hand under his pillow and slide in a coin.

He doesn't wake.

'Night night,' I whisper.

Pig Stew

It takes ages to die.

Screams like hot wire being yanked through your spleen.

Ingredients:

- 1 pig

Rufus found the piglet trapped between two tree roots.

We didn't need to speak because the same thoughts were hitting us. Like, ohmygodohmygod, *meat*. And: *who is going to do it?*

In the end it was Rufus.

I mean, he went to Gordonstoun, didn't he? He's practically spent his childhood rifle-shooting and horse riding and rabbit-snaring or whatever else the boys do in those woods they call *grounds*. Like, really.

We decided we'd go back first thing next morning, but we'd be more prepared this time. Rufus didn't talk much the night before. He just sat fiddling with some sort of knot-thing he'd made out of cord.

'Help me, Fran,' he says.

He's panting heavily and he's looped the knot over the poor creature's front legs and it's squealing like it's being branded.

'Christ,' I say.

'Hold the bloody cord, Fran. Don't let it get away.'

'Jesus.'

- A small piglet with squealing eyes.
- A dash of horror, pure and neat.

A stone is best.

And look away now.

Method:

1. Roughly chop your cabbage.
2. We have no idea if it's really cabbage, but it looks and smells like the stuff Rufus has grown and we've kept it down so far.
3. Rufus reckons it was planted by people who might have inhabited these islands in the past.
4. That would also explain the pigs.
5. Pull off the cabbage flowers and sprinkle in.
6. If you find any wild barley, sweet potatoes or ginger growing around the island, you can add those too.
7. We didn't.
8. Chuck in a load of water and, hey, why not a splash of coconut milk?

There won't be any pig-meat to add because you'll have snatched it off the fire –

the smell, the smell –

a nd torn into it with your teeth and drooled and mmmm–ed and *ohmygod* and wiped the grease off each other's chins and you won't have ever eaten such a meal as that, ever.

We finish off with the cabbage soup.

When we've mopped up the juices with our fingers, we just sit and look at each other and at the carcass, stripped bare in the pot.

'Bloody hell,' I say.

It feels so weird to actually have a full belly, like it's almost hurting. The grease on my lips feels so wrong. I wipe the last slick of fat from my lips with my finger and suck it.

'There's blood in your hair,' Rufus tells me.

'And above your eye,' I say.

'Shall we go and have a shower?'

We grab our washing stuff, which basically consists of the few rags that remain of Rufus's polo, and follow the path that leads to the waterfall.

And it's there that I peel myself raw.

Stupid me.

Rocks Don't Make Passes

So maybe it's all the flesh I've eaten.

All that blood pumping through my stony heart and turning rock into pulp.

Or something.

Whatever it is, it makes me creep out of my shell a crack; then flinch back inside like a limpet.

So at the waterfall this happens:

'Please could you pass me the soap?' says Rufus.

He's singing ever so loudly and untunefully, standing in the spray of the waterfall and rubbing his TeamSkill shirt-flannel all over his chest.

Of course we don't have any.

I pass him a pebble instead, wide and smooth and shiny.

'Why, thank you,' he says.

'No problem,' I tell him, 'and now could I have the Head and Shoulders, please?'

'Certainly, although I see you more as a Pantene sort of girl. Here you are.'

I thank him for the wet twig he passes me and rub its leaves into my hair.

The water gushes in a whoosh of spilling diamonds; it's clean and cold and fresh.

'Do you mind if I shave my legs?'

'Not at all, you go ahead.' He hands me a feather.

We're hairy as wolves, Rufus and me.

He once caught me trying to tug out my armpit hair with a mussel shell:

'What are you doing?'

'Passes the time.'

'Leave it. I like it.'

'Will you plait it for me?'

'Only if you plait mine.'

'Beardy Freak.'

'Wolf Girl.'

My legs and arms are covered in silky hairs bleached white by the sun. My hair is mostly dreads, which is cool. I close my eyes and let the whole force of the waterfall plunge down on my head. Stripping away the blood, the dirt, the sweat.

I'm very aware of Rufus next to me.

Sometimes our shoulders touch and it's a shock, this skin on skin.

'Do you want me to scrape the dirt off you?'

I open my eyes. Rufus is standing, grinning; he has a clam shell in his hand.

'It's doing wonders for my own stinking filth – look.'

He shows me how he's scraped away at his dirty skin and he's right; it does look kind of clean through his freckles.

'Are you saying that I'm dirty?'

'Well, yes.'

I splash water at him then and he kicks it back, both of us falling in the plunge pool, laughing.

'Come on then,' I say, when we've both emerged, gasping.

He coughs the rest of the water out of his lungs as I thump his back.

'Come on, what?'

'Make me clean.'

I lie back in the water and lift my leg up for him to wash.

He grabs it and pulls me round so I squeal; and then he places my leg over his knee and drags the shell over it carefully.

'Hmm, looks like you might need more than just a deep cleanse,' he says, frowning. He's about to plunge me under again but I stop him. His shoulder is both warm and cool and it's scuffed slightly with peeling skin.

'No, clean me again,' I say.

It feels nice, someone doing this to me. Stone on flesh. Flesh on stone.

With great care and attention, he drags the shell along my leg, from my foot to my knee, washing off the dried-on pig-blood with his other hand.

It feels so nice; I arch like a cat, melt like the moon.

'Other leg?'

'Other leg,' I agree.

And that's when my mistake happens.

He's midway through a scrape when I stop him; place my hand over his. He's staring at me; so close up I can see the swirls and flecks in his eyes.

'Cerulean, azure, sapphire, indigo, cobalt,' I say. I looked up words for 'blue' once, when I needed to describe the sea for my story.

'Fran?' He's watching me intently. He doesn't move.

Now I'm the flesh and you're the stone.

He watches me as I move my hands over his cool wet shoulders and then up to his face.

'The colours in your eyes. There's more of them but they're all the ones I know.'

'Fran –'

It feels strange and good, to be close to someone like this. There's never been a boy, not really. But something about Rufus makes me feel bold, and safe. And it's not Other Fran that's doing this; it's me. I trace my finger over his splatter-map of a face, over each and every freckle-island.

'We are here,' I say, 'on this island.' I point my finger to the freckle by his nose. 'And that one there is the one we're supposed to be on; it's full of fishermen and boats and chocolate bars and –'

And I lean forward to kiss the one on his cheek.

He doesn't move; just stares at me with his bluer-than-blue eyes.

So I trace my finger over his beard to his lips and they are soft and sun-scabbed and

> and I
> place my lips over his and
> kiss him.

Soft as Stone

'Please, Rufus,' I say, shaking him. 'Hold me.'

Why won't he kiss me back and wrap his arms round the back of me so that we fit together like a stone in a fruit?

For a moment, I hold his face and press it close and press my lips to his and just need,

> just need to be

close

to another human being.

But

when I draw back to ask,

'Why aren't you...why aren't you?',

he's just shaking his head.

'I'm sorry, Fran.'

I move backward in the water, shrinking, I am shrinking –

'I'm so sorry...' –

dying with shame.

I splash my way out of the plunge pool in my stupid bikini and I'm running, back up the path.

My flip-flop twists and I fall, landing on my hands and knees in the dead leaves. Bashing my knee, which is bleeding – so much for the shower.

I can hear Rufus calling me.

'It's not you, Fran. God, I'm sorry. Wait!'

But I don't wait.

I clamber up to the top of the ravine, where I know he can't follow me, and sit, looking down at his stupid melon garden, his pride and joy.

Smashed

I use the peepa pole.

Breath rasping, I seize it with both hands and smash and mash the melon head to jammy pulp.

THWACK.

I cringe at the memory of him staying still as rock. I

turned him to stone but this time I needed it not to work. I needed him to melt, to be something warm and soft against my lips; I needed his eyes to not be cold and frozen and *shocked.*

Glinting wetly in the headache-sun, black seeds slide down the headless pole. I seize his headdress and rip the feathers out, scattering them in the air like –

a murmuration. It's called a murmuration.

There is a mess on Rufus's bed –

he won't like that –

then I kick at the coffee drum we use as a table. It topples and rolls.

I stare around at our camp, think briefly of destroying it all – everything we've built together – but I won't do that –

I'm not frickin stupid.

And then there's Rufus beside me, and he's saying:

'Stop, Fran. Don't.'

And that irritates the hell out of me 'cause who does he think I am? Does he think I'll get to the melon garden and swing and swing the pole around like it's got a mind of its own? Send heads flying everywhere and, once they're on the ground, kick them and stamp on them and spike them?

Does he think that for one moment I'll give him the pleasure of shaking his head at me and saying 'Oh, Fran' in that patronising way of his?

'Oh, Fran,' says Rufus.

I can feel him walking around, touching his broken headdress, picking up the feathers one by one. He'll be arranging them, neatly, in our could-be pile.

In the stillness, the melons sigh as I wait.

'It's not that I don't like you. I like you an awful lot.'

He's looking at me with such an expression of – pity. That's it. He pities me. Poor Fran Stanton, unzips herself raw and spills out her insides so that all her heart and guts lie steaming on the ground.

My fingers squeeze on melon slime.

I'm not going to let him frickin pity me.

What Did They Teach You?

I stagger to my feet, head swimming.

'You're a liar, like the rest of them,' I shout.

He's flushing but I'm hotter. I glare through his heat, my fists clenched, waiting.

The air pants.

'Fran, let me just explain –'

Rufus takes a step towards me but I can't bear it, can't bear him to come closer.

I turn to go, to back away.

'Right,' he calls. 'Off you go then. Go and stomp in the forest to slash at some vines like you always do. Run away rather than confront things.'

I stop. We face each other across the ruined garden.

He's right and I hate him. So I hurt him.

'Think I care that you don't like me?' I spit. 'Why would I care? Why would I care that a stupid, stuck-up, little – what d'you call it? – *nancy boy* doesn't like me?'

I'm getting into my stride now; I know how to cause pain.

'You're a loser. Pathetic. Can't even climb a tree, can't even climb a cliff,' I taunt. 'Bet your frickin dad was glad to see the back of you.'

Rufus's face is stone.

'Please stop,' he says.

I'm being my worst self now, I well and truly am. It's like I've dug myself a great and stinking hole and am filling it with all the poison I can get my hands on. And the thing is, I can feel his pain. I feel all the little stabs I'm sending him and I still can't stop.

'Cause now that I've shown myself for what I really am –

a bitch, a monster –

there really is no point in holding back, is there?

So I really go for it.

'Sent you to boarding school, didn't he? Couldn't bear to have his boy who can't climb trees, can't climb rocks, can't jump off cliffs hanging around while he's making shitloads of money.'

Stab.

'And what did they teach you at that posh school anyway? To pretend you care about people when you only care about yourself and your uni place and being a frickin do-gooder medic? Oohlookatyou, you're on your gap year doing good and pretending to be nice to little crims, free-school-meal kids like me, so that it'll look good on your CV later and you can tell those uni interviewers that you're the good boy, you've done all that daddy told you, you've passed your exams, done your D of frickin E, been a goodboygood-boygoodboy –'

'Shut up,' he says, and his voice is low, dangerous.

But I don't stop, do I? Still I go sailing on.

Stab stab stab.

Hurt him while he's down, that's right.

How can a face be so white under all that sunburn?

'Daddy's boy,' I say. 'You're a frickin daddy's boy and always will be.'

His face twists. Then he's gone.

Fran Stanton's done it again.

Forget-Me-Not

I suck ice from the bottom of my Coke.

This is the poshest street in Brixton.

It's not raining like the last time I came here. Instead the sun bakes the pavement cracks and rises like steam from the tarmacked drives.

I settle down on a wall opposite the house and watch.

Angela looked very serious when I told her what I was going to do.

'Are you sure?' she asks, and it really is a question this time. 'Are you sure it's a good idea?'

'I'm only going to look,' I say.

'You could always wait, you know. It's not long. You have a legal right —'

'If you think I'm going to wait another month, when I don't know, I don't know…' I'm close to tears but I'm not breaking down in front of her. I'm not.

I have the address written on a piece of paper, neatly printed in Angela's writing.

I had to look all the way along both sides of the street before I found the house. It's not a place I come to very often. It's confusing because the numbers suddenly skip from odd to even and before you know it you're fifty numbers away from where you want to be.

I reread the address: *17A Bartholomew Lane*.

At first I think it's a flat; these houses look like they could have several flats in each one. When I ask a resident, she laughs, a high little sound, and looks shocked. She's squirting her roses with a green plastic spray-gun. Her hair is toffee-blonde highlights and she has her sunglasses on top of her head.

'We're all single dwellings here,' she says. She shades her eyes. 'Do you want somewhere in particular, dear?'

I shake my head and hurry away. I can feel her eyes watching me, roses forgotten.

These are the houses with the posh, painted doors. I name the colours: aubergine, vermilion, cyan.

Turns out the house I'm looking for is tucked away down a side street, and it's the biggest one of all.

17A Bartholomew Lane has a door of forget-me-not blue.

It's one of those Georgian town houses with loads of layers like a wedding cake. There's an iron fence painted in treacly black surrounding its front drive and there are steps leading down to its basement kitchen.

All the curtains look clean. There's no cardboard at its windows.

I slink back in the shadows and perch on the opposite wall, between a shrubby hedge and a parking meter. All the cars here have big yellow permits on their windscreens.

As I watch, the door opens and a lad a few years older than me comes down the steps and saunters over to a little Fiat parked on the street outside. He has his keys dangling from his finger and is checking his phone.

'Wait!'

A woman hurries after him; she passes him a wrapped

package and he laughs and kisses her on the cheek. She's tall and has iron-grey hair in a bob. She has a shin-length cardigan and boots the colour of cinnamon. I watch the boy open his package and tear at one of the sandwiches inside as he pulls away. The woman calls to him to drive safely.

I'm staring so hard that at first I miss him.

Then a movement in one of the upstairs windows makes me look up and there he is, my little brother, all serious-faced at the window, chin on hands.

I hiss in my breath and my heart's going *boomboomboom*, but then I remember he's not supposed to see me.

'Let him settle in,' Angela says.

I pull my hoodie over my face and stare at him so hard I swear I'll melt holes in the window.

He's lonely, I think. Must be, to be sitting there all alone.

His little dark head in that huge window makes me think of the princes in the Tower. Miss told us about them when we were doing *Richard III*. They were taken to the Tower of London 'cause they threatened his takeover bid for the throne.

Ended up smothering them, so they say.

But now Johnny's head bobs and he's gone.

Lights go on in the basement and I move closer like a shadow. Cross the street and shrink into the bushes spilling over the iron-fenced driveway.

It's a posh kitchen, one of those ones with an island unit and pans hanging from the ceiling. There's a great steel stove with a silver hood. And in front of the stove is a table full of people.

I pull apart the shrubbery and creep closer.

There's adults and kids, all helping themselves to something that steams in a big cream pot.

They're all happy, all laughing.

257

I stare and stare, swigging my Coke.

Where is he? I'm thinking. *Where is he?*

And then he's there, right in the middle of them all.

A woman with a smiley face ladles a huge pile of meat sauce on to his plate and he helps himself to spaghetti, struggling with the tongs.

A teenage kid helps him slide the pasta on to his plate. Gives him a friendly knuckle-punch.

The sun beats down on the back of my neck but still I watch.

I watch till the kitchen light snaps off, and then I wonder whether I even saw him at all.

Home Alone

He's gone.

Rufus has left me.

He's taken his bedding, his machete, his plaited flip-flops. And he's taken Dog.

I squat down and begin to pick up the broken post, the smashed pieces of melon. I scoop up a handful of mushy seeds and lay them one by one on the chopping boards to dry in the baking sun. It takes ages but it's good work. I'll plant them later.

It feels like hours have passed and he still hasn't come back.

I pull on a pair of Rufus's spare flip-flops to protect my feet from fire ants and take his second-best knife and a long stick. Next on, the grass skirt he's made me. After a pause, I put on what's left of Rufus's headdress. It's all crushed and broken but I'll look for feathers and repair it. I'll cut down a fresh melon pole too; make it a new head and re-carve its face with zigzag teeth.

It's calm here in the jungle. The oh-dear-me bird's calling away like an old friend and the *churra-churra* of the cicadas is sort of restful, comforting.

But it's so much harder without Rufus to help.

It takes me twenty thwacks with the knife to make a cut in the sapling, and then another twenty bounces up and down on the trunk to snap it in two. The trees here are iron-hard compared to the trees on the other side of the island. I can't do it without him.

I'm melting hot when the tree finally gives up its struggle and sinks with a sigh.

I stare at it, defeated; it's split down the middle and useless.

I put down the knife, take off my headdress and place it on a tree trunk. Then I break.

I break myself
     into little chunks, scatter pieces
     of myself over the forest, raw
     and open
     and glistening; a salt–wound,
     knife–wound,
     heart tattered
     like the tattered leaves and shreds of blue–sky
     flashing
     because if I
     pull myself apart like this then it means I'm sorry.
And I am so sorry.

This world spins around me: silver-green; lime-green; blue-blinding flashes of light; harsh throaty *caaaa-caaaaaaws* of far-off birds; endless creaking, hushing, sighing, hissing forest sounds. And I am nothing. But it's good, this stripping away of myself. I close my eyes and let it in; let it all in.

I get up, after a time, and stagger, disorientated; wander through the forest, gathering, collecting.

Scrubbing around on the forest floor, I unearth brownish withered stalks that turn out to be wild onions. When I tug at them, their round, white bulbs gleam like pearls in my hands.

I breathe deep their wild, strange scent and hang them by their stalks from my bikini bottoms.

I also find:

> Three green bananas
> Two giant stick insects
> Two handfuls of feathers
> A brownish piece of root that could be ginger
> One wild plum.

I find myself in Mosquito Alley, the grassy track which we avoid because of the clouds of bugs that always seem to attack Rufus but never me. His skin must be sweeter. I need poles, and here I find them: a whole thicket of tightly packed stalks with silvery leaves, stems musical as wind chimes.

Bamboo. I run my fingers along their straight, nubbled stems. Canes, like for my grandad's tomatoes. Much easier than saplings to cut.

This is a real find, but I have no one to tell.

I'll make a fence too, for my new melon garden, I think.

Somewhere in the back of my mind, a thought flickers.

Hollow. These stems are light, and hollow.

Like there's a much better use for them than a fence.

But the sun's sighing, and my ears are straining for the sound of a short, high bark and Rufus's voice saying something like, '*Where are you, Cow-bag?*'

I work hard, cutting down poles, as the shadows lengthen. Then I turn home.

They're still not back.

Visiting Time

Their eyes slide over me, twist like pins. Don't want to look too close or too long at Monster Me, do they?

Mr Nice has even bought me a Coke (ha! Like you can bribe a gorgon) but it sits where I've left it on the table, in a small pool of spill.

'He'll be along in a minute, don't you worry.'

'Found some new friends, he has. What are boys like?'

All the time Angela smiles and smiles.

I glare; burn through their tiny hearts and wither them into raisins. I bite my nails. I jiggle my foot and hatehatehate.

When Johnny sees me, what will he see? Will he see the change in me, what I've become? Will he flinch?

Mr and Mrs Nice are well dressed. They're mixed-race like Johnny; they've been carefully matched like paint samples. Their mouths move as if they're talking but I can't hear a word 'cause all I'm thinking is, when he comes, will he,

will he

see a monster?

Johnny doesn't come.

He'll be whispering about me to his new friends, hiding and watching. '*There she is, my evil big sister. She's done things you can't imagine. She's blown up the whole world. She set out one day with a thought that ate its way, like acid, into her till it was all she was, all she had.'*

Mr Nice is saying something. The word 'sorry' floats like charred paper.

I get up.

Angela touches my arm but I jerk it off as if scalded.

I need to get away from their curiouseyesconcernedvoicesfakesmiles. Monsters like me need caves to crawl in.

It's screaming loud in here.

'Johnny,' I cry, and my voice sounds all broken 'cause it's such a long time since I used it; this voice that once told stories is brittle as glass.

We're in Space City, a place full of kids screaming and pushing; hissing inflatables creaking and giant cages full of brightly coloured plastic balls. It's hell. Johnny will love it.

I think I see him then; a small figure in a red hoodie, spinning round and round on a rope. But the kid turns to face me and it's a girl: same eyes, same creamy brown skin.

I climb the face of the evil emperor first: a creaking, grinning monster with a giant purple face and giant red eyes. It sways as I grapple for a foothold on its silver horns.

'Johnny?' I call.

I can't wait to meet him. I am dreading meeting him.

It's been three weeks now. Three weeks of me refusing to go to school and the community-support lady coming round and counselling and That-Bitch-Angela trying to stick back together the pieces of our smashed-up lives.

Cassie has turned into a zombie. No, scrub that. She's become Queen Zombie; a zombie to beat all zombies. But it's fine because Wayne's found her some dog Valium to calm her nerves and that really frickin helps.

'Johnny?'

I leave the emperor and crawl through the net tunnel towards the space station. A woman is on her hands and knees, chasing her daughter. She catches her and tickles her and I see the mum's belly, stretched full and tight like an egg.

'They love it here, don't they?' She smiles at me. She and her little girl have matching My Little Pony glitter-stickers on their faces.

I crawl on, past the mum and her bump and her girl, to the creaking, blue and silver space station.

He's not in Minion City, nor on the Galaxy Hopper. He's not one of the kids lining up for the Plasma Swing.

Then I think I see him; he's darting away, down into a purple slide. He's quick as a whip, squealing.

I push past a load of giggling kids, past a dad on the zip wire, to the slide. It stinks of plastic and disinfectant; bounces as more kids scrabble on behind me.

'Monkey? It's me, Frannie.'

The slide is longer and steeper than I expected; it curves suddenly, knocking me breathless.

With a whoosh, I shoot out of the other end into a pit of balls. He's crawling through to the Star Raiders spaceship; a big inflatable sign points the way. Stumbling, I crawl through the netting and jump down on to bouncing yellow rubber.

He's here. I've found him.

Keeping Busy

I finish cleaning Rufus's hammock and carefully water the melon patch. I use a bunch of twigs as a broom and sweep the whole of our camp floor so it looks all brushed and soft and cared for. I straighten the knives and flip-flops and replait all the stray palm leaves on the roof canopy.

I line up all my finds on our coffee-drum table and put the stick insects in a coffee can with some leaves so they don't escape.

Then I get to work building a melon fence. Cutting through the bamboo makes my hands blister over the blisters but that's good because it means I'm working and keeping busy and it stops me thinking. I sharpen each post with Rufus's knife and bang it into the dirt with the biggest rock I can find. Thirsty work but I can do it.

Then I wait.

And wait.

When the sun slides behind Fear Mountain, I'm shivering even though I've stoked the fire and the flames shoot hot and high into the breaking-out stars.

What if he's left me for good?

I count twenty-nine more stars piercing the sky; then fifteen more, and then I can't bear it any more.

What if he's seen a fishing boat and they've rescued him and gone to a different island?

I edge closer to the fire, hugging my knees. The flames burn deep into my eyes, my skin, my bones.

But nothing warms me.

Speed Zombies

The spaceship walls bulge as we bounce.

'Fran.'

'Hi, Monkey, I'm so glad I found you.'

He's shiny-sweaty, hair glistening and cheeks flushed.

'Come and give me a hug, Monkey.'

He lets me hug him; the floor heaving as kids press and bounce and scream around us.

'Missed you, Monkey,' I say.

I breathe in his Johnny smell of grubbiness and warmth and sweat. For a moment he's all I can hold on to; I think I'm holding on to the last piece of myself.

'Is it true?' he whispers against my ear. His breath is hot and sweet-sticky. He smells of boy-sweat and cola bottles.

'What, Monkey?'

He wriggles away. 'Ouch, that hurts.'

He's wearing clothes I've not seen before: a Dark Knight T-shirt and brand-new jeans. He has his hair in cool braids like Jaden Smith.

Johnny's eyes are bright and serious as he starts to bounce in the spaceship.

'Is it true, what they're saying? Billy's sister says you burnt down the school and hurt all the teachers.'

Bounce.

'Why did you do that, Frannie? Were you angry?'

Bounce.

'I never…I didn't mean to hurt anyone, Monkey…'

But my words fall like stones.

They're hard and brittle like all lies. Because I did mean it. I meant to hurt from the moment I climbed those stairs. Rewind. From the moment I cleared Cassie out of vodka; stuffed the bottles into my bag.

And if you asked me: what was in your mind the instant you dropped that match?

Then the answer would be: I wanted to hurt and burn and kill.

In that instant I wanted to blow up the whole frickin world.

Johnny's still bouncing, those dark eyes looking at me, puzzled.

'So did you do it, Frannie? Billy says that you're a monster and I should keep away from you.'

'Who's...Billy?' I make myself say.

I'm not bouncing any more, but the walls and floor are still bellying up and down, up and down. My knees will give way. And I'm sinking, I really am. Because my match never blew up the world. It just withered the last piece of me that was still human.

Johnny bounces, arms and legs like a starfish.

Arms, legs, socks, kids, bouncingbouncingbouncing.

Are you a monster, Frannie?

Are you a
   monster?

Johnny's eyes flit past me and he smiles.

'Zombie attack!' he screams. He turns to go, still jumping as two kids jump down into the bouncy spaceship; the walls surge and hiss as I lose my footing.

'*Got* you!'

'No you haven't, Billy. You've got to blast me first an' –'

I'm getting to my feet; the noise from the air pump is deafening.

'Hey, Fran, I'm in the middle of a game – I'm being chased by speed zombies!'

'Wait –'

He's scrabbling back through the netting, the two boys close behind him. I stumble off the spaceship, wade through the balls to reach him.

'Monkey, see you again, yeah?'

'Bye, Fran. Oh, Fran?'

I look up hopefully. He's hiding behind a Minion, face pressed to the netting.

'Don't call me Monkey, OK?' he's whispering. 'An' if you buy me any presents, don't get me picture books.'

'OK, Mon–Johnny.'

'It's just that,' he says, 'they're for babies.'

The two boys chasing him squeeze through at last.

Johnny's eyes brighten.

And he's gone.

I wish

In the end I go to bed.

I get into Rufus's bed, after refixing his canopy and retying the drinks bottles under his palm-leaf mattress topper.

I wish Dog was with me. I wish Rufus would come back.

I can't sleep; images of all the people I've hurt keep pushing into my brain, squeezing out any chance of sleep.

Cassie and Johnny and Angela and Trish and Sally and Coral and Rufus and –

Miss.

I think I've only ever been nice to Dog.

It's too much, it's too much

oh oh oh.

'Shhhh.'

'Johnny?'

'Fran? Wake up and move over, Cow-bag.'

'Rufus?'

A face swims into the flames; pale, and smiling white teeth.

'Honestly,' the face says. 'You could have put dinner on.'

Less a Bitch

'You came back,' I say.

I wipe my eyes as Rufus climbs in next to me. Feel the bottles creak as he moves around trying to get comfy.

We both laugh as Dog rushes out of nowhere and jumps up too. I push him away as he tries to lick my salty face.

'Didn't think you'd come back,' I mumble. 'You were gone for ages.'

Rufus coughs. 'Couldn't bear the thought of all the tidying up,' he says.

I squirm.

We lie side by side, Rufus and me, as we gaze at the stars pricking out their dot-to-dot patterns in the shivering sky.

'Rufus?' I say.

'Mmmm?'

'Do you ever imagine that you're not you; that you're… something else?'

'Something else?'

'Like a monster or…a rock.'

'A rock?'

I'm glad it's dark 'cause now it's my turn to blush; I'm flushing like a frickin beacon.

'I try to be a rock,' I say.

'So, does it work?'

'Not really.' I take a deep breath. 'I'm glad you're back, Rufus.'

Rufus reaches for my hand and squeezes it. 'I've always liked rocks,' he says. 'They're solid and timeless and…interesting and – ugh!'

'What is it?'

He's snatched his hand away.

'You're all sticky.' He looks closely at me, as much as he can in the dark. 'Christ, Fran, you look like you've been attacking zombies.'

'I was trying to clear up the melons,' I mumble.

He licks his finger. 'Yum, all sweet and sticky. Mashed-up brains…my favourite.'

'That's gross,' I sniff.

He pushes my sticky hair away from my face. 'Trust you to get us all messed up after our shower. I don't know that I can use my special shell-cleansing technique again; it seemed to have a rather surprising effect on you last time…'

I squirm.

'Rufus, don't. I –'

'I mean, I know I'm devastating with my auburn good looks and my tall, incredibly dashing physique, but it's amazing what magic I can perform with just a…shell…'

I giggle, wiping tears and smashed melon flesh from my face.

'I can make a body go all of a quiver with my electric touch.'

He tickles my legs and I wriggle him off.

'Ugh,' he says. 'Ugh. Just look at my hands. I'm sorry. I can't go to bed like this. Let's use the cooking water.'

I watch him wash his hands and face over the seawater cooking pot. Then I let him wipe my hot forehead with what's left of his TeamSkill shirt.

'Rufus?' I say, once we've settled back to bed again.

'Mmmm?'

'Have you ever done something so bad that you're frightened to think about it?'

He's silent for a moment before answering.

'Sometimes I've thought things so bad, it's almost as if I've done them.'

'Your dad, right?'

Beside me, Rufus nods.

'Why am I such a bitch?' I say.

'Hmm. Less a bitch, more a cow-bag, I'd say.' Rufus turns to look at me. 'But you don't have to be.'

'I can't change the way I am,' I mumble. 'Not when I can't undo what I've done. It's easier to act like a monster. It's what everyone thinks anyway.'

'So what about the teacher? It said in your notes that she'd asked to see you. Have you said that you're sorry?'

I shake my head in his arms. 'I'm scared to – I don't want to look at what I've done.'

Rufus waits.

At our feet, Dog sighs.

'She was nice,' I say. 'Miss was just trying to help me.'

'So go and see her, silly. Just as soon as we've solved the little problem of how to get off this blasted island where we're marooned and all that.'

I laugh and snuggle down. It feels nice, him spooning me.

'So does this mean you aren't going to be such a cow-bag any more?' he says.

'Maybe. It'll take some practice though.'

'Now go to sleep, Rock Girl.'

'Night night, Rufus.'

Any Girl in the World

Neither of us is asleep.

Well, Dog is. I listen to his little pants from where he's

curled up at the bottom of the bed.

It's nice, spooning each other, and I can feel Rufus's hand on mine. His palm is warm and rough from all the log-chopping.

I sigh.

'I'm just not your type, right?' I ask him.

Rufus pushes hair out of my eyes.

'Little Fran,' he says, and he sounds like he's my big brother now, 'if I could see you, I know you'd have this look on your face like you're ready to retract at the slightest hint of rejection. But it's not you, I promise.'

'Sure?'

He squeezes me round the middle.

'Yes. If I could do it with any girl in the world, it would be you, Fran.'

'OK. Thanks.'

Pause.

'I've done it before with girls. Twice.'

I wait and listen.

'There was the girl at the summer social, when our house-master invited the local school over. And of course we're coed, which means we have girls and after Year Nine every lad goes a bit crazy.' He fidgets. 'I knew there was something different about me when I didn't. Go crazy, I mean. All my friends were, even Sebastian.'

'Sebastian?'

'My room-mate. He and I had a bit of a thing going; we had since Lower School. Nothing too serious, but we slept together sometimes; nothing out of the ordinary, but we did it more and more. It was just a bit of fun; I thought all the chaps did it.'

Well, what do you expect in an all-boys' dorm full of raging hormones?

'But there was something more. Sometimes, as we lay kissing and talking, I felt such a sense of calm, of peace, that I felt I could lie in Seb's arms for ever. Which wasn't how it was supposed to be.'

He sighs.

'Because of course, when we got a new intake of girls at Sixth Form, Seb, along with the other lads in Upper School, was off like a shot.'

His voice is low, his face flickering in the firelight.

'He'd done it officially with three girls by the time it was Christmas, and it was never the same between us. Seb didn't look into my eyes once after that. "That's not who I am. Sorry, mate," he said. I saw him stuffing his drawer full of condoms. He'd got his eye on Annalise, the hot one.'

Rufus gives a shaky sort of laugh. 'As long as my father doesn't find out.' Then he turns to me. 'Why are you crying?'

'What?'

For some reason my cheeks are wet. I rub at them furiously.

'I never cry. Crying's for sissies,' I say.

He sighs again. '"Course it is.'

Shooting Stars

Later, towards dawn, I wake.

Lie staring at the star-stabbed sky, and as I watch, one of them *moves*; I watch it etch its way across the world in a bright arc.

'Shooting star,' says Rufus.

'You're awake.'

'It's caused by tiny bits of dust and rock called meteoroids falling into the Earth's atmosphere and burning up. Those meteoroids are 4.5 billion years old. We're seeing something that is billions of years older than the ocean, older than rocks.'

I think about this. 'So are they happening now? Not like stars?'

'That's right. When we see real stars, we're seeing ones that actually died one hundred thousand years ago; but shooting stars are an event that's only one second old.'

For once, Rufus's encyclopedic knowledge doesn't annoy me. I lie back, thinking about all the layers of time that the sky has to hold.

Then.

'Ever played Shooting Stars?' Rufus says.

'What?'

'Don't say *what*, say *pardon*. Shooting Stars is a game of excellence and supreme skill. I'll go first.'

I feel him raise his arm.

'First you lift your bow, like so. Keep your grip firm and steady. Take your other arm…'

His hand digs into my side.

'Ouch.'

'Sorry. You take your other hand and pull back the string, feeling the arrow taut and quivering between thumb and forefinger. Got that?'

'I think so.'

'Then, with infinite care and precision, you position the arrow so it sits just above your target. The aim is to shoot a shooting star. Now…steady…steady…'

We hold our breath as he waits.

'There's one. *Now.*'

The star flashes in a perfect curve.

'Damn – missed it. Now it's your turn.'

He hands me the bow.

'It was a good shot though,' I tell him as I raise my arm.

'Why, thank you. Now careful, careful. Take your time…'

I take a breath; hold the arrow just so. I decide it's made of chicken feathers, my arrow, but it's a good one, finely weighted. I close one eye. Aim. Wait.

'Over there,' whispers Rufus.

Fire.

'I got it, I got it.'

'Beginner's luck. Now pass me the bow. Ouch, careful – nearly had my eye out.'

For the rest of the night, we shoot the stars till they fade away, one by one.

'Spoon?'

'Spoon.'

'Dog?'

He spoons too. Dog never needs asking twice.

Till morning, we spoon each other, Rufus and me; we fit together like a stone fits a peach.

Bottle-tops

'So what did you do when you disappeared?' I ask him the next day.

Rufus flushes.

'I went walking,' he says.

'Well, where did you go?'

'Nowhere in particular. I was looking for food. I thought

I might find more wild pigs.'

But he doesn't sound convincing.

'So what did you really do?' I ask.

'I made you something,' he says.

He roots around in his hammock and passes me something bright and plasticky.

'For me?' I say.

I turn it over in my hand. A necklace like no other. Its fishing-wire chain has been strung with bottle-tops, each pierced precisely in its centre. It rattles as I put it on. It doesn't matter that the bottle-tops scratch my sunburn 'cause it's the thought that matters.

'Well, it's beautiful,' I say.

'Simply stunning,' he agrees.

So all that time he went walkabout, he was making me a present. A surprise for me.

I could cry.

'The way the Fanta ones coordinate with the Sprite, that's really special,' I say.

'Just the effect I was aiming for,' Rufus says.

He winces as I hug him.

'Mind my sunburn, Cow-bag! I spent hours combing the island, looking for these. Found a lot of them washed up by our fishing rock, but some were on bottles floating in the sea. Had to swim out to get them.'

'I don't have anything to give you right now,' I say, 'but I'm working on something.'

Rufus bows his head gravely. 'Understood.'

'It would be kind of difficult to top — as gifts go, I mean.'

'Say no more.'

I squeeze his hand, and we go to get firewood, bumping hips, Dog running ahead, scenting every tree he can.

Barrels and Bamboo

There's something in the water.

I wade through the shallows and there are two of them: huge metal barrels, their letters blistered by the sea.

They're big enough for a water butt, or for making the coolest range oven, or maybe a beach barbecue.

I have to swim to reach them; each time I try to grasp the barrels, they roll out of reach. I hang on to one, kicking water till I get back to the shallows. It's buoyant, only half-filled with seawater.

I roll it upright and sniff inside. There's still a faint whiff of petrol, and I think how useful *that* would have been, for keeping the fire going, or if we found a boat.

When I've rescued its twin, I kneel on the sand and examine them.

The sea has made them beautiful; turned this trash into colours of violet and ochre and cerulean. It's streaked and blended the rust; worn away the branded letters till they're just a whisper.

'*Shellex Oil*,' I read.

I wonder where all the oil went; whether it cloyed its way into the ocean, leaving treacled beaches and glued-up feathers and rocks and beaks.

I stare at the barrels, and I think of the coffee drum we use as a table.

I think of the bamboo, long and strong and hollow.

Then I start to smile.

Because these barrels mean so much more than a water butt.

Rufus is finishing the melon fence I got bored with.

'You're not helping?' he says.

Dog's hovering. He doesn't like it when we separate into two groups.

'!'

'It's all right, Dog. You stay with Daddy.'

'Come on, Virgil,' says Rufus.

I give him the finger. Dog doesn't mind having two names though; I think he quite likes it.

'I think I've seen some more onions by Mosquito Alley,' I lie.

Rufus nods. He hates Mosquito Alley.

'Put the kettle on,' I call after them.

Each day I do a bit more: chop a couple of bamboo; forage for netting and rope; tie in another pole. And all the time I'm searching, searching for that fourth barrel, 'cause I can't finish the raft without it.

I haven't told Rufus because he'll go all sensible and frown and I can hear what he'll say: '*Water first, Fran. Then logs, then fishing.*'

I bet he'd say that, even though he took a whole afternoon to make me a necklace. I kiss one of the Cola bottle-tops and it bumps reassuringly against my chest as I work.

I need to make another frame and then sandwich the oil drums at each corner. Better still would be if I had six or even eight barrels, but I'll make do with what I have. Each time I'm done working on it, I heave the raft off the beach, tuck it away behind the bamboo.

It's hard to get it finished.

Fishing takes longer now; the fish don't seem to be so plentiful any more. Maybe it's the spring tide or maybe it's us, and we've overfished our little area.

We're getting thinner, and more tired, and sometimes it

takes all day just to keep the fire going.

But the raft burns like an obsession.

In my mind's eye I imagine it standing tall and proud on the water: a sail and a flag, and even a cabin to keep the sun from frying us 'cause there'll be nowhere to hide once we're adrift.

Adrift.

There's a word to make you shiver.

Fishing

We go fishing, Rufus and Dog and me.

We perch at the end of Fishing Rock and dangle our legs and cast out far with our hand-made lines and wait.

We talk, sometimes, of something or nothing.

Often we sit in silence, letting the world lap warm waves round us, in this endless, ceaseless sea.

'Cerulean,' I say once.

Rufus looks at me like he knows what I mean. 'Yes, it is. It is cerulean, it's exactly that. Cerulean as the sea.'

'And cerulean as a swimming pool,' I say, leaning back against the rock. If I wriggle, just so, it fits, like I'm part of it.

'Cerulean as a sandwich?'

'Well, maybe a mouldy sandwich. Maybe one of Cassie's sandwiches…'

'Why do you call your mother Cassie?'

'Cassie is a hopeless old prossie. I had to look after her, be her carer. Look after my little brother too.' I let out my breath; check to see if he's shocked.

The line twitches.

'So she's lucky to have you,' Rufus says matter-of-factly.

Really? But I'm a bitch. I'm cruel. I cut her a thousand times a day.

I turn my face away. Try not to think of great, fat, useless Cassie, with her arms soft as heaven.

'I never really had a mother,' says Rufus.

'Oh. I'm sorry.'

'I mean, she's not dead or anything. She left when I was a baby. Went to live in New York. I never see her.'

There's no fish on the line. Not yet.

'So what about your dad?' Rufus asks.

I shiver. 'Big Wayne's my mum's boyfriend. He's the one who made Cassie the way she is.'

Rufus watches me closely. 'He never – tried anything with you?'

I think of his smiling mouth. His hands holding my wrists.

'It was after they took Johnny away,' I say. 'It meant I didn't share my room with my brother any more. It meant that Wayne started to get ideas...'

I leave my sentence trailing.

'So what did you say to him?' Rufus cuts into my memory.

I laugh bitterly. 'I told him he was a fat, ugly, creepy wanker.'

'Did you really?'

'No.' I stare into the water. 'I said nothing.'

Dirty Sheets

It's been a week since I visited Johnny, and I can't stop hearing his voice –

'Did you do it, Frannie?'

'Are you a monster?'

I sit on the floor, back against the cold radiator. I clutch my scalding coffee and sip its bitterness and close my eyes. I can still smell him here.

Johnny smells of:

> Warm skin
>
> Scraped knees
>
> Dirty feet
>
> Damp hair
>
> Chocolatey fingers
>
> Turned pages.

I missed a few of Johnny's things when packing. There's his collection of Olympic Games fifty-pence coins in a Cadbury's Creme Egg mug, one of those cheap ones you get with an Easter egg. The planet mobile he made still hangs from the ceiling with Sellotape. It spins slowly now and then in the air currents.

There's something poking beneath his bed.

I slide it out and it's a picture book: *The Gruffalo*.

The others are gone of course –

> *See them shrivel. Watch them die.*
>
> *Rip them up, rip them up, rip them up.*

Johnny had lots of favourites: *The Runaway Train* and *The Gruffalo* and *Beegu*.

Beegu is about a little yellow alien that gets stranded all alone on Earth and everyone's mean to him because he's yellow and different and then he makes friends with some children but at the end his mum and dad find him and whisk him back up into their spaceship.

It's a nice story but the pictures kill me a bit and I never really liked reading that one.

Johnny liked it though.

'Again, again.'

'Only one more time, Monkey.'

We both knew all the words to *The Gruffalo*.

My coffee's lovely and muddy. I swirl the grindings around my tongue and hug my mug as I read. As always, the story and its rhythm calm me.

I turn the page. The book's nicked from Brixton Library. It's dated five years ago; we just never took it back.

I smile as I read the words aloud, and in my head my brother's voice mixes in with mine.

'Who the hell are you talking to?'

I jump and spill my coffee.

Wayne's blocking the doorway, his tiny eyes raking the room.

'What's it to you?' I say.

We stare at each other.

I stand up.

Wayne lights a fag and blows smoke.

' 'Course, it's better on all of us now Johnny's gone,' he says, eyes never leaving my face.

My nails dig into my palms.

'Messed–up kid, always wetting the bed. Always stealing food. "Send him to his dad," I'd say, but your mother wouldn't have it. Too soft, she is. Always has been.'

'Joel got married. Went to live in Australia,' I remind him.

'Should've taken his kid with him then, shouldn't he?' Wayne shakes his head, then walks over to the bed.

'Look at this. Dirty sheets. Stains all over the mattress.'

He's lifting the bedding, scenting the air, his fag wedged in the corner of his mouth.

'Get off his stuff,' I say.

Wayne raises his eyes.

'We all know it's difficult, love. But he's better off where he is. And you can get a proper night's sleep, not always waking to clean up after him.' He sighs out fag smoke. 'It's not right, love.'

I clench my fists.

Wayne makes a sad face. 'I know you meant well, with all you did for him. But did you ever think you might be making him worse with all that mollycoddling? Kids need to learn to grow up, sweetheart.'

He nods over to where I'm standing. 'All them stories, all them books. You gotta admit it's easier without him. You can be a proper teenager now. Got your room to yourself, like a big girl.'

He lets go of Johnny's bedding, wrinkling his nose.

'We could turn this into a proper room for you now. Get new stuff. Somewhere to put your clothes. A nice little dressing table for you to put your make-up on.'

He's moving around Johnny's room, touching Johnny's things: his coin mug, the mobile, *The Gruffalo*. Wayne smiles and smiles.

Then he comes closer.

He strokes my hair, turns me to face the mirror. 'You oughta smile more. You'd be quite pretty if you smiled more.'

He's pressed close behind me, so his fat belly's squashed against my back.

'There's ways you could start earning your keep,' he says, 'now that your brother's gone. Now he's not always in the bed with you.'

Wayne's smile broadens.

282

'You're a big girl now. I know people who'd like that.'

His hand's crawling over my leg now, like a giant crab or something.

'What d'you think, darlin'? You never know, you might enjoy it.'

Climbing fingers, breath quick and fast.

Snap.

What Then?

'So what did you do?' asks Rufus.

He and Dog are watching me seriously. Dog gives me a little lick on my hand.

'Not enough,' I say bitterly.

Revving Up

Wayne is staggering about, clutching his face.

'You little cow. You're unhinged, you are. Look what you've done – you've burnt me.'

There's coffee and granules down his face, his best shirt.

He's stumbling towards me now; he's going to get me for that.

I run, ignoring Cassie's bleats from the sofa, clambering over the boxes of crap in the hall.

Fumble with the door chain, pelt down the steps.

There's a lady struggling with her Sainsbury's bags.

Kids outside are revving their cars.

I want to run far, far away, but there's nowhere to go.

In the end, I just sit watching the ducks in Brockwell Park. I smoke one fag after the other till I feel sick.

Wayne won't come to find me; he's too lazy for that. He'll be spinning lies to Cassie, about how uncontrollable I'm getting.

Or maybe he'll be laying into her, taking his temper out.

I stub out my fag and watch a duck cleaning itself. There are terrapins by the edge of the lake; they're soaking up the sun, big as dinner plates.

So what if Cassie needs me? Sad, old, fat, loser, waste-of-space Cassie doesn't even try to hold on. Loses her son without getting up off the settee. There's nothing there any more, nothing left for me to hate. That's why I turned my hate to Miss instead. The one who started it all by telling tales.

Ten days till the court hearing, and then maybe they'll put me away in some institution for kids who've gone off the rails. Sometimes I think this would be for the best.

There's no way I'm going back to my room. Not when there's no lock on my door. I decide to sleep up on the roof tonight.

Angry Yowl

'So tell him now,' Rufus suggests.

'You what?'

'Tell him now – what you just said to me. Do an angry yowl.'

'What the frick's an angry yowl?'

'You know, like on *Dead Poets Society*. The teacher, played by Robin Williams, makes his student do one. You just roar out all your rage, get back to your primal self.'

'Like Medusa on the rocks?' I say. 'After she was betrayed by everyone?'

Rufus shakes his head. 'You're not quite right there,' he says. 'In Classics we learnt that she…'

I glare at him. 'I'm right,' I say. 'I know I'm right.'

I know about Medusa.

I know all about monsters, don't I?

Rufus shrugs. 'If you say so,' he says. 'Anyway, give it your best gorgon yowl.'

So I do.

I put down my fishing line, prop it carefully on the rocks; stand and face the sea. I lift up my face and shout, making the pelicans lift and the seagulls scream.

Below us on the sand, Dog barks and barks.

★ ★ ★ ★ ★ ★ # # # ? ? ! # ! ★ ! ! ! ! ? ? ? ' # ? #
? ? ? # ★ ! ! ! ★ # # ★ ★ ★ ! ! ! ★ ★ ★ ★ ★
★ ★ ★ # # # # ! ★ ! ! ! ! ! ! ★ ★ ★ ★ ★ ★ ★ ★
★ ★ ★ ★ # # # # # # # ? ? ? ? ? ? ? ? ? ' # ? ?
! ★ ! ! ! ! ! ! ★ ★ ★ ★ ★ ★ ★ ★ ★ ★ ★ # # # # #
? ? ? ? ? ? ? ? ' # ? ? ? ? ! ! ! ! ! ! ! ! ! ! ! # # # # ★ ★ ★ ★ ★ ★
★ ★ ★ ★ ★ ★ # # # # # # # ? ? ? # ★ ! ! ! ★ # # ★ ★ ★
! ! ! ! # ★ ! ? ? ? ? ! # ! ★ ! ! # # ! ★ ! ! ! ! ! ! ! ★ ★ ★ ★ ★ ★ ★ ★
★ ★ ★ ★ # # # # # # ? ? ? ? ? ? ? ? ' # ? ? ? ? ! ! ! ! ! ! ! ! !
! # # # # ★ ★ ★ ★ ★ ★ ★ ★ ★ ★ ★ ★ ★ ★ # # # # # # #
? ? ? # ★ ! ! ! ★ # # ★ ★ ★ ! ! ! ! # ★ ! ? ? ? ? ! # ! ★ ! ! ? ? ! ! ! !
! ! ! ! # # # # ★ ★ ★ ★ ★ ★ ★ ★ ★ ★ ★ ★ ★ ★ ★ # # # # # #
? ? ? # ★ ! ! ! ★ # # ★ ★ ★ ! ! ! ! # ★ ! ? ? ? ? ! # ! ★ ! ! ! ! ! ! !
★ ★ ★ ★ ★ ★ ★ ★ ★ ★ ★ ★ ★ ★ # # # # # # # ? ? ? ? ? ? ? ?
! ! ! ! ! ! ! ! # # # # ! ! ' ! ! ! ! ! ! ! ! ! ! ! ! ! ! ! ! ! ! # # # ★ ★ ! ! ! !
! ! ! ★ ! ! ! ! ! ! ★ ★ ★ ★ ★ ★ ★ ★ ★ ★ ★ ★ ★ ★ # # # # # # #
? ? ? ? ? ? ? ? ! ! ! ! ! ! ! ! ! # # # # ! ! ! ! ! ! ! ! ! ! ! ! ! ! ! ! ! ! # #
★ ★ ! ! ! ! ! ! ! ! ! ! ! ! ! ★ ★ ★ ★ ★ ★ ★ # # # # # # # ? ? ?
? ? ? ? ? ? ! ! ! ! ! ! ! ! ! ! ! # # # # ★ ★ ★ ★ ★ ★ ★ ★ ★ ★ ★ ★ ★ #
? ? ? # ★ ! ! ! ★ # # ★ ★ ★ ! ! ! ! # ★ ! ? ? ? ?
! # ? ? ? ? ? ? ? ? ? ? ' # ? ? ? ? ? ? ? ? ? ! ! ! ! ! ! ! ! ! ! ! # #   ★ ★ ★
★ ★ # # ? ? ! # ! ★ ! ! ! ! ! ! ! ★ ★ # # ! ★ ! ! ! ! ! ! ! ★ ★ ★ ★ ★ ★ ★
★ ★ ★ ★ ★ ★ # # # # # # # ? ? ? ? ? ? ? ? ? ' # ? ? ! ! ! ! ! ! !
! ! ! ! ! # # # ★ ★ ! ! ! ! ! ! ! ! ! ! ! ! ! ★ ★ ★ ★ ★ ★ ★ # # # # #
? ? ? ? ? ? ? ? ? ! ! ! ! ! ! ! ! ! ! ! # # # # ★ ★ ★ ★ ★ ★ ★ ★ ★ ? ? !
! ! ! ! ! ! ! ! ! # # # # ★ ★ ★ ★ ★ ★ ★ ★ ★ ★ ★ ★ ★ ★ ★ ★ ★ # # # # #
? ? ? # ★ ! ! ! ★ # # ★ ★ ★ ! ! ! ! # ★ ! ? ? ? ? ! # ! ★ ! ! ! !
! ! ! ! ! ! ! ! ! ! # # # ★ ★ ! ! ! ! ! ! ! ! ! ! ! ! ! ★ ★ ★ ★ ★ ★ ★ # # #
? ? ? ? ? ? ? ? ? ! ! ! ! ! ! ! ! ! ! ! # # # # ★ ★ ★ ★ ★ ★ ★
★ # # # ? ? ? ? ? ? ? ? ? ! ! ! ! ! ! ! ! ! ! ! # # # # ! ! ' ! ! ! ! # # #

Scribbles in the Sand

Rufus stares.

'Um, Fran. I think you might have frightened the fish away.'

'There's quite a lot more where that came from,' I pant.

'Well, maybe when I'm doing my yoga, you can do your yowling,' Rufus suggests.

Dog is delighted that I've stopped; he drops a pebble on the sand and rolls and rolls on it, wriggling and scratching with a demented look on his face.

'So are you still afraid of Wayne?'

'No,' I say. 'He's just a sad old loser with his sad old songs.'

'Definitely a wanker,' Rufus agrees.

I sit back down; pick up my line.

'What are you going to do, if you ever get off here?' asks Rufus.

I consider. 'Well, I'm going to get me and Johnny a little house by the sea and it's going to be whitewashed, very simple, and there'll be shells leading up to the front door, and a tiny little front garden, just enough to sit in, and…'

I blush.

Rufus doesn't laugh.

'Me, I think I'll buy the house next to yours. And paint. I've always wanted to paint. You could do your writing and I can do my painting.'

'And Dog?'

'Virgil will be inside both our houses, hogging the beds and the sofas. What about Cassie?'

'Maybe Cassie could come and sit on a chair in the sunshine with her tinny in her hand. She always did like the sea.' I frown. 'I'll have to get her into Turkish coffee though. A can of Kestrel doesn't really fit with the scene...What?' I demand. 'What's so funny?'

The float dips.

'Got a catch?'

I wind my line a little around its jam jar. 'Nah, frickin fish has taken the bait again.'

'Frickin fish,' Rufus agrees.

I wind it all the way in and catch the hook. It's a good one; made with a ring pull from a cast-up Cola can. I've broken it and bashed it into a mean, sharp point.

I smash another limpet with a stone and jab its flesh on to the fish hook. Limpets here are bright yellow, like pollen.

We're fishing for snapper.

When we catch them, they shimmer in the plastic peanut-butter tub like they're mother-of-pearl or something. Rose and coral coloured and tastes like heaven.

Except we've only caught two.

The shallows burn blue-white below us. Above us only sky.

When we're thirsty, Rufus opens us both our 3,799th peepa (or something).

Then:

'Fancy doing some sand-doodling?'

I leave off prodding the fish and look up, squinting. My Ray-Bans got lost long ago. Rufus says I have white lines around my eyes from screwing them up so much against the sun:

'You'll get crow's feet like knife-cuts,' he warns.

'Sand-doodling?' I say. I'm feeling drowsy and peaceful, resting here against this warm rock which moulds just so around my back. The sea has stars in it; it winks at me with infinite eyes.

Rufus is in one of his energetic moods. I wedge my line in the rock and trail after him to his favourite part of the beach.

He's sort of dancing, is Rufus; swaying and curving in slow motion, he's drawing crazy patterns with a stick in the sand.

The tide is lowlowlow and has left us an empty page.

Laughing, I pick up a stick and join him.

It's the best thing ever; we twist and spiral and loop the loop till the beach is covered in one giant doodle.

'Let's fill it in,' I suggest.

This time I choose a broken shell 'cause it has lovely jags and thicknesses, which make interesting lines like calligraphy. I spend hours hopping from shape to shape, filling them in with wiggles and whirls and coils.

Time passes; the tide turns.

Rufus takes my hands and swings me round and round on our beautiful patterned floor. The sunlight is spinning and our smiles are flying and just at this minute, this moment, this exact moment, nownownow –

I. Feel. So. Happy.

But the tide is coming in.

It sucks at the sand, at our beautiful scribblings.

'Fran?'

I can't bear it. I can't bear it.

'Silly old Cow-bag.' Rufus puts his arms around me.

'It's all going to go – it'll all be washed away,' I mumble. Inside his arms, I feel safe as a crab in its shell.

'But that's all right, Fran. That's the way it should be.'

I pull away. 'It's not all right. It's never all right to have something you love rubbed away.'

We watch the sea as it licks and nibbles at our drawings.

Rufus starts to cut up the fish on a flat stone.

'So what did your brother look like when you last saw him?'

I consider. Think of his bright eyes, his sweaty hair. 'Happy,' I say.

'Ah.' He busies himself with the snapper and I wish he'd skewer himself with the frickin stick.

I wish he'd stop sounding like Sally-the-counsellor.

I wish he'd tell *me* more.

He hands me a piece of snapper, fresh and raw like sushi.

The fish tastes good today.

We sit for a long time on the edge of the shore, and watch the tide lapping slowly inward, closer and closer, licking the tip of the picture delicately, till it kisses the top of our drawing, then trickles into each line, each curve.

And now a third of it is gone. And then a half.

And then.

And then.

I suppose Rufus's right; it is kind of beautiful.

Beautiful as an ache.

Almost There

Only one more barrel to find.

Just the second frame to finish now.

Smiling, I take what's left of the TeamSkill polo shirt and rip it into two halves.

We never wear clothes now, not really. Our skin's kind of used to the sun; my legs and arms are brown and hairy as coconuts. Poor Rufus will never be sun-friendly; he's just one big freckle nowadays, but he covers his blistered shoulders as best as he can with his feathered headdress.

So we can spare half of this polo shirt.

Carefully, I fold up the second half and tuck it in with my knife at my hip. We'll need it for washing, bandaging, as a sun hat, dishcloth and a tool-bag.

It's just the piece in my hand that I need now.

I take a piece of charcoal that I've saved from the fire and draw a large face: coiling snakes for hair, and a fanged mouth. Then I nick my thumb with my knife and splash in two blood-spots for eyes. Suck my wound quickly to keep it clean.

I tie my work of art to a thin sapling stem and stick it in the sand.

There.

A flag for our raft.

The raft of *Medusa*.

Long may she sail.

Lists

'OK,' Rufus says. 'If you could eat anything right now, what would it be? Make a list.'

He's always doing this: thinking of games to distract us from hunger or boredom. In a way he's like Miss but somehow less annoying.

Mine goes like this:
- Fish and chips
- Quarter-pounder, no cheese

- Snickers
- KFC bucket
- Triple vodka and Coke
- Turkish coffee
- Haribos

'And yours?' I ask him.

Rufus's list:
- Couscous (I have to ask him to explain and spell this)
- Moules frites (and this)
- Guacamole (and this)
- Bouillabaisse

'Oh for frick's sake,' I say.

Stick Insect Banana Surprise

Ingredients:

- 3 green bananas
- 1 wild onion
- 2 giant stick insects
- A handful of snails
- A brownish piece-of-root-that-could-be-ginger
- 1 wild plum

Method:

1. Chop onion finely and add to coffee can, together with the piece-of-root-that-could-be-ginger.
2. Dry-fry to release the flavours then add a little seawater to stop it sticking. Add the chopped plum.
3. Ignore any growling noises in your belly.
4. When softened, throw in the stick insects and snails.
5. Try not to think of big blue fish, fat as cushions.
6. Debate it for a moment, then add chopped bananas. Yes, they're hard, but the cooking will soften them.
7. Definitely don't think about wild pig.
8. Take a deep breath.
9. Eat.
10. That root-thing definitely isn't ginger.

Rockfall

Maybe it's because the tide's turned.

Or the season's changed.

Or we've overfished this little cove.

I untangle Rufus's line for the eleventh time.

'Snails?' we say at the same time.

Rufus is right when he says they're scarce too.

I remember when the rocks were heaving with snails, tucked like wet stones under the ridges and crinkles. Now we find nine.

We're running out of food.

We're getting weaker, though we don't admit it to each other.

Rufus is thin. I'm thin. Dog too.

Dog's ribs show sharp through his fur and he no longer dances around the sand. None of us do. The fish have left One Tree Beach and the rocks; I think we're all fished out. Every limpet has been picked, every crab, every snail.

Neither of us has the energy to go clambering after wild pigs. There are hardly any peepas except in the trees; most of the ones left on the ground are rotten. We try hacking into them every so often but there's a stink when they crack open which makes us retch.

Dog spends most of the days in his favourite shady spot by the hammock. His tail still thumps when you say his name and he has learnt to answer to both Dog and Virgil. He doesn't get up much now though.

'The forest?' I ask again.

Rufus shakes his head.

'There's nothing, Fran. Everything's been used up.'

'No more onions?'

'No more onions.'

Neither of us mentions the melons. They ran out ages ago. I've watered the seeds I planted in the new garden I made, but they're spindly and exhausted-looking, like us.

One day we decide to look for better fishing grounds. This means climbing rocks.

Rufus is uncertain.

'Too dangerous,' he says, when I show him where I mean.

I shrug. 'It's the only place we haven't tried. What choice do we have?'

I start to climb the rocks but he stops me.

'They're too green,' he says. 'And the sea's too rough. We'll wait for a better time. Maybe later when the sun's dried them.'

But I'm stubborn. My stomach growls for fish and I just know they're out there somewhere, waiting. All we need is a couple of big ones, maybe snapper, and we'll be set up, at least for a day or two.

'It's fine, I'll be careful,' I say.

I slip.

Oops. My leg throbs but it's fine, there'll just be a bruise later.

'I'm fine,' I call.

I pick my way over the drier rocks, the ones that are still crisped by the sun. I no longer bother with shoes; my feet are like toughened leather underneath.

Vaguely, I'm aware of Rufus following. Dog doesn't bother to join us. I'd hear his little claws tick-tacking on the rocks if he was. He'll be lying in the shade somewhere close, listening and waiting.

Soon there's an overhang and a crevasse. It's deep and slick with green weed. To get to the other side, the rocky outcrop that juts over the sea, we'll have to climb over. To my right, the sea throbs; it's absolutely filled with fish, I'm sure of it. Below me, the deep crevasse, which is beginning to fill as the tide comes in.

But there's the rocks and the fish-filled sea.

And it's not going to be dark for hours yet.

'It's OK,' I call, ignoring the thudthudthudding as I place one foot and then the other on the driest rocks first; begin to descend the crack before I can get to the other side. I wish I wasn't so weak and hungry. My legs haven't always felt as shaky as this.

The sun wobbles.

'Fran – stop.'

Rufus sounds determined.

I sigh. 'I'm fine,' I say.

I watch him approach, face clenched and resolute. He's shaking his head at me, hesitant as his foot feels for the next rock.

'I'll climb across. You wait here,' he says, when he sees the crevasse. The skin between his freckles is pale.

'Are you sure? You don't have to prove yourself to me,' I say. 'Honestly. I can do it. It doesn't matter.'

But it does matter to him, I can see that. And it's not me he's proving himself to.

I sit on the rocks and watch Rufus climb down. Try not to feel a flash of impatience as he takes his time; takes a million years to place each foot before continuing.

His foot slips and my stomach lurches.

Avoid the green, I'm thinking. *Avoid the green rocks.*

Rufus is over now; he's reached the other side and is starting to make his way back up, to the high rock in the sunshine. The perfect fishing rock.

He's nearly there. I watch his foot move around for a ledge. Just one more push and he'll be up.

I see his foot move in slow motion; in slow motion I see the rocky ledge give way.

And that's when Rufus falls.

He falls awkwardly, his hand still scrabbling for something to hold. There's a sort of terrible pause. And then he lands. He actually bounces a bit first. That's how hard he falls.

He lands on the jagged rocks which are deadly with slime. There's an awful cry, hoarse with pain. And Dog's there at once, on the top rocks, barking and barking.

I'm screaming; I think I'm screaming. I'm saying:

'Rufus! Rufus?' and 'Are you OK?' and 'I'm sorry, so sorry.'

I have no idea how I get to him, but I do; I'm there beside him, shouting at Dog not to follow.

Rufus's eyes are staring up at me and he knows
   he knows
   that everything's so not OK.
'It's my leg,' he says.

Not OK

So.

Where there's his shorts, there's a gash. It's on his leg and it's a real biggie, torn into his skin all right. It's deep and wide and bleedingbleedingbleeding. And through the blood, there are things exposed.

I heave with horror.

'Tendons,' he says. He's strangely calm.

We both stare. Dog's still barking from the top of the crevasse. I wish he'd shut up. I can't think straight, can't get past this tide of fear.

Everything's changed now, in just a click of the fingers.

A foot wrong and whoosh. Your whole world comes slithering down.

'What does that mean?' I say, but we both know, 'course we do.

It's the thing we've tried to avoid, ever since we came here. The big *what if*.

What happens if one of us gets ill? Has an accident? Gets appendicitis? What then?

'Cause you can plan and you can build and you can collect driftwood all you like but nothing will help you once illness happens. No matter how many shells you collect to decorate your home camp. No matter how many water bottles you fill with charcoal and socks to filter it. In the end, you're just kidding yourself.

We've both been waiting to die ever since we came to this island, this little rock in the middle of the ocean. In the end we're all just spinning and waiting.

We can't fix it. Can't mend the tear.

It means that Rufus will die.

But still we pretend. I have to turn away from the knowledge in his eyes.

I take my T-shirt from around my waist.

'It'll stem the blood,' I say.

Rufus nods. He shows me where to tie it so that it acts as a tourniquet, and all the time he isn't gasping and crying. Just a slight hiss when I force it tight.

'Bind it up so it doesn't get dirty.'

We both know this is ludicrous. We're so filthy that all the scrubbing and scraping in the world doesn't come close to making us clean.

I pull the T-shirt tight, and my fingers are slithering in his blood –

there's so much blood.

Then we both look up, to where Dog is running back and forth. He's frantic.

'I'll help you,' I tell Rufus.

He nods and I want to die, right there in the bottom of this slime-filled chasm. It's all my fault – everything. If only I hadn't made us both come here. If only I hadn't let him climb up.

If.

'I'm so sorry,' I say.

Rufus's teeth are gritted.

'It's me that should say sorry, Cow-bag,' he says.

We begin the long climb, and each time we get to a ledge I have to pick up Rufus's foot and place it. And he leans heavily on my shoulder and his breath is hot against my neck. I point out dry rocks and Dog is quiet now, waiting.

The blood's seeping now, under the makeshift bandage, on to the rocks.

I don't know how things will be any different when we get to the top.

If we ever get to the top.

Red

'It doesn't hurt,' says Rufus.

His eyes are bright.

I've propped him up on the bottle bed and rebound his wound –

don't look, don't look, don't look –

so that it looks neat on the outside. It's tied with what's left of Rufus's TeamSkill polo, which we use for washing up. I've rinsed it best as I can and hung it to dry but it's not clean, 'course it isn't. What else can we do?

Rufus's eyes are closed now. He looks fine. Much better than you'd expect after such a shock. He's just sleeping it off.

'You've got to wash the wound,' he said, as we staggered back to camp. That meant a trek to the waterfall, and him screaming in pain as I made him stick his leg under the tumbling water.

The water ran red after that.

Can't think of his pain.

He's sleeping. He'll feel better in the morning.

Please be better then.

Perhaps it can still heal, even without stitches.

Rufus does look better. He does.

Treasure

Rufus grips my arm, suddenly desperate.

'Fran, I don't want you to go.'

'Don't be daft.'

'Fran, I don't want you to die.'

I stare at him; he's slumped on his bed, panting.

'Can't be left here alone again,' he says.

I know how he feels.

'Don't be so stupid.' I plant a kiss on his clammy forehead. 'Think of all those fish I'll catch.'

And he watches as I attach the hook to the line. Tug it to check it.

'OK?'

'OK.'

I leave Rufus propped up in his bed, untangling fishing net. I make my way back to the rocks, determined to catch something, to feed us all.

It's slow-going. Not only am I weak and tired from our near-starvation diet, but every time I find a foothold on the rocks, I'm reminded of Rufus's fall; of the sickening sound he made when he landed. It can't happen to me; if it does, there'll be no one to look after Rufus, no one to feed Dog.

I'm giddy with relief when I reach the first outcrop.

I'm about to climb up to the crevasse when something catches my eye.

A much bigger treasure, washed up by the sea. Another barrel, bobbing in the shallows. I grip my fishing pole firmly and climb back down.

So now we have four.

I wade into the sea and use the pole to pull the barrel nearer, then drag it in out of the waves. Even that small effort makes me exhausted. We're so tired now. Dog no longer follows me to the beach on my fishing efforts, preferring to lie by Rufus.

Rufus – well, he sleeps much of the day. I clean him and make sure he drinks enough, and help him out of bed when he needs the toilet. It's been two days since the accident and that wound's not getting any better.

But we need to eat. Rufus needs to eat to get his strength up, so I try not to think of the way the wound smells bad when I change the dressing. I try not to wonder if Rufus's eyes should be so bright and his cheeks so flushed.

This barrel is wooden, and smells of wine. I peer inside, breathing in the faint fumes. There's something inside the drum. Something waving at me from just inside the rim. It scuttles deep down when I reach for it. I get down on my hands and knees and peer into the shadows. Suck in my breath.

It's a lobster. It grabs at my hand with one of its giant claws but I hold it out of danger's way and pull it right out where I can look at it. It's a monster; there's enough flesh here to feed me, Rufus and Dog for two days. Heart skipping, I bind the lobster's claws quickly with twine from the fishing pole and hang it at my side.

I roll the barrel to the back of the bamboo grove, where the rest of my raft lies. And I spend a long time then, just looking and thinking.

I need to find the energy to finish this.

Rock Lobster

'So we can use the barrel to finish the raft,' I chatter, aiming the point of the knife at the base of the lobster's head and smashing the rock down. I'm hoping that my revelation will spark some interest in him. 'There's only three barrels, but we've got this coffee drum we use as a table. I thought maybe if lashed them all together, like with creepers or something?'

Rufus has been quiet since I got back. He's sitting in his bed, staring down. I've giving him a couple of limes to chop on a board. They go with fish so maybe they'll go with lobster.

I place the lobster upside down straight into the embers. It'll be only minutes till it's done. I look around for the rocks we used to use to get meat out of crab claws. When we could find crabs. I've never tried lobster but I'm sure it's delicious and those claws are thick as bricks.

Rufus doesn't answer 'cause he's probably feeling bad he never let me try to get to the fishing boat all those weeks ago. Or else he's annoyed that I've started building a raft without him.

The lobster hisses and I turn it over. Think of all that fat white flesh.

I use the knife to crack it into sections and my cheeks start to ache as I see how much meat is inside.

I pass Rufus his tin and a rock. Then I fall on to my portion, moaning.

'Oh my God, Rufus.'

Each mouthful is crazy-gorgeous.

'Mmm-mm,' I say, digging at the claw with the knife.

It's made Rufus speechless.

'What do you think?' I say, looking up at last.

But Rufus's just sitting there, staring down at his leg. His face hovers in the shadows.

'It's worse, Fran,' he says.

Spreading

He's left all that lovely lobster on his plate. The board of limes unchopped.

It's bad, really bad.

The edges of the wound have peeled away and they're reddened. The flesh around them is hot and throbbing.

'Why's your leg all hard?' I say.

'It's the infection. It's spreading.'

His skin's all tight and he flinches when I touch it. It's burning too.

I make myself say the words.

'So what will happen if we don't treat it?'

Rufus tries to get comfortable, and hisses with pain when his leg moves.

'The poison seeps into your bloodstream. And it spreads and spreads like curdled milk. And then, unless it's treated – unless all the pus is removed –'

'Yes?'

Voice so low now it's just a murmur, and it might be the

sea or it might not.

'Rufus – talk to me.'

'Septicaemia.'

I don't want to know what that word means because I can tell it's hissing and evil like a snake. I try to get Rufus comfy and it's difficult 'cause he can't move; he can't 'cause every tiniest jolt hurts – I mean, *screaming* hurts – and in the end I have to prop him up in bed with anything I can find. He was terribly thirsty before, but now he half sits, half lies, watching and not watching me.

I imagine the poison welling inside him and filling his poor, aching body –

how can it all end like this, in this stupid, stupid way? –

seeping out yellow goo and infecting his organs, infecting and burning with throbbing, pulsing pain till it reaches his blood –

how does it reach his blood? How?

Septicaemia.

Sounds like a kiss of death.

Scrambling

I scramble down to the beach, dragging our coffee-drum-table behind me, feet skittering on the scree. The world lurches as I throw it down; watch it bounce on the sand and wedge to a standstill. I hold my sides, gasping. I feel sick with exhaustion, with hunger. I walk to the edge of One Tree Beach and they're still there, the other barrels; I can see the marks in the sand where I rolled them. Just need to get back to Mosquito Alley.

Just need to get the frames now, after I've checked on Rufus.

From the bed, Rufus's breath is catching, but it's OK – plenty of time.

There's no time.

Use the old fishing line.

Drag the bottle mattress from the other bed.

It'll do as a base till we get to the nearest island. And if there's no other island? Well, then we'll just stay on the raft, wait for a boat.

We'll not go without a fight.

It feels good to be active. I may be skin and bones but fear pushes me.

Grab all the rope you can get; pull down the poles from the shelter. Now for the peepa pole.

Rufus half opens his eyes, but doesn't ask what I'm doing. Beside him, Dog's tail twitches.

Balancing the poles on my shoulder, I sway and almost fall. *Almost.*

One foot in front of the other, I force myself to walk in the direction of the beach.

One more step.

And another.

Nothing Between

Take a breath.

That's right. And again.

I've made it to the sea.

I open my eyes and there's nothing between me and all that blue; nothing between Rufus and the poison seeping into his blood but me.

I take the first pole; place it over the barrels. Pull the ropes taut, lash them round.

Building, lashing, tying.

This will not defeat us.

I am strong. I will save both Rufus and Dog and all those I care for.

For I am a rock.

Pulling, dragging, tying, lashing, heaving, panting.

Just hang on in there, hang on, hang on, hang on.

For some reason I'm thinking of Cassie, slumped on the settee. Grasping at me, at Johnny.

She tried.

She tried to grab on to what she loved, but she just didn't hold on tight enough.

I'm not going to let that happen.

I feel around with my foot and there's the next pole; I move it towards me, which means I can keep the rope tight with my hands.

And so it continues. The heat presses against me like a heavy dog panting on the back of my neck but there's no time to stop; no time to take a drink; no time to let go of my concentration for a moment.

Keep lashing.

Keep fighting.

By the time dusk falls, I've run out of poles. I need to save one for steering. But there's more bamboo.

My machete's good and sharp. I place my foot on to the cane till it snaps; finish off the job with the knife.

I don't stop till night comes 'cause we're fighting for time now. We need to catch the tide. It'll take us in the rip current; sweep us far away. And there'll be other islands out there, hundreds and hundreds, just like there are stars in the sky.

There'll be fishing boats, out night-fishing. They'll see us and pull us in, net us safe.

Not long now.

A little white shape appears in the darkness.

Dog scampers in and out, curious, bold now.

He's woken up

and it's time,

it's time to grasp everything I love and hold on tighttight-tight till the bitter end 'cause really that's all there is to this world.

Grab that hand and clingclingcling.

Hands reaching out like stars

rising from the sofa, like a terrible fish.

'Love you, baby.'

'Love you more than sky and sea and stars,' I whisper, to Cassie, to Johnny.

I drag the finished raft to the edge of the ocean, where the water laps and sighs. Lashed to it are bottles of water, the last of the peepas, a fishing line.

Please let her float.

Praying hard, I crouch down and ease myself on board, slowly, gently. Water seeps, cool between the poles and net, but the raft stays buoyant. Her flag flutters. She is strong.

The moon waits.

It is time.

Escape

Rufus is worse.

His skin's shining but his eyes are dull.

'I can't move, Fran. Don't make me move.'

I have to lean forward to hear him and his breath is sour-hot.

'I'm thirsty.'

I pour water into his mouth and he swallows gratefully, but almost at once he sicks it up; a thin stream trickles out of the side of his mouth.

'I'm so sorry, Fran,' he whispers.

'Don't be stupid, Posh Boy.' I'm making my voice all jolly like I'm Santa or something, and he knows and I know that it's all an act because we're both

scaredscaredscared.

'The raft's ready,' I repeat.

I brush Rufus's hair out of his eyes and try not to see what a skeleton he's become. His eyes stare back at me, blue-bruised.

'I'll help you down to the beach. You can lean on me, and I'll lay you down on the raft, nice and comfy, and I'll take us to another island.'

'Another island?' Rufus is slipping back into that half-sleep again; he's so still that for a moment I panic and think —

'Rufus?' I say, shaking him gently. 'Rufus?'

But he opens his eyes again and tries a smile. 'I'm here, Fran, I'm here.'

I take his damp hand and squeeze it tightly.

'It's OK, Rufus, I've got it all sorted out: we'll get to the edge of these waters, and there'll be tons of other islands – remember me saying? And there'll be a fishing boat or something.'

'A fishing boat?'

'Yeah, someone will see us and bring us ashore and there'll be…there'll be someone to help you, Rufus.'

And I do believe it.

I do.

But Rufus is asleep. His chest rises and falls the tiniest amount and it hurts to wake him but I have to – I must.

'Rufus, wake up. You must wake up.'

It's an effort but I manage; I make him sit upright even though the movement makes him bellow with pain.

'I'm sorry, Rufus. Christ, I'm sorry.'

I'm sobbing by the time I finally get him standing. He's hanging over me, gasping, too exhausted to scream any more. He weighs no more than a –

fistful of twigs –

and his breath pants light and hot and quick on my shoulder.

I swallow to get myself together. Make my voice calm and even.

'We can do this, Rufus. Just walk with me – that's right. I'll carry most of the weight…'

Each step is knives; each breath is a sucked-in scream. Dog runs back and forward, anxious to keep his pack together.

We are tatters by the time we get to the beach.

Rufus sags, moaning. But there is the raft, silhouetted against the shimmering water.

'We've made it, Rufus.' I try to smile.

Moving

I don't think about how I got Rufus on.

I've made him a nest from our softest, wornest clothes and all the dry grasses I could find. I've put rolled palm leaves under his head to support him.

On board I've packed:

    5 bottles of fresh drinking water

    Our last 6 peepas

    A fishing line and hooks

    Plastic bags to make solar stills

    A tub of limpets for snapper bait.

    My rucksack, with my knife and Rufus's machete inside.

We're very low on carbs but that's how it's always been; we'll have to survive mainly on fish. And anyway, when we reach civilisation we'll get all the carbs we can eat.

Rufus is too exhausted to open his eyes. But he's here. And I'm here, and the raft creaks as I push it into the breakers. Dog hops on obediently and knows to avoid Rufus's leg.

Sighing with relief, I use my peepa pole-oar to head the raft straight for the horizon.

Rocking

We lose the fishing line a long time before dawn.

I'm pulling in a snapper when it tangles on some flotsam and gets yanked out of my hand. I can still see it, snarled over the rubbish, bobbing out of reach.

'*No!*' I scream, and the wind takes my words and scatters them like crumbs. 'Nononononooooooooooooooooooooo!'

I fight it; I scream and howl and kick. If I could bite something I would bite.

All this time, Rufus is lying at my feet, eyes half-open, watching me.

'Let it be, Fran,' he says quietly. 'Let it be.'

'I will *not* let it be,' I rant, grabbing the pole.

I paddle with wild fury, digging in the pole on both sides like I'm stabbing that stupid silent sea, jabjabjabbing. It's not till I rest a while, exhausted, that I hear Rufus gasping.

'It hurts, Fran, it hurts.'

'Oh God – it's me. I'm rocking the raft. Rufus, I'm sorry.'

I place the pole carefully down the side, hands trembling. Sit back down and watch the flotsam drift away, a small heaving shape in the slapping water.

Rufus sleeps; he's burning to touch but peaceful now. I hold his hand and watch the flickering stars scratch out their distant patterns.

And all the time the water slaps.

Time Burns

The night is clear, the sky salty with stars.

We lie on our backs on the raft, watching. I'm careful not to jolt him.

'That's *Caelum*,' Rufus says. 'Its name means "chisel" in Latin.' His voice is quiet as the breeze.

I watch his finger trace its outline in the sky.

'Do you know, like, everything?' I ask him.

'Practically everything,' he whispers.

'That's what I like about you,' I say. 'You're so frickin modest.'

But Rufus is asleep again.

I doze fitfully in shreds of sounds: the whacka-whacka bird bawling its call; the *ting ting* of the tin cans on their bamboo sticks and somewhere I hear, too, the sigh and hiss of splitting melons.

Around us, the sea lops and slaps in the rustling wind.

Rufus's hand tightens on mine as he stirs in his sleep. He's peaceful now, but it's an uneasy peace; it's a giving-himself-up-and-accepting kind of peace and I don't want that.

I. Don't. Want. That.

We spin, Rufus and Dog and me, in the star-stabbed sea. Time burns.

Dog

'Dog – don't!'

He's barking at a seagull that's standing bold-eyed at the end of the raft.

Each little movement jolts Rufus; I can tell by his wince. He closes his eyes.

The sea's picking up now; we're on some rolling waves, swelling and surging. I use creepers to tie down the last of our stuff: our water bottles (two), our last remaining peepas.

I don't know how long *The Medusa* will last. It creaks and

squeaks with the bottles. If it stays fairly calm, everything will be fine, but what if a storm comes?

We'll never survive a storm.

We can survive three weeks without food though, and that's an awfully long time. So I just need to keep up our water supplies.

Carefully, I pour out the water that's collected from the seawater in the stills. I've set up four, one on each corner of the raft. Beneath the plastic, the water's warm and pure and life-giving.

I make Rufus drink first, even though he shakes his head; tries to push it away.

'No. You,' he says.

I press it back to his mouth.

'Drink up. Don't be daft.'

I can only just hear his words as he drinks and closes his eyes.

'Silly old Cow-bag.'

I smile and let Dog lap up water from a peepa shell. He finishes it double quick and still pants.

'Move over, Dog.'

His stinky breath's too hot against my skin.

Heat shimmers, but the waves are swelling.

The seagull is back. It stares us both out, bold as anything.

'!' warns Dog. He doesn't like seagulls.

'Quiet, Dog.'

I'm dry-mouthed 'cause I didn't get anything to drink myself; I'm waiting for the other still to refill. I'm tired and crabby.

So I forget to check on Dog. I don't see him hop on to the barrel, the oil drum that's always been a struggle to lash in close as the others. I feel his little feet scrit-scat on to the tin; sense his warm body has left mine.

So I don't see the wave come.

And I don't see the creepers unwind.

The barrel takes the wave surge, and I see it almost in slow motion, the lazy surge as it breaks over Dog's end of the raft.

I see the seagull lift its wings and fly, soar into safety.

I see the barrel detach and take Dog with it.

For an instant he's there, little legs scrabbling frantically to keep his balance.

And then the barrel rolls and a wave sweeps Dog off.

Can't

'Fran, please, you have to leave him.'

There's no way –

no way –

I'm leaving Dog alone in all that wide, open sea.

I'm in the water and I've remembered to wind the rope from the raft around my hand.

I'm scooped up on top of rolling waves huge as houses, and from there I look and call, over and over:

'Dog!'

'DOG!'

'DOG!'

And there he is, his black nose pointed up to the sky, front legs scrabbling. He's seen me; he's trying to come back.

'Come on, boy, come on –'

But as I watch, the swelling wave behind him breaks over his head and he's down; he's sucked under, a tiny form. He can't do battle with all that weight of water.

I dive down, eyes stretched as stalks, and in the sudden silence, with only the whumpwhump of my heart in my ears, I see his little pale body, legs circling, slowing.

Things touch and swirl. I push back water and yank my neck up for gasping breath and I *will* get to him.

I will save him.

Keep hold of the rope.

I can see him; he's trying to keep his head up,
his little nose is just peeping out
of the water.
I will not, will not let
Dog go.
I'll not give up.
Sinking bright water spins
him under.
I dive, and through water bubbles slow and cool
    I see him.
He's still paddling.
His little feet going.
Sinking, he's sinking.
Sobbing, gasping.
I grab his collar, the scruff of his neck.
Oh oh oh.

Still

Please move, Dog. Please breathe.
The white shape of Dog lies still at our feet.
A hand finds mine.

'It's not your fault,' Rufus whispers, soft as moth-breath.

His little body couldn't cope in all that water.

'No!' I say. I retch over the side, all that seawater out of my lungs and stomach.

I press down on where I think Dog's heart may be, and seawater streams out of my eyes, my mouth, my hair.

I howl, and all the pain in the world is in that cry.

'Please don't, Fran. Let him go.'

I'm sorry, Dog, I'm sorry.

I wail out my pain, over his little drenched body, so still, so —

shivery.

'Dog?'

His body heaves, and he's coughing, retching up seawater all over my feet. Then he opens his liquid eyes and looks at me.

'!' he says, in a tiny voice. His little tail thumps, just a little.

'Oh, Dog!'

I pull him into me and whisper 'Sorrysorrysorry' into his sodden ear and he wriggles free and gives a huge shake that flings water like diamonds over Rufus and me and the raft.

I laugh and laugh

and Dog's hard little head is butting me; he's licking me with hot stinky breath, licking away the tears, making me laugh, making me —

'You're crying,' Rufus says.

'I never cry. Rocks don't cry,' I say.

But I make his words all wet, and my whole heart is being pulled out, uncoiling and unending. And my tears are warm and endless, spilling my cheeks, my hair, my neck.

Dog and Rufus try to kiss them all away but each shudder brings more as the sun turns to stars and the moon smooths and cools.

Tap Three Times

I dream of Rufus.

'Come on, Fran,' he says, covering my eyes. 'I have a surprise for you.'

He's holding something wriggly in his arms and when I open my eyes it's Dog but his eyes are different; they're Johnny's eyes.

'I'm back, Frannie,' says the Dog that is Johnny.

We're on the beach and it's a party; everyone's invited, they're all here: Trish and Steve and there's Cassie, waving from the settee by the rocks. Coral is dancing with a little girl and they're spinning, spinning on the sand till the sun flings out of their hair and eyes.

'Come on, Frannie. What are you waiting for?' asks Johnny-Dog. He leaps in to join the party and his tail is spinningspinning.

Rufus pushes me gently into the very centre.

He points to my feet and tells me to tap my heels together three times. 'It's all you've ever needed to do to go home,' he says. And he floats off in a bubble like Glinda the Good Witch in *The Wizard of Oz*.

Scorching

'I've had such a funny dream,' I say to Rufus with a smile. I shift around to look at him.

He's already watching me, just one eye open the tiniest bit. His breathing is very fast and shallow and he's burning-hot.

'Fran,' he whispers, and his voice is the smallest thing.

I'm scared of the hand that scorches me, and I chatter on 'cause talking pushes it away, this fear.

'We were all on the beach. Everyone, even TeamSkill, and you were there and –'

'Fran.'

'Have some water, Rufus. It won't be long now till some-one will find us and –'

'Fran –'

This time I lean close as a whisper to hear him.

'You have the water,' he says.

'Don't be stupid, you've got to have some. You –'

'You…have…it.'

I stare at him then. He's flushed all over, hotter than I've ever seen him, and no amount of wiping with squeezed-out seawater cools him down. His one eye is burning at me, forcing me to –

'All right,' I say. 'Just this once, I'll have yours.' I take a tiny swig of water and he seems to relax. 'OK? Happy now?'

Rufus's hand tightens on mine. I put my arms around him, spoon my body around his like he always did to me. An owl in its hollow; a nut in its shell; a butterfly in its cocoon.

'Silly old Cow-bag,' he whispers.

Spinning

I thirst.

The last peepa is at the back of the raft, green and full of liquid. My knife lies beside it; Rufus's machete. But I don't take it; I can't move from here, where I lie, because Rufus is beside me, like he's always been, and if I move – if I leave him for a moment – he might leave me, I might break our connection.

My will is all that's keeping him here.

I look past where Rufus lies burning, eyelids flickering in fever-dreams,

and for a moment I look beyond to the scratched barrels of our little raft and they seem to bulge and bend into yellow rubber; it's not wood, it's rubber. Yellow raft, yellow bouncy spaceship.

I blink –

make it come back –

and it is our raft again.

But if I squeeze my eyes tight I can see our story. I can replay it over and over again.

Rufus and me: spinning for ever on the scribbled sand; in this spinning sea.

A voice, posh as plums and husky from disuse.

'Do you want me to scrape the dirt off you?' Rufus standing under the waterfall, a clam shell in his hand.

Rufus taking my hands and swinging me round and round on our beautiful, patterned beach. The sunlight is spinning and our smiles are flying and just at this minute, *this moment, this exact moment, nownownow –*

And Monkey…

I close my eyes, smiling, soaking up every millionth of the moment of memory.

Then I kiss Rufus's poor, burning lips and reach for his machete.

Brighter

The peepa tastes good.

I drink, deep and full, and the liquid fizzes sweet against my tongue.

I chew shark meat slowly and feel strength come back.

I take the pole and measure my rowing, pulling twice, slow and steady, before swapping to the other side.

After ten pulls I rest. I cover my head with my T-shirt and try not to squint. I set up my solar still.

'Getting better at this,' I tell Rufus.

He's lying beside me, leg outstretched and red-throbbing. His freckles have finally won the takeover bid for his skin. He's Robinson Crusoe, a hobo, a wolf-boy. His face is fever-flushed but smiling.

And I am strong.

And I am rock.

And I will not stop till I've saved him.

Faces shimmer in the burning sun.

Rufus becomes Cassie, soft and plump and sleepy, care-worn eyes bright with booze, bright with love.

Monkey's cheeks burning, flushed as he races to escape zombies, as his breath catches, as he's caught and his eyes flit past me, to his friends, and he's happy.

And I did that.

I think what Rufus would say; what he'd tell me to do.

He'd say: go to see your brother, Cow-bag. Be the best sister you can be.

He'd say: look how he's growing up, look how he's happy. You did that, Fran. You did that.

If I get out of here, I will:

Be nice to Cassie.

Buy a lock for my door and practise my angry yowl.

Ask to take Monkey out for the biggest pizza and make him wide-eyed with my adventures.

Visit Miss and say that I am sorry. Write her a story to try to explain.

Night comes and the sky's stabbed with stars now, moon-cooled.

I lie back, reach for my bow.

You can always shoot the stars. There's always the stars, Fran.

One star is brighter. It hovers just above the water, bigger than the rest.

'Shall we?' I say to him. 'My turn first?'

This star winks as it burns and grows.

On. Off. On. Off. On. Off. On.

'Do stars blink?' I turn to ask Rufus.

Do stars grow bigger and bigger? Do shooting stars do that?

And Rufus's hot hand squeezes mine.

So, I draw back my hand, *steady now*; lick my parched lips; grip the arrow more firmly. It's a good, straight arrow and I've made it with pelican and gull feathers, exactly like Rufus's headdress. Closing one eye, I gaze at the approaching star, take a deep breath and aim.

And then.

And then.

And then.

Acknowledgements

They say that every book must have a controlling idea. And that you should stick this at the top of each page. Plaster it over your wardrobe. Tattoo it on your forehead. I eventually whittled this one down to: 'No girl is an island'.

Well, it seems that no writer is an island, either.

So thanks goes to my lovely and wise agent, Clare Wallace, and the rest of the hard-working Darley Anderson team. To my editor, Sarah Odedina, queen of mechanics. To Juliet Mabey, Cailin Neal, Margot Weale and the rest of the fabulous team at Oneworld. To Madeleine Stevens, for incisive copy edits. To Paul Nash and Laura McFarlane on the production team. To Nathan Burton, for that wonderful cover.

To my very first reader, Sarah Dukes, for constant encouragement and bubbly optimism. To Cathy Knight, for meticulous close reading (no one can spot an errant apostrophe like you). To Ellie and Tim, fellow writers and Scribblers. To Mike Woods, wordsmith extraordinaire. To Jane, Bron, Penny C, and the rest of the readers in my English department. To Penny Bates, for all the *Bookseller* articles in my pigeon-hole. To my teenage readers, especially Joe Xia, for your boy's perspective, and Lauren (Spoz) Carter, for sending me my very first fan mail. To Bex Triffit, for no-nonsense advice when I was wrestling with early chapters. To Paul, Chris and Andy, for patiently answering all of my Facebook messages about machetes and engine fans. To my Baps book group, for treating me like a real author, well before I finally became one. To the SCBWI crew, especially Clare Bell. To Melvin Burgess for patiently Skype-sharing your wisdom.

To my family, especially my husband, Jim, for supporting me when I took a year's sabbatical from teaching. That was the year that started everything. To my long-suffering sons, Sam and Louis, for putting up with microwave meals. My mother, Judith, for giving me my first pencil and a book-brimmed childhood. My step-dad, Stephen, for all of your support and hand-selling.

To my brother, Greg, for years of long country walks and plot talks. And Fliss, for the loan of your Brixton flat. To my little sis, Sophie, for sharing my book on your very own island.

To my own Dog, Basil, for constant support and licks.

To Lucy Irvine, and your incredible true-life account as a *Castaway*.

Oh, and to Joanna Lumley. You don't know me, but thank you for turning your bra into a caveshoe.

www.rocktheboat.london